LIBERTY AVENUE

Other Worldgig.com editions

JAZZ AND THE ABSTRACT TRUTH
ARCANIA
OMUSONGU
TAKE MY HAND AND LEAD ME TO THE STREET
THE LEOPARD AND THE CADILLAC
ALPHAGIRL
MOODSWINGER
LITTLE DEVIL IN PARADISE
DONNA DONNA DONNA
SUPPERTIME
BRISTOL GARDENS

Max Fabian

LIBERTY AVENUE

worldgig.com

Dedicated to my friends the Russian family
who always offered shelter from the storm.

TABLE OF CONTENTS

A GIRL, A PIANO AND A DOG

New York City - 1993

The town I discovered was far from what I had imagined. Skyscrapers, yes. Big money, of course. Powerful cars, screaming headlines at Times Square, and people of every description. Guys, running, talking, hustling, disappearing fast, always in many languages, and wearing crazy, outlandish clothes. Cafes reverberating with dozens of voices. Banks with doric columns, built like churches. Glamour girls and teenage vixens, with huge price tags. Non-stop hustling. Pretty soon I had only one thing on my mind, which was to keep searching for money and work, and never to stop moving.

I had arrived with no money, actually a debt. I had a girlfriend, a music keyboard and a big black dog. Flying in from London, ready to make it as a musician, or die.

Travelling from Kennedy airport, on the subway, as it rode over ground, I stared out at concrete blocks and tenements, and suburban streets with pick-up trucks and parking lots. All the love in the world for America was in my heart at that moment. I had no idea of the teeming cauldron of madness I was diving into. As the train dived underground, I could imagine the pounding throbbing heart of the animal that was America.

I was there. This was it. How could I fail?

Within a few days we had moved in with Jean, a generous, motherly black lady who lived in Flatbush, Brooklyn. We shared with four or five other characters who would creep in late at night to bed down wherever they could find a spot.

We slept in the middle of the living room floor, and grabbed kitchen time when we could.

Each morning she gave us advice.

"Going out to hustle for a dollar? Well dress up right! You gotta be looking good!" She was soon proved right. It was all about how you looked, how you spoke, where you were from, who you knew. And yet, because this was New York, it was about how you played most of all. They had the best here, and knew it, and wanted the best, and would take nothing but the best. We soon learned to exaggerate who we were and where we were from. Pretty soon we were describing ourselves as some kind of jazz royalty. There was no room for modesty here. Either you were the greatest, or forget it.

A man was shot dead right outside the very first night we arrived.

Our days were always the same. Get up. Bagel and coffee, although soon the coffee was changed to decaf because we were eternally screaming at each other from an overload of stress. Then, dress up really well. Try to make it to the subway in one piece as the gangs of black kids eyed us carefully, as they prepared future scams and attacks. I soon learned to be the chameleon, to walk to the subway in my tramp outfit, then actually change clothes right there on the subway train into more classy stuff. Nobody batted an eyelid at this. I was not the only one doing the on-board wardrobe swap, it seemed. Then we would get out at Wall Street, just to feel the rush of status and power as we took our second bagel and coffee break-fast amongst the crazy, stressed melee of business men. I'll never forget the glossy marble floor of the huge arcade, the perfumed, air-conditioned scent, the shining eyes of the Arab coffee man as he served us the steaming cups. We would grin and swap know-ing glances, luxuriating in the knowledge that all of our hopes and aspirations were focussed here in this enormous hall, charged by destiny and empire, and the might and the glory of the American dream.

For ten years I had been fighting, hustling and scratching my way up and down Europe, playing thousands of gigs, always in semi or total poverty, but living the dream, never ever doubting that I was a true artist, that this was the path to making it, and that we had something worthy to offer the world.

Sitting here in this Wall Street emporium right now appeared to justify everything, since all roads had lead to this point. I had finally arrived in America. My years of effort had not been in vain. I knew that we had become legendary amongst all our friends back home. We had dared do what no others could. To leave for America forever, with no mon-ey and nothing but our music talent, whatever that might be, was impossible and insane. People in Eu-rope were not ignorant about this. They knew all the details about how, if you simply packed up and left for America, as an artist, without support from management and record label, that nothing good would ever happen, that you would merely be set upon and torn apart by terrible unseen forces which would grind you to dust under the brutal steel wheels of the machine.

But I didn't care. I had already been through years of hell in Europe and felt I was tough enough. I'd endured begging by the side of the road in many different places, often in Italy, once when we were stranded in a petrol station under the merciless August sun for a week, another time in the mountains on the coast in the north, and sometimes in Rome itself. There had been good times too, playing big gigs, or TV or radio, plus being reviewed and talked about in the press, but I valued the tough moments also, because I knew it had turned me into a man, and hardened me in preparation for America.

However, even with all my courage and new-found experience, I was not aware that the oncoming rain of destruction in New York would be insidious, invisible and mental, or how thoughts themselves would become twisted, or how people would lose nearly all memory of who they had been previously, or where they had come from. Perhaps not lose memory exactly, but certainly discard that part of their life as being worthless. All of this I was about to learn. The great battle for survival had begun, and it was to be against an enemy who would never show his face. You had to have enormous reserves of inner strength, intuition and psychic power to survive such a conflict. It was essential to have discipline like no other being. You had to believe in yourself, but also there was more. You had to know and remember how unique you and your culture were. You must continually treasure all these things. And finally, you had to put yourself, and your work as an artist, higher, far higher, than any other consideration. You had to be able to carry on creating your art, continue writing your music, arranging your band, playing your gigs, however tough the conditions became. Sometimes there would be no food, and no money either, but you would have to carry on anyway. Occasionally there would even be no place to live.

You would have to learn never ever to spend money, not to look at any shop windows where products were laid out enticingly in rows, as though some evil magician had been weaving his spells and laying a trap. However New York is nothing but stores, cafes and restaurants, and things for sale. All of this consumerism you must ignore, forever. If you strayed from this precarious path, you would be lost for good. You must forsake capitalism and all its trappings.

Much of this was in my mind as I looked around the luxurious hall, soaking up all that I could from the perfumed air here, the scent of comfort, success and the allure of the big money world.

Scanning the crowds I perceived that whereas that some of these crisply suited, business people appeared polite and cordial, however most were stressed market traders with desperately unrelenting schedules, who talked fast, barking out orders for coffee and snacks, then rushing out, bearing all the troubles of the world on their shoulders as they went. I was grateful not to be one of these.

First we tried landing a gig in the Wall St area itself. There were lots of wealthy characters around. Suave places. Expensive decor. Plenty of pastries behind the glass. And we were hungry.

"Maybe there's a chance here," Marina said.

The first place was an elegant cafe on the corner. It sold alcohol too. "That's a big clue," she whispered. "It's probably an after-hours place."

She reached over to straighten my shirt collar, and brushed down my jacket. Then we walked in.

Immediately Marina locked on to the man, grinning like crazy, gesturing with the arms as Italians do, making her proposal seem absurdly attractive, as though he would be swimming in cash the moment he hired us.

The owner was Swedish, and rather dry and straight to the point.

""Yes, I do book duos occasionally," he said. "But do you have a pull? I only book acts if they bring people in." Then we made the mistake of letting him know we couldn't guarantee that. His face hardened.

"Can't do it," he said. "Sorry. No go. Come back when you have a pull."

It was like this for five or six more places. My

brain started to hurt. Each rejection was knocking me down slightly.

"Let's try the Village," I suggested.

"Yeah, but it's high pressure there," she warned. "The whole world wants a gig in the Village."

The next few hours we walked thirty or forty more blocks, asking a gig from every possible place. I reminded myself that we had a good chance. Being a jazz duo meant that we were cheap to book. I had also learned to be adaptable, mixing in more popular tunes, rock and blues too, into the repertoire. But even with these advantages it was hell to get a booking, and the constant refusals would gradually hit into your confidence and wear you down.

Marina never tired. She walked fast. Her long brown hair occasionally gusted in the fresh ocean breeze. Suddenly I heard her familiar big laugh in my ear.

"Max, we're gonna make it, do you know that?" I grinned back. I was not totally sure, but I liked this dedication of hers. Plus, she did everything fast, and confidently, and this attacted me too. She knew where she was going. Right now she shook her head impatiently and marched on into the sunlight.

New York is not like other cities, where you have to ride around in buses, trains and cars to find the gigs. In New York City everything is all laid out, block after block, thousands and thousands of places, all compressed together, bars, clubs, cafes, halls, theatres, community centres, hotels, auditoriums, a seething, sparkling monster of music and theatre, but all live, all happening now, hiring and firing fast, shooting the best to the top and condemning anything less than great to a hopeless small town circuit, or worse, the madness of grey and total obscurity.

So at least you could walk, and search, non-stop. Walk till you drop. It was a hustler's paradise.

The first day we must have asked at about fifty places. Later, when we developed the 'New York muscle', it would be more like 100. The great thing was that you could just walk in and ask. There was none of that dreadful British formality, *'Who do you think you are?'* and so on. America had been built by guys in rough clothes and hats, hustling and shaking up and down the strip, and we knew it, and them too. New York might be elegant, but it was also real, and in your face, too. We valued that.

They all liked that we were from Europe, and admired my British accent. I told them I liked their accents. This was true, although some could only speak a few words of English. But I was excited by the spirited way their voices rose and fell, specially when talking about music.

It was soon discovered that I had played gigs in England, and that Marina had an extensive CV, including theatre tours and also residencies at her father's theatre in Rome. This helped a little, but never as much as I was expecting. Marina herself was resourceful and full of drive and initiative, and she was great at sheer hustling. She never ran out of energy. We argued a lot, and this new town we were in seemed to make this even worse. Every day we were talking big and thinking big, and ready to bite each other's heads off.

In any case, she was an explosion of energy and she knew how to make things happen. I respected her for this. As for me, I was still learning.

We tried jazz gigs, bars, clubs, cafes. Within hours we understood that to get a gig at a real New York jazz club, you needed a CV as long as your arm, plus actual records, and a substantial press kit. We had some material, but never enough. And if they were interested, the gig might be for the following summer, or even next year. December, you didn't even try, as the entire scene would be booked solid.

After a few hours more, and many breaks for muffin and coffee, the caffeine overdose began to make us truly crazy. This helped in a way. Finally we started to look like real New Yorkers, a high octane comedy team, sharp like a knife. In this city, craziness and eccentricity were everywhere. We started getting advice from hoodlums, hip-hop kids, buskers and tramps, and hustling for gigs in the most unusual places.

Within a few more hours, a hat shop had said OK. It was a bucket gig, meaning we'd work for tips only. But she'd done it. A gig had been booked on the very first day! This was unthinkable. After twelve hours of non-stop walking, arguing and hustling, we finally got back on the subway somewhere around

120th street. I was groggy, almost unconscious.

Some of the gangster kids circled us as we stumbled back to Jean's apartment. They sensed we were almost down, but at the last moment, with a superhuman effort we trudged past them, looking away.

"Put your hand half way in your bag, Max," Marina said quietly. They backed off. Gratefully, we crashed into our foyer and slumped into the freight elevator. A few West Indians scanned us thoughtfully. They'd already figured out I was British, and knew we were musicians. They also understood that we were living with Jean, and this fact protected us. Nobody messed with Jean. She was physically big, and a psychiatric nurse, and would just slap down anyone if they got out of line.

She ruled the whole area.

After a few months the cash situation got so desperate that I started taxi driving. Jean and Marina spent a long time dressing me up to look my best, with a decent pair of pants, a shirt with a trendy collar and a pair of Italian suede shoes. I felt good and after a short subway ride to Cobble Hill, she showed me a storefront where the window sign requested drivers.

The Arab boss took me immediately.

"Can you drive an automatic car?" he demanded. Marina giggled.

"I'm sure I can," I confirmed. He grabbed my license and examined it.

"Take it for a spin," he said laconically.

"See you later," shouted Marina, and disappeared.

It was such a relief to nestle back into the soft plush upholstery of the luxury sedan car. For a while I began to imagine I would make good this way. It would be a pleasure to get to know this area, Cobble Hill in Brooklyn, a dreamy little back-quarter, where life was mainly routine and tranquil.

For a few weeks things worked out fine. There were some interesting fares. I drove film people, musicians, media people, all kinds. However quite a few just carried a large, brown paper bag on their lap, and told me to step on the gas in a hard, determined voice. The money was low but it was a survival.

However one day everything changed. One of the Arab drivers had begun to argue over money with the taxi chief. The two were standing outside, on the sidewalk. It was broad daylight. And now, as if in a dream, I saw the boss whistle and instantly a huge figure, dressed all in black, began to cross the road, heading towards us. As he reached us, the offending driver saw him coming and fell to his knees in fear. The huge man reached down and hit the side of his face, hard, with the back of his hand. In a second the driver was running away, never to be seen again.

Quietly, the other drivers went back to what they were doing. Well satisfied, the boss returned to his compartment, inside the store.

For a few weeks I drove customers all around Brooklyn and the city, often to the airport. However the car had no radio connection with the office so I had to go back to base every time to pick up another customer. My earnings were so low that we were in despair.

"Just give it up, Max," Marina told me one morning, so I did.

One evening we stopped to sit outside a cafe on the edge of Soho. The sun was going down behind the enormous buildings above us.

I was utterly exhausted. We had just walked all the way from 120th street, searching for work all the time. But the day had not gone well. I was not desperate or angry, just vacant and exhausted. All I knew was how much my feet hurt, and how much I needed to climb on the homeward bound subway train.

Then I pricked up my ears. Two men were talking music at the nearby table. I quickly heard enough to understand that one was a record producer. I whispered in Marina's ear and she immediately introduced herself to the pair. The moment they understood that she was Italian they were all smiles. Now Marina had passed her headphones to them such that they could hear our music.

Incredulously, I began to understand that an actual record deal was being sketched out between Marina and this tall, dark Ital-American, whose name was Roman. Before I knew it the two had scheduled an appointment for two day's time, where Roman would listen to more of our demo tapes.

The ride home was a joyful moment. We talked excitedly of where all this might go. Marina's eyes were shining as the train rocked and rolled into Brooklyn. Her voice was rising and falling dramatically. She didn't care who might hear. We were lost in our own success.

Before I went to sleep that night it occurred to me that there was a true justice, or kharma, in what had just happened. In all the occasions we had walked all day looking for gigs, this one had been the longest and the hardest, and the most fruitless, until the moment we met Roman. I felt proud.

A few months later we bought a car at a police auction. Marina suggested I try the taxi thing again, at a different base this time.

"You may make more money if you provide the car," she pointed out.

The new taxi base was not far from Atlantic Avenue subway, and the boss was a friendly man from Sudan. He immediately gave me a broken colour TV as a present.

"You'll do good," he promised. I looked around. Twenty three Arab drivers stared back. The place was dingy, with a carpet that smelled, and a horrifically filthy toilet, but to me it looked neat and logical and the start of something good.

A girl arrived and talked to the boss through the glass window.

"I need a car. Do you have a car?" she asked. "And can he drive me?" she added, pointing directly at me.

"There's a strict order," the boss said. I felt relieved. The other drivers all stared back at me with sinister expressions. But as soon as they realised I was not jumping the queue they relaxed.

The days passed in an easy manner. It was nonstop talking with the customers, and then, back at the base I began to make friends with the drivers. And finally, at sundown, all of them would have their heads down on the floor, praying.

And yet our poverty increased. The dog was injured in a fight with another dog and the vet's bills were sky high. The anxiety and paranoia became extreme. I felt that I could personally take any amount of suffering, but if the dog was in pain, then that was unbearable.

One day things came to a head. We were driving in Manhattan. I knew that neither of us had any money left, not even enough to buy supper. The gas tank was low too.

Suddenly Marina reminded me that there was a political meeting we had to attend. Something about anti-racism and left wing politics. I told her that she should go, but that I had to go to the taxi office. I reminded her that we were desperately low on cash and that we didn't even have the money for the evening meal.

Instantly she went beserk. It was awful because I so much wanted to support in all of her left-wing principles, but had reached my breaking point. Seeing her chance, she now went for the kill, telling me I was a guy with no morals and no conscience, and that I was a lousy right-wing racist. Her jibes hurt. My stomach began to go acid. I wanted to slap her, but restrained myself.

Now she ordered me to stop the car, and got out at a dangerous corner, smashing the car door behind her as she did so. I was left scarred, and speechless. She had brought me to my knees, and I felt ashamed. At this moment I had finally come to agree with what she believed, that money was dirty, meaning that the entire system was corrupt. Now I knew myself to be the guilty one as I cruised over to the Brooklyn taxi base. But there was nothing else to do. I felt wooden, like a zombie, or a man with no emotions, no feelings, and no future. She had finally brought me right down.

However hell now turned to heaven extremely fast. New York was lithe and professional to turn the tables like this. She constantly took you by surprise. You would never know if you were standing on your feet or on your head.

The day of the recording session arrived and things went very well. Although I had played mainly funk, rock, jazz, blues and latin up till now, this song was to be house music. I knew the kids were crazy about that stuff, and that Roman was a talented, well established producer, so I found myself enjoying the style more and more. It sounded like the future.

We arrived into a large, spacious studio in lower Manhattan. The two of us were broke and almost starving, but the love of the music kept us more than good. The session lasted all night long. Every second felt great. Calculating the pitiful finances carefully, I was able to ride the elevator eighteen floors down to the all-night deli enough times to keep us fuelled and inspired throughout the whole thing.

Roman's spirit was cheerful and positive, plus he was intelligent and reasonable when discussing which instruments to record and when.

He had a way to ride the gigantic mixing desk like a horse, stretching his tall body all across the sliders and knobs, grooving and moving, and dancing in time with the music. As we worked the thing got better and better, until at 6am it sounded like a dream. However I was so high on caffeine and excitement, and lack of sleep, that by this time I was starting to hear things that were not even there.

I'll never forget the ride back to Brooklyn. Life had become a full-on, burning, American success story, right in front of my eyes. I knew I was *the one*. In my head, I had made it. I was looking down on America from the highest show-biz mountain possible. The feeling was noble and gracious, and I knew that life was going to be OK from now on. We had done our thing and made our mark. I could die happy now. We had come to America for this, and now it was in the bag.

Back at Jean's apartment I slept like a log.

However after a few days, we crashed down into a new, sobering reality. I now understood that, although the record did sound like a hit, we would need intensive promotion to sell this thing. And one thing disturbed me. How to survive financially? How would we even stay alive? How would we eat?

But then a further miracle occurred. News of my keyboard playing had travelled fast around the local gang of record producers. The phone started ringing continuously. I was being offered recording sessions by many new producers. For several weeks I then trailed into Manhattan, carrying the keyboard wrapped in bubble wrap to prevent it being stolen in Flatbush.

Each studio I recorded at was more luxurious than the last. Big names were working in these places. You could read all the details on the wall calendar. For a while I understood the thrill of success. The money began to pour in. It was a powerful feeling.

Yet one week later Jean told us we could not stay in her place any more. A new fear gripped my heart. Where would we go? The session work had not yet paid enough for a down-payment on an apartment.

"There's always the basement," she pointed out. "Talk to the super. Hand him a dollar or so. He'll let you stay."

We knew the super by now, a wiry, tough Colombian.

He took us straight downstairs. Then unlocked a massive room, hot, filthy and dark, with massive engines pumping away in the gloom.

"You'll survive," he said. "Fifty dollars. For the month."

As he handed us the key and closed the door Marina and I looked at each other.

"I don't know," she said uncertainly. "Maybe just for a while?"

Within a few days an entire family had moved into a tiny room just down the hall. They were all dealing hard drugs, even the nine year old child. They were black, and the child had one eye that was not working.

Our mood soon deteriorated to total depression. Roaches were everywhere. There was filth and human waste all over the bathroom floor.

Every morning, after waking, we would have to catch the D train into Manhattan and find a cafe, just to feel human. The alternative was to become a mental casualty.

The only ways in and out of our basement was either the freight elevator, or a side door to the street. Both of these were controlled by the super. Sometimes locks worked and the elevator could get you to the basement. But other times nothing worked and we were stuck, either inside, or outside the building. There were nights where we could not get back in at all. The super was a heavy sleeper and only rarely heard you call.

Many months passed. Marina and I were arguing intensely now, mainly over money. The heat in the basement, combined with the filth and the roaches, made us both crazy. Often in the evening we would be crouched on opposite sides of the enormous dark basement room, holding our head in our hands, sobbing, or just slumped in the depths of depression.

One morning Marina snapped.

"OK, enough," she shouted, kicking a chair upside down. "We're getting out. Come on, pack your bags."

We ended up in a cheap hotel in the East Village. It was an insane, desperate move. Our last cash reserves were being burned out.

The following night as the sun started to go down, we were washed up on the sidewalk, at an intersection in Alphabet City. It was getting colder. Knowing I'd have to sleep outside, I bought a beer and drank it down.

Now I was terrified. I understood that this was the way to go crazy. I knew what would happen. Your mind would start to go, bit by bit. Someone would rob us as we slept. There were thieves and hustlers everywhere. I prayed. It was a horrific moment.

It was getting darker. Marina was jumping around, talking to people, asking if they knew any place we could sleep, a shelter or whatever. Also we'd heard there was a squat somewhere close by.

Now I saw a guy smile at her. After a long moment she turned and beckoned to me. As in a dream, I saw they were already tight together, discussing something. He had a leg that didn't work properly.

"He says we can crash with him," Marina sang out.

"Thank you," I stammered. I was overcome with emotion. "I'm Max," I told him. "We're musicians."

By now I was taking in his rugged brown latino features. There was a scar above his left eye, and a dark handkerchief tied loosely around his head.

"My name's Pedro," he said. "I'm a heroin dealer," he added, grinning broadly.

"That's fine," I told him. "We all gotta do

what we gotta do." Marina chuckled wickedly.

"C'mon," he said. "It's getting cold." As we set off as I saw that he limped.

We walked rapidly towards the place. It was two blocks east. There was a fierce joy in my heart. Pedro was a saint, I was sure of this. He had saved our lives. What did I care how he earned his money? I blessed him in my mind.

"Here it is," he said, as we crossed the last intersection. We had arrived at a building surrounded by an extra wooden wall, with a special door covered in chains and padlocks. Pedro spent a long time unlocking all this, and finally we moved through, and then he unlocked the inner door. Once inside he lead us through gloom and shadows and then up three flights of steps. It was mainly dark except for an occasional naked light bulb hanging from the ceiling, here and there. A few figures passed us on the stairs. One of them was smiling. The desolation was so extreme that it was almost comical.

Now Pedro halted.

"You sleep here," he commanded, pointing a finger at a wicker basket crib in the centre of the landing.

"This is my room," he explained, as he unlocked another door. "Nobody comes in here." We said goodnight, thanking him.

Marina looked at me.

"Well, it's something," she said.

"It's better than where we were," I muttered.

"Let's try it out," she said. "For a while we

experimented. It was hard to make our arms and legs fit together in such a tight little basket, but in the end we found a position that worked.

"Now, nobody move," she said. I was so relieved to have been saved from the street that pretty soon I did fall asleep. But then whenever Marina moved I would wake, and have to find a way to fit again. It went on like this for a few hours.

Then suddenly I woke. It was deepest night. Absolute silence. The air was dry and thick. My skin was crawling.

Then I realized that somebody was with us. I opened my eyes a fraction. A figure was creeping up the stairs and had entered the landing. He was hunched and had one hand held out in front of his face.

"F***," he said. Now I understood that Pedro had opened his door and was advancing on the intruder through the darkness.

"Dime bag," said Pedro, shaking an object at him.

"F*** off!"

"Dime bag?"

Now the two figures repeatedly cursed and swore at each other. They had moved closer and closer all this time, and had reached the two sides of the basket in which we slept. At this point the obscenities increased and a forest of arms flew out, almost grappling with each other over our heads.

Marina squeezed my arm slightly. I closed my eyes. The two carried on their struggle for another minute, then the unknown figure slowly retreated down the stairs, still spitting venom as he disappeared. Gradually I nodded off to sleep again.

In the morning I could hardly move. With an effort we managed to climb downstairs and then wait for someone to let us out.

Across the street there was a place to get a bagel and coffee. I started to come back to life.

The following night was a little worse, with more junkies prowling all around us as we slept.

The next morning I heard two men talking on the floor below. All at once I made out the sound of a British accent. Racing downstairs I introduced and introduced myself to a rough, bearded guy wearing a flak jacket.

"Excuse me?" I started out.

"Well what do we have here? Another Brit is it?" he chortled. "Fancy that!" There was a fantastic blend of welcome and sarcasm in his voice.

"Yes, I know," I said. "What a place to meet, eh?"

Within minutes I had ascertained that he was a fire-eater by profession. Then came the golden discovery.

"You sleep where?" he shouted. There was an incredulous glint in his blue eyes. "Up there, in that old place? On the landing? Why, that's where all the junkies do their deals and shoot up all night! My, oh my. Look, it isn't much, but I can offer you my room." I almost wept as he told me this. By now Marina was by my side, jumping from foot to foot in ecstasy. He pushed open his door.

"There's not much here. It's very rough," he exclaimed. "But if you want it, then you can sleep here for a week. I'm going away on business."

"Fire-eating business?" I asked.

"Yes, that's right." We all chuckled together at this odd little notion. He patted the bed. It was rough and dirty but to me it looked as good as anything I might find. We hugged him.

We walked out together. It was a fabulous, sunny morning, with all the hope and good intention that New York mornings are famous for. My heart was singing.

At the intersection, the fire-eater suddenly reached down and hugged a huge, washed up, homeless man who was sitting surrounded by black plastic rubbish bags, various filthy objects and clothes.

The big man grinned wearily as the fire-eater stood up, then suddenly rolled to one side and vomited. Then he sat back up again.

"Sorry guys," he said, with a quizzical expression. "But that's how I start my day."

We walked on.

When the fire-eater finally returned from his trip we moved into a dead-end hotel in the Times Square area. It was expensive and as such, an insane, illogical move. I think our minds had gone. It was painfully obvious that what tiny cash reserves we had left would soon be squandered.

Every moment I took the elevator up to our room on the fourteenth floor I would witness an African woman loading a supermarket trolley packed with black plastic rubbish bags containing all the little African curios they were selling outside on the sidewalk around 42nd street. I could make little sense of it all. Hotels were not like this in England.

When at last we found a duo gig in the area, the Turkish owner would only give us one night a week, Saturday. But the money from this was only enough to pay one night in the hotel. Financial disaster was looming. It was at this point that I began to chant mantras and meditate, and remember to do the yoga exercises I had learned in the past. The fear was a desperate, binding thing. I knew we were finished, and as the sun went down over the skyscrapers each night I prayed to whatever higher power might exist, desperately hoping that this would somehow save us. I could see how fast we were running dry of cash. There was no escaping from the fact that we were going down, and fast.

After a few more days and nights of acute tension, and anguished chain-smoking, we found a cheaper hotel in Chelsea. The dog had to be chained outside the hotel on the sidewalk, all day long. At night, against the rules, Marina would whisper in his ear to be quiet as a mouse, and then she would sneak him into our room when no-one was looking. The dog understood perfectly and there was a certain sweetness to see him instantly curl up on the warm carpeted floor under the desk, and not move an inch until the morning.

Yet the pressure never let up for a second. One afternoon I was returning to the hotel room with a bottle of milk, and suddenly there was a man screaming with rage. I looked up to see that one man had raced up to another car which was waiting at the lights, and he was holding a gun to the driver's head and screaming something so fast I could not understand the words. Then suddenly he jumped back into his car and raced away.

By now I had become fairly detached about the street violence that went on around us. There would be calm days where life looked almost normal, and then for some reason something would snap and there would be a scene. Passersby wouldn't hang around too much when the violence occurred. Police went around in groups, often not even wishing to get involved. We discussed this sometimes.

"There are people here who will kill you for 10 dollars," Marina told me one night, as we were getting ready to sleep.

"Yeah, crackheads and maniacs," I agreed.

It was soon established that if some desperate, suicidal junkie attacked, it was better to hand over 5 or 10 bucks, and stay alive. Why fight with someone so low? It made no sense.

After a few weeks more I bought the paper and showed Marina apartments to rent in Harlem at a really low price.

"I know Harlem," she whined. "It's not what

you think. You're gonna go down low there, Max. Forget the romantic legend. I don't want to live there." I didn't understand this mysterious, garbled story of hers. Go down low? How could I ever go more low than I already was? What was this sinister side of Harlem she was so scared of?

So I kept quiet for a few more days, then one morning I checked my bank account and told Marina we would be out on the street really soon if something didn't change extremely fast. By now I was exhausted, and deadly serious. Finally she consented.

The place was a basement apartment on 148th street, close to Broadway. The landlord was an elderly black man, called Mr Carter. Once inside his apartment he took a good look at us, and made a few jovial comments as I handed over the money.

"What did you say you were?" he asked. "Jazz musicians?" I told him yes. "So get on the piano! Give me a tune! Sing me a song!"

It was all suddenly so intimate that I now felt a little self-conscious. With mixed feelings I sat down at the grand piano.

"St Louis blues," Marina whispered to me. I rolled into the introduction, knowing that I never really played this one right. As she sang the first verse in her high, little girl voice, Mr Carter's ancient eyes narrowed with pleasure and he rocked a little harder in his rocking chair.

"That's really something. Ain't that something," was all he would say.

Later, as we crunched out along the gravel drive outside his house, I finally understood one thing. That song had been written just around the time he was born. We had chosen the right one for him.

That night I felt calm, proud and with my feet finally on the ground. With my own Harlem apartment I was walking tall.

Now I knew myself to be on the level, up there with all my grand parade of jazz and blues heroes from the past. Even Marina appeared satisfied. We immediately made friends with the old black lady who lived upstairs, whose room was packed with fabrics and materials, lace and calico and suchlike. She liked the sound of our music too.

"You're in the right place," she observed, dryly. "Welcome to Harlem."

However the easy Harlem life I dreamed of was not to be. What happened next was the very worst thing I could ever have imagined.

An army of every kind of insect now descended from the walls, the floor, the garden and the air. I had never known that fleas, ants and roaches could all attack at the same time, with such a ferocious intensity.

The first night we never slept. I scratched and scratched at my arms, legs, head, neck and back. Soon there were bloody areas of skin everywhere. We drugged ourselves with painkillers, but could not stop the agony.

Grudgingly I admitted that Marina had been

right about Harlem. She had correctly predicted trouble, and now here we were, deeply in it.

In the morning I raced for the pharmacy and bought all kinds of powders and tablets to decimate the insects. I also set off bombs, cannisters that sprayed out toxic gases. Nothing worked. The insects left, then immediately returned.

"They're immune," Marina told me incredulously one morning, after yet another sleepless night. "The insects are winning. These chemicals can't get to them any more."

"But they're getting to me," I howled. "You know I'm always allergic to everything!" It was true. I was a medical case by now. Yet we were trapped. There was no question of leaving. We would have to learn to live with the insects. There was no other choice.

JAZZLANDS

It was 9am. The dawn was a majestic explosion of blue and scarlet. Jet airliners hurtled down through distant cloud banks and then queued up, mid-air, for the JFK and Newark airports. The helicopters were out, police and tourist, buzzing the sky, while on the ground the city was coming to life. Beneath the earth a mournful blue train, loaded with yawning commuters, rolled into Grand Station.

Cars streamed across the Brooklyn bridge into Manhattan. On Park Avenue, the hotels were busying themselves for the day. A flock of gulls passed the 93rd floor of the Empire State building, calling out with raucous cries. Down inside the TV studios at Rockefeller Plaza, computer monitors flicked on, while executives prepped themselves with vitamin packs in the luxury bathrooms. An enormous liner at the sea-port was pulling anchor and blasting her foghorn.

All across the tri-state area, housewives cleared breakfast tables as their husbands scrambled into vehicles, groggy from stress, junk food and too many late nights. In Tribeca, established fashion executives and film operatives munched healthy sandwiches and checked electronic agendas.

In the West Village, the cleaners were filling bagfuls of trash from the previous night's revels. In the Lower East Side, store-owners were raising their metal shutters with a crash.

Up in Harlem, two cops had twelve latinos with their hands against the wall, and were patting them down, searching for drugs and weapons.

I awoke cursing. My arms and legs were covered with bloody scabs. But I was used to this by now. I got up, made coffee, did some work on the accounts, then started to practice piano. Then I opened the sliding door and looked outside, past the long, wild grass of the garden. I could hear a few kids playing not far away. The sky was blue and there was a fresh wind. I knew it would be many hours before Marina woke.

During the next few weeks we grabbed every duo gig we could get, but I found them almost impossible to play, since I was half-poisoned by the various chemicals we had used against the insect attacks. I had become a pitiful wreck of a man, desperately hoping for any other option, any way to get out of this horrific death trap of an apartment.

Things were so desperate that at one stage we headed down to the East Village and kissed the brick wall of the house of a world famous jazz saxophone player in the blind hope that this might bring us the luck we so badly needed. But nothing did change, at least for a while, and many days later I laughed savagely at how superstitious I had become.

As for our career, the struggle for survival was so intense that it was hard for me to know if we were really getting anywhere. This was the town where you were supposed to make a million, but the bitter reality was that most musicians I knew were scrabbling around for dollars and dimes every second. All else was fast being blanked out.

Everything and everyone was for sale. After a year and a half of desperate hustling for cash, gigging, making hats and selling them in the East Village, then taxi-driving, and finally being thrown down to the level of having to collect used cans and bottles from the sidewalk, in the manner of a homeless tramp, I made a courageous, yet financially dangerous career move. The idea was to start a music club.

In the midst of all this grinding poverty, a substantial cheque had just arrived in the mail, a late insurance payout from England. Our plans now took shape fast.

I had a distant relative living in Boston and soon we pinned her down on the phone. We needed someone who was a US citizen to sign the lease, so that all the legal stuff would go through her name. I'd seen this procedure happening all around. The relative agreed and soon she had travelled into the city, and we'd met the landlord, signed the paper, and I'd slapped down a hefty deposit on a cafe lease.

It was a place in Ludlow Street, just below Delancey, in the lower east side of Manhattan, a dream spot for jazz musicians, but a nightmarish address for everyone else. We were bang next to the poverty of Chinatown, with their dreaded "Tong' mafia, and right opposite our front door was a needle exchange where heroin junkies would slink in and out all night.

But it was a jazz club, and, what's more, it was totally ours.

Two big rooms, front and back. A big glass window so that passersby on the street could see inside. A yard at the back and a basement below for storage. We would sleep in the rear room. The rent was $700 a month. This was the standard price for an apartment at the time. To get a club or cafe for that low figure was a fabulous deal. They could easily be five or ten times as much, even in this miserable area.

To celebrate we made a huge sign saying 'JAZZLANDS' and fixed it in the window. It took three weeks to tidy up and repaint the place. We built a low stage for the music performances.

Finally we opened for business. The plan was to sell pastries and coffee, plus small, easy meals like eggs on toast. Almost immediately the daytime cafe business failed. However by this time we were rehearsing our band in the back room, and locals started to poke their nose inside the door curiously. Word started to spread like wildfire.

And now an enormous procession of musicians and bands began requesting bookings. In the beginning we took everyone who asked. One by one they trooped in, delivering rather nondescript or lack-luster performances to an almost empty house. Yet we cheered them on, and gradually people began to buy and consume tiny little snacks, a biscuit or two, or a soda for example. Pretty soon, new musicians appeared, and performed and they were good.

Then a few more arrived, and these were excellent.

The whole thing started to take off. Many nights a week a bunch of black, free-jazz musicians would troop in, usually with beads, dreadlocks and suchlike. They knew all about communism, anarchism and conspiracy theory, and we would lock on to these topics for a while. Then they would get onstage and blast their horns all night, or at least till 3 or 4am. I would be on keyboards, and Marina singing with her microphone. It was fabulous, intuitive, spontaneous music, right from the heart, the real thing, the truly free New York spirit, but rageful too. Then suddenly after midnight there would be wrangling over the pros and cons of communism, and also discussion regarding the massive corruption and imminent collapse of the USA. I noticed that this music, and the rebel anti-politics, had become one and the same thing.

Spring began to move into summer. By now I thought I had seen every possible kind of act. Wearily I hung on, still desperately broke, yet with some kind of a communal, artistic, creative vision, waiting for something or someone to come, someone who was totally outside the box, someone who defied all the logical rules of the music business, someone to believe in, someone to be real friends with.

And now Leo arrived.

One rainy afternoon he walked in with two young kids, all grins and elbows on the counter. We saw eye to eye immediately.

He had long red hair, a beard, an iron physique and a roaring laugh. I stared at him and the kids in wonder.

"What, they play?" I asked. "With you? The blues? Honestly?"

The deal to have them perform at the club was done in a flash, after which the three, much contented, disappeared into the roar of the midday traffic. There had been a knowing smile, a particular, roguish glint in Leo's eye, and then a military cut to the three of them as they filed out all in a silent line, back to the street again.

The kids had been charmed by our animals. By now we had the dog, a cat, and also a pigeon who had damaged a wing and was waiting to heal. All three animals constantly wandered the floor, keeping out of each other's way, never fighting. After the cat and pigeon had been rescued from the street, they had learned the house rules by which Marina kept them in check.

Three days later the Russian family showed up. Leo kept an eye on everything as the kids set up their heavy gear. I offered free drinks. The room was packed with new faces. The club had never been full like this before.

Now it began. It was nothing I had ever heard or seen before. Yet the intensity was overpowering. They were dressed rough, yet colourful, a blend of gypsy and prince, with Leo and Irene in military fatigue pants, and Maya in a long ornate Russian robe. It was a glorious, crazy, carnival of rock.

The children handled their instruments with casual professionalism, occasionally glancing at a parent for musical cues, like starts and ends of numbers. The audience were smiling and tapping their feet, cheering loudly, and then applauding after the solos. The feeling was all about family, and it was infectious. We all sensed that we were part of some kind of a tribe, something vaguely Russian, something different from the idea of family as we knew it. You felt you liked these people, and were being drawn into their wild, free expression, which broke all the rules. There was a sense of something flying. There was no keyboard or guitar, no middle part of the band, and this fact merely increased the sense of dreamlike euphoria, or empty skies, like someone is offering you the whole world, but it has been cleaned out, there is almost nothing there, and in particular, all the pain and the discomfort of your previous world has been washed away. And all the while there was an angelic look to the children, and something devilish about Leo, and also Maya was wearing an expression much like the Madonna in a certain painting that I remembered. So this was almost a religious moment, and yet always with that roguish glint in Leo's eyes, or the mischievous glances from the choir boy face of Serge.

I scanned the faces of the audience. They were evidently enjoying their own sense of confusion. I felt good about all this. In particular, financially desperate as I was, I was also very relieved to see how many sodas and pastries they were buying. All in all, it was turning into a wonderful evening.

And then it was over. I fixed up some music to play through the house system, and then the kids, flushed with satisfaction, marched through to the counter in the front room, immediately badgering me with requests for various confectionery. Then came the questions. There was plenty they wanted to know.

How long had I had this place? Would I jam with them? What was England like? I asked them how their lives were going, and what did they think of this constant gigging? They told me they liked it, that it was fun, but Serge said it got tiring sometimes, and occasionally he got sleepy but that was all.

By this time Leo had strolled through.

"Great gig, anyway," I told him. "You filled the place more than any other band we've had here." It was true. They'd made good money for the club and we now split it according to what had been agreed. The kids were packing up their gear, looking weary but satisfied.

Leo and I returned to the stage.

"We can do good things together," he told me, as he began to dismantle their sound system. "I like this place," he added.

"But where are you really from," I asked.

"Odessa," he told me, searching my face for a reaction. "Then later it was St Petersburg," he added. But I felt something good straight away. My parents had been communists for many years. They had met each other at Cambridge university in the 30s, and half the college had been communist at that time. So there was common ground here.

I looked at this strange man, who right now was running a hand through his beard in a thoughtful, quizzical way.

"But did you grow up in Russia in the communist years," I asked?

"Yes I did," he replied. And that was it. I told him I was fascinated by that, and wanted to hear all about it.

He began to explain how he had played many gigs, but that on many occasions they had to be undercover, because the authorities were not allowing such music. This opened my eyes. I was surprised he'd dared to challenge the authorities in this way.

We lit cigarettes and sat down at a table close to the wall. He was flushed and triumphant with the thrill of the successful performance. I looked him up and down with admiration. In front of me I saw a man who was clearly on the same path in life as myself, and made from the same stuff too. A curious blend of gypsy and aristocrat, artist and scientist, a symphony of opposites. His eyes were warm and friendly, and yet they bored into mine with an almost medical precision. His long red hair and beard were all-dervisher. I had seen him operate the sound equipment with the expert hands of an engineer, and yet I knew without being told that Leo, with his hypnotic stare, was a visionary from another dimension, a twilight land of strange beings and mystical, arcane forces, untouched by wanderers from the west. He sensed all that I was thinking and his mouth teased into a grin of recognition. I shook myself awake.

"You played actual blues and rock gigs, in Russia, at the communist time?" I asked. He nodded emphatically, shaking his enormous beard to emphasise the point.

"It was not easy," he admitted. "If you played blues, that was seen as freedom music by the KGB. It was a threat to them. As soon as there was a big gig, it got very dangerous." I nodded sympathetically.

"We were being watched," he continued. "A close friend of mine was shot dead. He was at film school with me and he was out one day filming a demonstration. It was the time of the big change. So I told Maya to go to New York, with the children, and then I followed a few months later."

It was getting late. Outside cars, taxis and cyclists careened around. The club was full, but people were beginning to filter outside slowly. I poured Leo another beer.

We talked on. He spoke of the strangest things, Vikings and Indian philosophy, and the gypsy folk of the Ural mountains, and shamans too. Then how he had played, as a child, in deserted lots with other kids, finding guns and grenades from WW2, and firing them off at imaginary enemies. As he talked, he rolled his eyes and drew pictures with his hands in the air, and I was struck by his sense of old world honesty and obvious sincerity, things which were largely missing in this new American jungle I had landed in.

"You fascinate me," I said. "Here in the west we had an idea of Soviet Russia, you know, long grey streets with faceless people, and always the threat of jail if you said the wrong word?" But he said this was nonsense.

"That's not it," he told me, shaking his long red hair. "Life was colourful. Things were happening. You know, we had rock concerts going on in Soviet Russia. You would see a long line of western journalists standing there at the edge. One of them would phone his editor and tell the story, and the editor would say that he could not sell that story because no-one would believe it."

The waitress brought us tiny cups of coffee, giggling at the sight of Leo's wild hair and grizzled face.

"So news is news only if it can be sold?" I asked, mouth open with disbelief. This was a new concept to me.

"Exactly," he replied. We both smirked. Now I felt we were getting somewhere, bonding on the uncomfortable and frightening reality of modern life in America. Suddenly I was viewing the place through Russian eyes, and found this refreshing.

In the backroom a few people had started dancing, and the dog was barking with excitement.

"They are lying here, aren't they?" I agreed.

"Everything is for sale," he confirmed. "It is the land of Mickey Mouse."

Now Serge joined us. He put one foot on the stage and stared at me.

"I like playing here," he told me. "Can I have some more chips?" he begged Leo with a cute expression.

"No, you've had enough. We're leaving anyway," Leo barked.

"Oh, please?" Serge whined.

"OK," Leo said. "But no more after that." His son scurried back to the counter.

As I watched Irene and Serge pack up their bass and drums I wondered if they really understood how very different their lives were from other children. Born in Russia, and now touring America playing gypsy rock and blues at the ages of ten and eleven? What on earth would they turn out to be? I'd never known a family like this before. I shrugged and walked away.

It was well past their bedtime. Maya, the mother, gave me a weary smile as she lugged some instruments out into the night. I knew I had to find out more about these people, and I hoped also to play music with them.

Having lost my ex-wife and house in a bad divorce in London many years before, it felt good to be making friends with this strangely mysterious family. They had a way to be very open, simple and generous, in the Russian style, and I appreciated that.

New York is normally an ice-cold world. Nobody gives an inch. There are hardly any true friends, and very little love, or trust from anyone. You see only the money. People get wounded by this process, but try to pretend it's not happening.

Right now I sensed that this meeting today meant something special. I knew I was close to total burn-out in this city, but finding these people had made a difference. Now I knew I could carry on a while longer. They had given me that extra strength.

"Maybe I could come and visit you in a week or so?" I asked Leo finally. "I want to hear more about Russia, and also we should talk about press and media, and stuff. You are the best outfit I've ever had here."

"Thank you," he said. "Of course. You're welcome to visit any time." At that, we said good-night.

That night I fell into a restless half-sleep. And as I tossed and turned, I dreamed a man with red hair and a beard playing a harmonica, leading all the rats out of the city. Was this Leo? Was he the Pied Piper, returning finally to clean up New York City?

THE LITTLE BOY

It is several years earlier. An eight year old boy has received a drum kit for his birthday. He sits down and plays, on and on. He is so small that we can hardly see him behind the kit. But the pounding rhythms are full and strong, the drum-rolls rich, powerful and true, sophisticated polyrhythms played with all the panache and expertise of an adult.

Serge doesn't smile. He never looks at his mother and father, who glance at him occasionally as they move around the faded, East New York apartment. The minute hand of the small clock on the shelf gradually completes a complete circle. Finally the boy looks up from the drum kit, and lays down his sticks proudly.

The mother tells the father that it's time for her to leave for the subway. They will be playing as usual, performing for tips, in the busiest possible location. She calls to the daughter to get ready and to pack her tambourine while she herself checks her trumpet, then slides it into a bag.

The son complains. It's his birthday, he reminds his mother. He wants to come. He wishes to play the subway. He has never ever done this, whereas his mother and elder sister do it every day.

The mother tells him no. She has a hundred

reasons why. She knows her son is wild and fear-less, and will make trouble and get into trouble. The family understand only too well the danger of the New York subway. All of life is there. Not only com-muters and regular people, but also the worst types, desperate hustlers, addicts, thieves, con-men, people you don't want to know or to have your children ever meet.

But the son persists. He has a strong argu-ment. He knows he is already good at the drums. He wants to get at that crowd. He'd heard how huge the crowd can get down there. He knows his drums will be loud, far louder than any tambourine. He wants to help his mother. He remembers how much the family needs money. He presents all these arguments.

The mother is wavering. She starts to see some truth in his argument.

Gradually the son finds the weak point open-ing up, and cunningly and expertly he drives in his final argument.

The birthday! His birthday! The birthday gift that cannot, that must not be refused. He demands the birthday subway gig!

The father is smiling now. The mother looks at the father. The son makes a pitiful face, pleading for his life, but with big eyes and a tiny smile.

The mother knows her son is growing up. Fi-nally she relents. He hugs her. The father laughs out loud, but tells him to be good. He promises. The little girl has a quizzical look. She's happy for her brother.

They head down into town. Soon they have

found the spot. It's busier than usual. A large crowd appears instantly.

The son knows what to do. Quietly, scientifically, he sets up his drum kit. The band begins. It's loud and furious. The people are entranced. The mother goes from number to number. Sometimes it's just free improvisation. The crowd love it all. The son never tires. The sound of the drums booms and thunders and echoes, like a vast roaring tide of primal joy, all the way along the many tunnels and corridors of the New York subway.

Serge is now almost a man. Nothing can stop him. He has learned his power. Nobody will ever be able to take that away from him.

It's over. The family pack up. Not much is said, but as they ride the train home, their hearts are overflowing with happiness, and they have the satisfaction of having achieved something worthwhile, in the face of danger. And they have done it together, as a family.

New York - 1995

For the next few days as I went about my business, this meeting with Leo constantly came back to me. It was the strangest feeling to be friends with a Russian family. Who were these people? What kind of hell had they been through? I had to know more.

The fear of the USSR, in Britain, had been enormous, all my life. The newspapers and TV had talked of dark, secretive, brutal goings on, and above all, a totally alien mindscape. The threat of nuclear attack had been constantly with us. There was a continuing psychosis and horror of everything and everyone Russian.

However my parents, being socialists, had been less extreme in this way. But the main point was that almost no information about actual life in Soviet Russia had ever reached Britain. It was a dark, sinister wall and we could not possibly imagine what lay behind, and whether Russian people were merely programmed zombies, or in any way recognisable as the kind of people that we might understand or be friends with.

Meeting Brother Kharma had vastly increased my sense of confusion, but this was also something pleasurable. I'd once heard someone say the words 'a problem is a gift.' I knew I would have a lot of fun figuring exactly who these people were. Right now they looked unreal, like people in a film, or a legend. Almost angelic. From another time, for sure. A better world, perhaps?

And what was this *Kharma* word in the name of the band? I remembered that it was something to do with Buddhism, and possibly reincarnation also, but that was all.

I also knew that life, for me, in New York, had reached some kind of breaking point, that I was not really born for such a mad, crazy, rat-race, and that deep down I was waiting for something to happen. Could Brother Kharma be that thing? While watching the band perform I had been reminded of certain pictures of Indian gods and goddesses, but also Vikings, a curious mixture.

Certainly Leo had appeared to be not of this world, or from our time, but more like a whirling dervisher, a chaotic, transcendent presence, forcing us all into another reality, whether we liked it or not.

I also knew that he had an enigmatic attitude to money and success. Could it be that he did not want any of these things? I began to see that where he was going was a different path entirely. And within all of their inexplicable behaviour, eccentricity and madness, Brother Kharma appeared to be beckoning, daring me to enter their wonderful exotic land of gods and devils.

I didn't need much pushing. I was finished with the material world. Things were simply too savage by now. I was on the run from drug addiction, a bad divorce where I had lost a fortune, and then, under Marina's questionable guidance, too many years of begging in the streets, rubbing elbows with famous musicians for sure, but always desperate, semi-homeless, prowling around the club circuit in countless European cities, never losing the dream, but at the same time becoming bitter and fatigued by the new reality where businessmen used machines to make music, and musicians earned almost nothing as a result. My soul was aching and I was half ready to quit.

I longed for a monk's cell in the mountains, some ancient books of wisdom, and a chance to slow down and feel the essence of the world.

Also, deep within my troubled soul was a need to believe that this Russian family were channeling something sacred. Kharma, reincarnation, spirituality, all these ideas were like manna from heaven for me. I was fully ready to enter this alternative dimension.

Brother Kharma looked like something outside normal reality. Why not believe that they were? The thing was fixed in my mind. Something precious had arrived for me, in this sad, lonely city, and I was not about to let it go. From now on I would always carry a little part of the *Kharma* essence everywhere I went. I took much comfort from the fact that my new friends would always be around, to reassure, to comfort and to guide me.

In particular, I would occasionally hear Irene's or Kira's voice whispering across the subway tracks as I waited for the train. Occasionally I could make out what they were saying, but sometimes it would just be a dull murmur at the edge of my mind.

I no longer felt so alone.

Marina soon learned that I had made friends with the Russian family. This was not at all to her liking.

"Lousy tramps," she raved at me, one evening, when I was washing dishes at Jazzlands.

"I don't want you visiting them again," she continued, fixing me with an angry eye. "Who do they think they are? They have no talent! And that

Leo, he's vulgar and crude. He may be dangerous. Just stay away from him, if you know what's good for you!"

I fobbed her off with a few idle words. What did she know about anything? And who was she to tell me what to do, or who to be friends with? Yet she had been trying to do that for years.

She was a manipulator, that was for sure, I now understood. However, at the same time, she also had a good side, which was why I stayed with her.

It was hard to make sense of who Marina truly was.

Still fairly young, and quite pretty, she had a lithe way to move her tiny body around, and was hyper-active, and also a workaholic, like myself. She always appeared to know the scene, even before arriving. She dressed, walked, and danced attractively. Supremely fashionable, she often donned a slinky leopard-skin top, camouflage jungle pants and brightly coloured sneakers. This raised eyebrows.

I never minded that she was eleven years older. Always with a jaggedly convincing rap and patter, she knew the entire world of culture forwards and backwards, and spoke at least five languages with ease.

However soon after meeting Marina I had discovered that she possessed a wild gypsy streak, meaning that she could never remain too long in one place. Many times we'd suddenly jumped on a plane to another land with no money at all to speak of. But she had always hustled her way through somehow.

After the inevitable shock treatment, I usually ended up enjoying the entire process, and felt proud to have survived the ordeal, yet also knew I could not match up to her level of 'front' and 'blag', or 'bottle', as they would say in England.

I'd been attracted to the tomboy in her, right from the start. She was without fear, in all situations. It was like being married to a pit bull. I'd seen her arguing with club security men, and even mafia figures, and get away with it. And when she sang a blues number, she had one hell of a chainsaw sound.

So right now I pretended to comply, but secretly ignored her usual, manic rant.

However my head hurt from this latest onslaught. Right now I needed to get outside into the fresh air, and walk a few blocks. That's what you did in New York, when your head was jammed with bad stuff, you would simply escape outside and walk for a while. The non-stop action and energy in the street had the power to wash most of the pain and confusion away.

Right now I wandered up to Houston Street, then headed into Alphabet City. On my right, just next to a deli, a guy with a mohawk was surrounded by a mound of boxes and bags on the sidewalk. Having just been evicted he was arguing with a yellow cab driver who was refusing him.

"Are you crazy?" the cabbie shouted. "I ain't putting no fridge in my cab and that's it." I walked on through the late afternoon haze, watching gorgeous violet clouds strafing the highest edges of the high rises.

Where to go? Too late for the central library, or the music stores. I bought an energy pack, vitamin pills, and various extra stimulants, flushed it down with a bottle of water, lit up, and continued on my way.

A beautiful black girl in a bikini was at the lights, hustling drivers for sex work. A couple of cars were hooting or shouting compliments.

I walked on. The sound of hip-hop percolated out from a convenience corner at Third and Second Avenues. A few bikers roared by. An elderly Jewish lady gaped at them from behind her elegant parasol, then nearly dropped her large paper bag of groceries.

"Hey Max!" I looked up. It was an old friend, a wiry session drummer called Bill. It was great to see him. I knew he was one of the best. We punched fists.

"What are you up to? What's happening?" he demanded.

His rugged jaw was clenched tight in a welcome smile. There were people carrying gear into a club all around him.

"Are you playing here?" I asked.

"Yeah, but later," he replied casually.

"I guess you're too busy to talk?" I queried.

"Not at all, cob," he said, pulling a sturdy, brown leather jacket closer around his neck. "My guy over there is setting up my gear." I was impressed. He had a roadie. It was years since I'd had a band with a road crew.

Now he drew me over to the side, patting my back.

"Max, my man! Are you still with that woman?" He scowled. I knew what Bill meant by this. He had not got on with Marina. She had mis-hit badly with him, and didn't even regret it, not knowing that he was one of the best drummers in New York.

"Yes, I am," I said. "But to be honest, things are not looking good for us." He smiled in a big-hearted way.

"I've been through it," he said. "It's not easy." He had always been quick to the point like this. We moved on to other things. I started to tell him about the Russian family.

"Them?" he asked, in much surprise. "You play with them? I'm teaching those kids. They're really something." We stare at each other in delight.

"Irene," I say. He nods violently.

"That girl," he exclaims. "She's just so pretty," he groaned. I took a step backwards.

"And she's only twelve," I agreed. "More than pretty, she's totally beautiful," I reminded him. "Her eyes are almond-shaped, did you notice?"

"Yeah, I've been teaching them a bit," he repeated. There was a pregnant pause. To our left the roadies continued to wheel amplifiers and drums on trolleys into the club.

"Everyone I know has fallen in love with Irene!" he yelped.

"I know. What is it exactly?" I asked.

"It's everything," he said. "We're all in pain when we're jamming with her, or being close to her, or even thinking of her."

It was true. I knew what he meant. It wasn't just admiration, love, or desire, when you were close to Irene. It was something so big, that you couldn't think about anything else. It was almost as though she were some kind of goddess. But she was just a child. So you just had to shut up, and forget it.

"And she's only twelve," I reminded him, slapping a mosquito off my wrist.

"I know," he moaned. "It's awful."

"What's coming later?" I asked. "What about when she really grows up to be a woman? What then?"

"She shouldn't be allowed to walk the streets," he decided.

"And you're playing with the band?" he wanted to know. "Trying to," I said. "But I have to do other sessions too."

Who was Irene, I wondered, suddenly awe-struck? It wasn't just beauty. Not just physical, either. I remembered how she would appear to me as a presence sometimes, caring for me, keeping me on the path, helping me do everything the right way. I would even dream of her sometimes. She was something innocent in a world of dirt. Like a guiding light.

Then all of a sudden he became serious.

"Listen, Max," he said. "You know, it may not be good for her music, the fact that she's that pretty," he added.

"What do you mean?" I spluttered. "She's out there, selling the band! She's helping them by looking good... or am I wrong?"

"Yeah, but just think about it," he continued. "It's always the same thing, always about how she looks, instead of how she sounds, and how she plays. Yes, they book her, and pay her, and the band too, but what is it all really about?"

"But she can truly play," I shouted, getting emotional now.

"Max, my man, calm down! Yes, I know she can play. Serge too. They all can play. And I know the whole family is good looking, not just Irene.

Now he put one hand up against the hard cement wall.

"But what about when they get older?" he continued. "And even now, does she have the inner fire, that unstoppable thing?"

I looked him square in the eyes.

"I say she does," I answered. Then I let him go, since I could hear them calling for him inside.

Later, when it was dark, I returned to check his gig. You didn't want to miss a chance to see Bill play. Tonight it was a smaller club, so I knew I would be able to watch him close up, and study his style.

The band were in the middle of a jazz fusion jam when I returned. I grabbed a seat near the bar, and started watching, concentrating on Bill's drumming.

He was wearing black jeans and T shirt, with

a denim hjacket and a black baseball cap, and from his look you could see that he meant business.

It was quite hot in the club and I needed a drink but it was hard to pay the inflated bar prices.

As the groove eased into higher gear it was a miraculous thing to see him in action. His boxer's rugged form was 'all in one piece' as the Italians say. The beat was absolutely solid, tight, dependable and in the pocket. His tom tom rolls were fluid and crystal clear.

Watched so closely as I did made me understand one thing for the first time about him, and also about drumming in general. Bill's greatness was all about what he was not doing, rather than what he was doing. There was none of that verbose, busy, show-off stuff that too many drummers fall victim to. It was all just crucial, essential, solid playing, yet with an intention and conviction that you could not miss. He was playing less deliberately so that the other players could sound their greatest.

He had authority, in his delivery. The drum-set was never too loud, which is the huge problem that besets most drummers all their lives, often without them even knowing it. He had everything a band needs from a drummer. And now a question formed in my mind. Had that enormous power, dexterity and control come partially from his boxing years maybe? And was it also something to do with his cockney London roots? I felt proud to be a Londoner, as I watched him. It was obvious he could outplay anyone in the business. Suddenly I wished I was cockney too. There was no-one like Bill. I'd played so many incredible gigs with him, back in England. And now, today, I was living for the moment I could get to play with him again.

I'd seen enough. There was a huge pain in my heart to be witnessing the great drummer that I had now lost. I knew that it would be too painful to watch any more. I paid my drink and slipped back out into the street.

THE RHYTHM OF LIFE

The rhythm of life was very apparent in New York. Every second I could feel the pulse of the city, beating inside me, and pushing me along. As the days went by, this sensation became stronger, and more urgent.

The mornings could be hard. I would wake to the sounds of sirens, traffic, and even distant screams occasionally.

By this time I was changing. I was no longer the same man I had been back in England. Also, my sense of time was being twisted out of all recognition.

Definition drops away. What's going on? Are we in the present, the future or the past? Or is it all just one moment? Consciousness, and thought, and most of all language, is changing so very rapidly, becoming chaotic and fragmented.

This is an odd moment in my life. New York has turned everything upside down. Nothing is as it was, and everything appears disconnected. Perhaps I am not in my body any more. For a split second I have the sensation to be high in the sky, actually watching myself as I start the day. It is as if my world has suddenly become a theatre, and that I am living on the stage.

Try to focus. It's a bright new morning, and there's a fresh wind off the Atlantic ocean, and the city is pushing you in the small of your back, telling you to wake up, move your ass, get working.

So you go out running across the Williamsburg bridge for exercise. Got to stay fit. Get a grip. Don't become soft and flabby. The city is getting harder and harder. Keep up with the race, or get wiped out, and end up like the derelicts and street people you see sleeping on every corner. Either that or you'll go down low like the desperate immigrants who come begging for the right to sweep and wash the club floors, and don't even want any money. You say you have no money but it's coming. They say OK, they can wait, but they work anyway, hoping desperately to secure some permanent job position. You tell them you may never pay them, that the club may not even make it. They say that's OK, they will work anyway. You love the latinos, and their fabulous, burning, salsa fusion jazz, and wonder if you'll ever play that stuff.

Just to celebrate you stop off at a latino cafe and get more coffee, and hear more salsa pumping, and get yourself a bar stool, then bring out the notebook, and write down things that have to be done at the club.

And now it's Leo's vision that locks in your mind. 'Very simple', is his favourite phrase. And then how will he explain it all? His way to be? His formula? The answer comes back in a flash.

Just work, work and more work, playing the

music. Keep on gigging. Never forget to be yourself. Don't play the cheap, sugary stuff they do here, the cover bands, the show tunes, the recycling of a culture that was already rotten sixty years ago. Trash it all. We don't need that. We do our thing our way.

I almost choked on my drink at this revelation. The juke box shifted to a faster tempo as a huge jet growled over the bridge.

I sat up fast. Leo was right. It was the only way to be, I figured. All at once I was grinning through sunlight and cigarette smoke, as I understood that Leo's way was the only chance to fight the New York demons who were twisting and smashing my soul, and anaesthetizing my mind.

Because what was so impressive was that he obviously had the key. It was so very simple. And now his words were in my mind constantly.

Be yourself. Never give in. Fight to the death. Everything is in the music. Because it's all about the music. The story of who we are. Why we are born. Why we are alive. And what we're here to do. It's got to be our music, and no-one else's.

He had the formula. This was truly something to believe in. Him, a figure who was real, defiant, threatening, taking on all of New York City before breakfast. You had to admire this guy.

I gulped and slushed my coffee, spilling quite a bit, but not caring. Fire was burning through my veins. Then it was back to the club.

At the door the landlord, a short, bald man, saw me bringing a heavy old plank of construction wood into the club.

"Hey, I don't want that thing in my building," he barked. I tensed up, ready to fight, confronting him. We shouted at each other. I was about to lunge at him, but suddenly he went wild and I backed down. Then he demanded his rent. I told him he'd get it later.

Inside the club Marina was on the phone, lining up more bands, booking gigs for our band, searching for a new bassist. She was expert at this.

Now a semi-famous jazz drummer of the old school visited. Delightedly, she brought him inside, and showed him round the place. They talked about old times. They had been friends since many years before.

Right now he was proud of us, and what we'd done, getting this place. I was impressed by his look, black leather from head to foot, including cap and boots. I'd never seen jazz musicians dressed like this back in England.

When he asked who was playing this month, Marina proudly showed him the list of names. Then she begged him to play here, but he told her he could not. At this she persisted, hustling him to come and jam anyway. He told her maybe.

There were a few weeks of incredible heat. Sometimes we drove to Coney Island and laid out a bunch of gadgets on the sidewalk for sale. There were plenty of people doing this. Anything to raise a buck. It was electronic gear, books, records, magazines and cassettes, covering block after block, as far as the eye could see. We arrived home exhausted, having hardly made anything, knowing there were only a few days left before rent day.

Now I discovered that Brother Kharma were booked to play at CBGB's, and immediately phoned a couple of friends.

Kaspar Weintraub, who worked in broadcasting, and also Bill, the drummer.

It wasn't far, so I cycled over.

In his long black leather coat, Kaspar was easy to spot. He had the look of a CIA man with his circular steel-rimmed glasses and attache case. Now I could see Bill there too. In marked contrast to Kaspar, Bill, in his short brown jacket was all muscle and sinew, stocky and alert, ready to kick ass.

As I moved closer Bill turned and punched my hand brutally with a warm cry of recognition..

"Ouch," I said, backing off. "Hey, Bill, I know you're an ex-boxer but go easy, OK?"

The guys chuckled amiably as we strolled towards the club, passing a group of Tibetan monks on the other side of the road. It was getting late and a few cardboard boxes were being blown around in the wind. I kicked one out the way.

Kaspar had a new cell phone and was making calls as we walked. He looked nervous and was twitching his fingers constantly. I watched him enviously. I needed one of those phones so badly, but how to pay for it?

Naturally we began to discuss the Russian family. I remembered that Bill had already hooked up with them, and had been teaching the kids music. But right now Kaspar wanted to know what this family band were all about.

"Just some friends," I remarked, offering him a stick of gum. A husky dog was pulling his owner along beside us, panting with the heat.

"You say they have their kids on bass and drums?" Kaspar probed, straightening out his tie and smoothing back his long blond hair impatiently. "Can they truly play, for real?"

We hustled along, avoiding a drunk, homeless guy, stretched out on the sidewalk, face down. Incredibly, he had a beeper strapped to his hip.

I turned back to answer Kaspar.

"Of course," I told him. "It's a Russian family. They've survived Soviet Russia, KGB threats, poverty, squats, shelters and all kinds of attacks." Bill chuckled, wiping the sweat from his hands onto his tropical shirt and military fatigues below.

"They must be pretty tough by now," he muttered.

"Yeah, but you wouldn't know it when talking to them," I confided. "Listen, they've already played at my club and I got to know them all. They're easy going and gentle.

"Except of course Leo is hard as iron," I continued. "He has to be. They've only got him. He has to protect them, night and day. The mother and the young girl are incredibly beautiful. It's beyond anything you can imagine. Everyone is falling in love with them, all the time. It's not just their looks. There's something deep and mysterious here. Probably because they're Russian, I think. They have something we don't have. Maybe it's to do with innocence and honesty. All the good things, all the stuff we don't have, because we lost them. So obviously Leo has to fight for them night and day.

"Christ," muttered Kaspar. "This is unique. There's a lot of big issues here. It goes very deep. Are they getting any write-ups yet?

"Yeah, and there's something else. You know what I think?"

"What?" He fixed me with his eye.

"They are also gradually being damaged, even destroyed by New York," I complained. "It's the same old story. They're too fresh, too innocent, too different. With them it's all about the family. But families so often get torn apart here. Too much pressure. It's only money that matters."

There were various grunts at this. Bill spat into the gutter.

"So something here is eating them alive, " I continued. "They may not last too long." We walked in silence for a bit. A slight wind rustled my hair.

"Hey, we're all being trashed by this place," muttered Kaspar, staring at the horizon, where smoke was rising and tiny clouds were forming in the east.

"And I'm not getting any younger," he added ruefully, drawing his jacket up around the neck.

As we reached CBGB's I could hear the band had begun. Pretty soon we'd paid our tickets and were making our way inside. The place was almost full. Bill bought a beer. Kaspar offered me a cigarette. All kinds of punks, goths, freaks and oddballs skated around the place. A few people were dancing wildly near the stage. A group of bikers huddled around the bar. The walls were scrawled with graffiti.

Serge was doing a drum solo. We could hardly see him behind the kit but nobody could ignore his huge rolls on the tom-toms, punctuated by cymbal crashes. The bikers seemed to like this, and one waved his arms around, mimicking Serge's attack on his drum kit. Leo and Maya smiled at Serge from opposing sides of the stage.

Suddenly I saw a gang on my left videoing the band. There was a big guy, all in black leather, with long dark hair, oiled and tied in a pigtail. He was filming with a couple of others, and I could see from the expensive and bulky broadcast-quality gear, that he and his friends were part of some hefty media operation. When they paused from filming for a moment, I explained that I'd already booked the band, and wanted to know if this footage was about to be on TV?

"Could be," the guy snorted. "For now it's an independent documentary. We're a set-up from Hollywood."

"You've come from LA?" I asked.

"Sure. To film Brother Kharma and a few

other acts. With any luck this will be edited, sold and aired within a few months."

I told him thanks and his team sprang back into action.

Shouts and a primitive scream told me a small fight had broken out between two wizened old gaffas near the toilet. A large black woman tore them apart. Several latinos in the crowd laughed openly at the skirmish. A guy passed close to where we stood, selling small electronic items, phones, watches and stuff, but I refused.

The drum solo had finished to a deafening applause. At this point Irene began her solo.

"Dammit, the bass is bigger than she is," snorted Kaspar. But I could see he was fascinated. "They're like pixies or leprechauns, those kids," he chuckled.

Irene was dancing around as she soloed.

"It's like a bass has grown legs and is walking," someone snorted.

"They are magical," I whispered... "And just you wait. That walking bass is going to walk all over the world!"

Near the back of the club someone had collapsed, and was being carried out. As she passed I saw to my amazement and horror that it was a young punkette girl, covered with tattoos. She was far too young to be in the club at all.

"The Bowery," said Kaspar despairingly. "They just overdose all the time here. It beats me, why this has to happen."

"This is New York," Bill said. "What do you expect?" For a while we became mesmerised by the music.

"How much do these kids practice?" he wanted to know.

"They never stop," I told him. "But I reckon that they don't call it practice. It's their life. Music never stops for them. They're right in it."

"I guess they're lucky," Bill added, breaking out a new pack of cigarettes. "My old man doesn't think much of me drumming all the time."

"Most parents are like that," I admitted.

"But with Irene and Serge, and the other kids, who knows?" I continued. "Time will tell. Some people think Leo is harming them with all this non-stop gigging. But what's the alternative? They're poor. And they're immigrants, and pretty desperate. I reckon they can get down on their knees and thank God they're alive, and that they have Leo to protect them, and that they have music in their lives.

"Look at the millions of other aliens here," I added, warming to my argument. "Their work is nothing to do with live music. It's just endless factory jobs for them, punching the clock, or working in coffee shops, or construction work. Their entire lives can come and go without them ever knowing about any of this professional music stuff."

"Gotta go to the can," growled Kaspar suddenly.

Now Leo was on the mike, calling for applause for Irene. He needn't have bothered. The

73

whole place lit up as everyone roared their approval. Irene smiled and bowed. At twelve, she already had figured out how to solo on bass effectively. I felt emotional. Maya was smiling as Leo picked up his harmonica and the band blasted into a heavy, rocking blues that lasted fifteen minutes. More people were dancing now.

"These guys are gonna make it," Bill shouted in my ear. "They've got it. I've never seen anything like this before. Kids playing blues? It could be the start of a whole new thing."

I finished my drink and turned and faced him.

"You're right," I replied. "It's a new style. They've broken through. Now we're gonna see kids everywhere, playing blues and rock. Watch out. It's all gonna be different after this."

By now Kaspar was back.

"Christ, this is really something," he hustled. "Max, I need to know more about these guys. Hey, I'm going to grab a pizza. Come on out. I need you to explain who the hell they are." We followed him to the street. The last thing I saw was Leo and Serge doing a wild kind of extended solo together. I'd never heard blues so raw, so earthy and so real. The women appeared to be entranced and some were visibly emotional.

Outside it was raining slightly. I pulled my jacket tighter. In a minute we were a block to the south, ordering pizzas.

A huge black limousine prowled slowly past the glass window as we ate at a table.

"So how long have you known these guys?" Kaspar wanted to know. "That's a very powerful front-man there. Leo, you say his name is?" He took a big bite of the oily pizza slice, and wiped his mouth with a shirt sleeve.

A gypsy woman with her hair tied in a red handkerchief, sidled up to our table. Her baby was tightly wrapped around her chest. With a routine smile she offered a flower for sale. Kaspar waved his arms in despair, telling her no, and she moved on to the next table.

"OK, about Leo, yeah. I first met him a month ago," I informed Kaspar.

"He's wild, that guy," Bill growled. "You know those raging banshees figures?" We nodded with much grinning.

"You gotta love it," he continued. "All red hair and wild beard, he is. God, the energy he's got. To push the whole band along the way he does. Are all Russians like that? He's scaring everyone."

"Yeah, he's tough," I admitted cautiously. "The Russians are made that way, apparently. Can you believe they were our deadly enemies until just a couple of years ago? Thank god the Berlin wall came down, and the cold war ended when it did!"

"Americans are tough too," Kaspar pointed out.

"The British were, but our empire is over," I chipped in. They both guffawed.

"We're your colony," Kaspar joked, with a mischievous glint in his eyes. "You should be proud."

"Yeah, but you threw us out," I complained, only half-joking this time.

"That bass player kid is absolutely ravishingly beautiful," moaned Bill, slamming a fist into the table. A couple on our left looked up in alarm, then continued talking.

"Yeah, and Leo has to protect her nonstop," I told him. "They live in East New York."

"Oh no," groaned Bill. "I couldn't do that." He wiped his brow.

"I know," I said. "I'm lived in Flatbush for a while."

"You were in Flatbush? Why? I couldn't live there," Kaspar said. He shot me a weird look. "Did you survive there OK? It's real rough in that area. My friend got attacked at Ocean and Caton. The conversation froze for a second. I stared at my feet, took a huge swig of coffee, then suddenly had a thought. Bringing out out a bunch of watches from my bag, I set them on the table, and made one talk.

"Cute," Bill commented.

"Ten dollars," I said. "I've sold eight this week." They writhed with indecision.

"OK, gimme one," Kaspar barked finally.

"How is your lady doing," I asked him, as I pocketed the banknote.

"Lady? What lady?" he snorted.

"Sorry," I said. "I thought you were with someone."

"No, that was long ago," he muttered. "She was way too expensive," he added. "She threw me out in the end," he confessed sheepishly.

"Are you still with your Italian mafia b****?" he demanded.

"I'm not sure," I said. "Things are weird right now. New York has made her so tough she's not even like a woman any more."

Kaspar made an incredible grimace, and stirred the dregs of his coffee with a finger.

"Join the club," he announced.

Bill slithered out to fetch a coffee refill.

"Are Brother Kharma signed to anyone?" Kaspar asked, narrowing his eyes.

"They're negotiating with everyone," I replied. "Not just labels, but TV too. The kids are sessioning with quite a few people, doing videos and recordings and stuff," I added.

"Sessioning? At eleven years old?" This, with a stunned look.

"Ten and eleven, yes."

"How do they do all this?" he probed.

"Energy. Russian energy. They never ever stop."

"Don't the kids get tired?" shouted Bill, returning to the table and struggling to fit himself into the confined space.

"I've never seen that," I told him. "Leo has a very strong sense of discipline," I added. "He can talk quite sharply, and shout sometimes. I'm aware of that. And I know he's slapped them a few times."

"That's not good. The police will be called," Bill said bluntly.

"I know. I've talked this out with him. Don't worry. He loves his kids and he would never do them any real harm. I got slapped as a child. We all did," I pointed out, holding my hands out in despair. "That's life. It happens all over the place. What can you say?" And then I had a thought.

"You know what's really behind this slap-or-no slap issue?" I demanded.

"What then?" Kaspar exclaimed.

"It's all one big smokescreen," I said. "The real question to ask is why a man cannot slap another man?" I argued. "Why is it against the law? How can it be morally acceptable that we citizens pay money to legally install nuclear weapons, and yet if you slap a man's face you go to jail? Who are these modern laws really helping? Who created this nightmare agenda? Tell me that? You want a nice clean slap or do you prefer guns and knives? Answer me that?"

I was almost shouting by now. Bill rushed to my aid.

"Calm down gov," he grunted. "We've heard it. Here, take a hit on this." He pulled out a wicked little silver flask. I swallowed a few mouthfuls and coughed.

"What is that?" I asked. "It's wonderful. Thanks."

"Cognac," he said. "Keeps out the cold."

"Oh you chaps are just too British for words," said Kaspar. The amusement was written into the many furrows of his brow. We all calmed down. Then I continued my drift.

"I reckon Leo has to be pretty tough," I rationalised. "You know, I'm from London. It's not like this over there. This is like a war, this animal we call New York City.

"I guess," grunted Kaspar, looking out the window.

"In a war, you need a good leader," I continued. "Leo is that guy. He's exactly like an army captain. He's protecting them."

"And on stage he's a demon, the red devil," Bill said. "Yes. It all fits together."

"I guess he's training the kids, bringing them up in such a way that they will have a chance to survive in a city as tough as this," I added.

"A baptism of fire?" asked Kaspar. There was a look of wonder on his face. "Like an Indian, throwing his babies in the water to make them swim?" he added.

We stared at each other for a long moment.

As night fell, and the stars came out above the rooftops outside, we agreed that Leo's discipline was the Russian way, and how it was something we were losing here in the west, and also that it was actually a precious and necessary part of the old world.

Ordering beers, we bonded over the idea of the previous, patriarchal style, and how the idea of male wisdom used to be celebrated in the west, and yet was so often derided today.

"If it's over and finished with, then what is replacing it?" I asked.

"Nothing any better," laughed Bill.

There was the sound of heavy funk starting up on the radio.

"It's true that things are becoming too politically correct," Kaspar chipped in. "You're not allowed to say if someone's black any more," he confided.

"Or fat," Bill added. "Like you, Kaspar." There was a pregnant silence.

Suddenly we all roared with laughter. Then I became sober. Something was nagging at me.

"Sorry guys," I told them, "But to me, being British, this America I'm seeing looks pretty unreal. Leo says it's the land of Mickey Mouse."

"He's probably right," Bill grunted. "It's just kind of useful for the music, but that's about all."

"Welcome to the madhouse," Kaspar grinned. "The American world of 1995. Of course it's a mind game. Do you think that I don't know that?"

"Well many Americans don't seem to," I butted in.

He ignored this comment, and lit up another cigarette, greedily sucking smoke in, and then exhaling behind his hand. With some irritation, I swept smoke away from my face.

"This is gonna get a lot worse than that," I continued. "Total disinformation. Complete chaos. A *smoke and mirrors* landscape. Nothing will be real any more."

"Just look at Leo's journey," said Bill, with sudden awe in his voice. "He's just climbed out of one mind game, Soviet Russia, into this! Another mind game."

"Maybe worse," I said.

"Poor guy," said Kaspar. "I'm bleeding inside for him."

MARCELLO

Back at Jazzlands I found myself looking at a photo of Brother Kharma for a long minute. Irene's enigmatic, sad face stared back at me.

It was hard to sleep for an hour or so. I slept in my clothes always, just with one extra leather jacket over my body. There were no sheets or blankets anywhere. This was my style. I liked things this way.

When I finally did fall into a troubled sleep, I immediately began to dream. The phone was ringing. I was answering. It was Marcello.

"Hi, it's Marcello," he said. "I need your advice on this project we're doing. Can you come over? I'll pay your time." Then the dream ended.

The following morning the phone did ring, fairly early. With a strange feeling I reached out for it. Then heard the familiar deep voice on the line.

"Max? It's Marci here. The guy who filmed Brother Kharma last night? Remember we talked?" Now I was fully awake. The dream had come true. It was astonishing. All my senses were alert.

"How did you get my number," I wheezed, grabbing a tepid bottle of water and knocking some back.

"Leo gave it. I was on the phone to him just now. He wants you to come and see the footage we shot." I woke up fast.

"When? Now?"

"Yes," he said. His voice was hard. "Well, soon, anyway. In a few hours? There's a tight schedule. I'm gonna have to mail this off to the boss in Hollywood by 5am. and we need a reaction from on the ground, like from Leo."

"So why doesn't Leo do this?" I blustered.

"He says he's got too much on his plate. There's several new gigs plus a label, and also a management company that he has to see today."

I told him OK and put the phone down, then crashed back down on the mattress.

"What did I do to God?" I muttered.

Within a few hours I was climbing out of Pleasantville station. After a quick phone call a chauffeured black Mercedes transported me effortlessly to a large mansion house close to a lake on which three large swans were gliding. Marcello met me at the door, ordering two pit bull terriers to lie down.

His living room was vast and full of antiques. An enormous painting of two boxers hung near the window.

He was still in black leather. I noticed how his jaw was so square, and eyes fixed and without emotion. In the corner was his own, private cocktail bar. Carelessly he rubbed and patted my shoulder with a huge hand, then waved me to a silver stool.

"So you play music also," he enquired, offering me a shot of spirits.

"Thanks, but I don't drink," I told him.

"What are you, some kind of weirdo?" he snorted. "C'mon!" Something in his manner was disturbing. I accepted a shot.

"Good boy," he said. "Don't mess with my head now, OK?"

I thought it better to get back to the music.

"Yes, I play," I said. "Piano, and guitar too."

I writhed on the stool, feeling way too rough and ready in my Vietnam-style leather jacket, jeans and sneakers. This place was so elegant, wealthy and spotless.

"Pretty nice house," I marvelled. You've got your own bar here, and an indoor swimming pool?

His gravelly voice was unmoved.

"It's my uncle Giuseppe's place," he admitted "I'm from Hollywood, remember?"

"What are all these guns on the wall?"

"He does a lot of shooting," he growled.

"But what's his profession?" I began to feel something wrong.

"Oh, he does deals. Bits and pieces. You know, restaurants and clubs and things. He looks after me and I'm always there for him. He's in a little bit of trouble right now actually."

"Oh, what kind?" Then I bit my lip, seeing the suddenly rageful look he threw at me. Quickly, I changed the subject.

"But I love Italian culture," I gushed. "My girlfriend is Italian. Look at all those marvellous painters and film-makers. I lived five years in Rome, you know. By this time I had figured out he was Sicillian, but wasn't about to mention the fact.

The phone rang. His whole body tensed up as he strode to the window, muttering a few words in Italian. Then he turned to me with a hard face.

"I have to take this call," he barked. I nodded.

Marcello strode into an adjoining chamber, and before he slammed the door, I caught a glimpse of a life-size stone bust of Julius Caesar, a stately desk, some scarlet curtains, a large bronze set of scales and three enormous metal safes stacked on top of each other.

Once safely inside the room Marcello lowered his voice.

"Uncle Giuseppe?"

"Yes, my son, it's me. I'm not dead yet."

"Please. Uncle? Don't talk like that. The whole family is fearful about you. How is everything. Are they treating you OK in there? Do you have your heart pills?"

"Marcello! Don't worry so much," Giuseppe shouted. "Enzo and Mario have everything organised. Don't think I am knocked out! The meals are wonderful and I have all I need. Hopefully my case will come up for review in about 2 years. How is your little film going? With all that music and this new Russian gang of ours?"

"Last night the video shoot went real good," Marcello said. "Uncle, they are the right band. And this little girl, Irene, she is the one. She's f***ing beautiful. She has the killer face. With her face we can trash every other movie corporation. She's ours.

I'm gonna make her mine. Take her to Sicily, alone with me, probably. Give her the full treatment. What do you say?

"I've been waiting for a face like this for a very long time," he continued, raising his voice with emotion. She gonna f*** up the world. Put us back to where we used to be, when Severio was in charge..."

"Don't mention Severio!" roared Giuseppe suddenly. Marcello instantly regretted his deadly error.

"Sorry, uncle, my mistake. I won't ever mention him ever again," he whined desperately.

"You better not. Otherwise you're finished for Hollywood. I'll put you in charge of our setup in Bogota. You want that? Ready to look after our lousy, filthy restaurants down there? All twenty six of them? No? I thought not. So shut your f***ing face and listen when your uncle is talking."

"Yes, Giuseppe," Marcello whispered, crossing himself.

"You got me angry, *stupido ragazzo*. Your father was always dumb too. You got me mad now.

"*Cazzo de porco dio*! And when I'm mad I think of Echoes. That place of ours in the West Village. What the f*** was he called? That little bastard? Ah yes, Bert. That's his name. OK, now tell me. Has he paid his rent yet?

"No, uncle," Marcello trembled.

"And why not?"

"He's about to. I guarantee that. He'll have it for you by next week, I promise."

"You better, or it's Bogota. Got it?"

"Yes, uncle." Each man now took a deep breath. The line went silent for a moment.

"Now the girl," Giuseppe continued. "Tell me more about her. What you want for the girl?" he asked, sounding tired.

"If it's not too much to ask, uncle, then give us the best recording studio in LA? A mastering studio too? Special grooming for her film career. How to walk, how to talk. How to represent the family.

"She's going to be a star, our star," he added. "The biggest the world has ever seen.

"She'll be the face in our movies," he continued. "The face of the family, our face. She will be our girl, to do whatever we want with, to make sure the family stays on top, forever, no question. She has that kind of talent, that power, that attraction, that look."

"And what about the rest of the band?" grunted Giuseppe.

"Flush them," said Marcello. "Don't worry about those guys. Oh no, none of that hard-ball stuff. We will shelve them, with no fuss. They'll be paid enough to shut them up."

"I want to meet the girl," said Giuseppe.

"Meet her? You're in jail. It's against the rules."

"F*** the rules!" the old man raved. "I said I want to meet her. And you're gonna fix it for me. Or it's Bogota."

"Yes, uncle. I will do it."

"Goodbye, kid."

"Goodbye, uncle."

He put the phone down and walked back into the sitting room. Taking a deep breath, he leaned against the counter and put an arm around me.

"This Leo," he said. "I don't really under-stand him. He's a tough guy, right? Band amazing. They not Italian, but still great. My family ready to put big money in them. We not here to f*** around. We go to the end. Anyone who gets in the way, sorry but he is out. Finish. That's the only way. You under-stand, I'm sure? You lived in Rome. You half Italian! Little *Pinocchio*, that's who you are. You cute guy. Come on, it's OK. Be happy! You under my protec-tion. You not here to f*** around. I can talk straight with you. More whisky?" I held out my glass, unable to reply. He poured out another shot, stretched and yawned.

"Let's go," he urged. "We watch video and then you go back and tell Leo we gonna blow this thing sky high, OK? Anything Marcello do, is like that. I am not here to waste your time. Got it? That's right."

I told him OK.

He took me to the cinema room and we watched the video. Marcello occasionally glanced at my face as the video played out.

The raw footage was astonishingly high qual-ity. Irene's face was huge on the screen. Now Leo was there. Then Maya, Serge and the rest. There was something mystical and trance-like about it all. A sensation of power, of affirmation, yet artistic, Italian and stylish.

With a certain shock and awe I understood that Marcello, with all his sinister talk, might actually get them to the top.

"It's fine," I muttered. "You did a great job."

The chauffeur was summoned and he drove me silently back to Pleasantville station.

I had been playing this music game for quite a while.

Working as a musician for years, playing keyboards, based first in London, my native city, then later in Rome, and now in New York. This was the place where you could really make it big, but the price was high if you failed. I had done sessions with all kinds of bands, every kind of music, and often worked alongside talented players, but the reality was that for most of us here in New York, life was basically just a bitter, savage fight for survival.

Yet the crazy paradox was that we all loved this place, even though no-one truly understood why. I'd talked with homeless people on street corners. They were addicted to the city, and ready to die rather than leave. Some brandished American flags. All loved New York. As you talked with them they would have manic, burning eyes, full of a wild kind of belief. So, if you failed to make it here, you might never know it, and be trapped here forever.

This place was a one-way street. No going backwards. No escape. Thus the relentless dog-eat-dog struggle continued.

In Brooklyn I'd heard guns firing outside my window most nights and getting home from the subway each evening I was having to pay a few dollars to mafia kids on the sidewalk, otherwise things would get physical and very ugly. I needed New York for the music and the dream, but knew I was burning out. Other people were in a similar condition. It was common to see a guy freshly evicted, standing on the street surrounded by all his possessions, not knowing what to do, or where to go.

People wonder why go through all of this, just for music? The world of today doesn't understand why we suffered all this hell. However we were following a dream, and as such we lived and died for our music. Nothing else existed in our world. I don't know exactly why it was like that. Actually, we lived inside our own self-created legend. It's true we were not major-label icons playing stadium gigs, but a part of us felt that we were, or that we had that potential. New York audiences helped with this. They were hugely sensitive and responsive at that time. They knew what it meant, and what it felt like to be a musician. They made you believe.

New York the black music was powerful and real. To me this style was the greatest of all. The rhythms, the gospel feel and the fact that it was all born out of slavery, had fascinated and enchanted me from an early age. I resented the fact that some people objected to the idea of a person or a music be called 'black'. I was proud and protective of black culture, even as a white man, and was not going to let these terms be white-washed out, by those who were obsessing with the negative side of it all. After all, we were happy to call sunshine golden, roses red, or snow white, I argued. Even knowing that I looked like a crazy loner to many others, to think in the way I did, I was not about to change. Finally, both Leo and me were convinced that there were secrets encoded into black music, secret intelligence, survival techniques and so on. After all, the drums had been used in Africa to convey military messages and other secrets too.

The thing of 'making it' and big and small, and how high up the ladder you were, was very hallucinatory in New York. You could not trust your own eyes. Famous musicians could often be seen, sitting in at tiny club gigs where the wage was only a pittance.

So in this city we lived in our own microcosm, meaning that everything felt big, including ourselves. As a result our playing was always in peak form. Constant jamming with top players meant you were high on music, all the time, but also primed and ready for action.

The money thing was all different to normal, too. If you got paid a decent wage for a gig, the cash like much more than it actually was. Specially if you were broke. The focus was always on music, and music gear. Many times when I carried my amplifier in the street in Brooklyn I would often hear a shout, either to ask where the gig was, or alternatively how much I would sell the amplifier for.

Basically, the music scene was one big family. You'd see musicians who were total strangers suddenly get down to talking on the subway, or in the street, just like old friends. It was one big club. Maybe you couldn't trust them for lending money, but you could trust them on things like where to jam, or where to buy gear, or who was the big new sound of right now.

Record companies could be phoned direct and they would give a meeting, one on one, in their office, and take you seriously. The memory of the sixties musical revolution was fresh, only 25 years back. Music was life, it kept you high, it gave you reason to live, to carry on. And yet, you had to love it like nothing else, because at the same time, being a musician felt like trying to dance on a giant ball that was spinning faster and faster, or attempting to survive in a room whose walls were closing in on you. The money issue too was a toxic, brutal thing. Everybody was desperate for a dollar each second. All were broke and hungry for fast cash.

And yet by contrast, many New Yorkers appeared to be high on life itself, and would express their feelings in a dramatic and public way. I had seen this in Rome and always enjoyed the free performances, although if the mood turned ugly you would have to escape fast.

Although fairly worn-down, I had become alert and even a little psychic from endless busking in the street back in Europe. I thought I knew how things worked by now, and thus could assess people, and figure things out fast. Not so with the Russian band. With them, nothing made sense, but it did so in a magical, almost beautiful way.

Who and what were they, I asked myself, for the hundredth time? A family from Russia who played music and gigged non-stop? That much was becoming clear. And yet from this point onwards, things became mysterious. I still had no idea of who they really were, or what their plan was. So where would they be going next? We were all about to find out.

FIRST VISIT TO LIBERTY AVENUE

The weeks rolled on. Our music sessions at Jazzlands continued, day and night. Hardly any money was coming in, however.

We made up for it by doing other things. It being the dawn of the video age, we managed to get a few jobs videoing jazz performances or fashion shows. Sometimes I would go and work out at the gym, or swim in the pool at the community centre. There was an internet computer freely available at the library, and I went in and sat in front of a screen for the first time ever, trying to figure it out, awed by its obvious potential, yet frustrated by my own lack of knowledge.

A theatre company moved in next door and then repeatedly called the police, complaining we were making too much noise. When a few officers arrived, I got a little fed up. After all, we had been here before our rival.

"OK, I'll just take the five grand I ploughed into this dump of a place and go straight back to London and start a club there," I told the three cops. Hearing this they backed off fast. I knew what I was talking about. The landlord was lucky to have us paying rent at all for such a junkie-infested spot.

At this time, the question of legality in New York was highly elastic. At a certain point I visited another club owner to ask advice.

"An artists co-operative cafe in Ludlow St?"

he asked. "So do like the rest. You go for 18 months without paying licenses. Just pay the fines, that's cheaper than the licences. Then, after 18 months you make the decision to go 'legit' or fold. Simple."

And now came the day to visit Leo at Liberty Avenue. This was the legendary 'East New York', in Brooklyn. The place you don't ever want to go. The area taxi drivers won't take you to.

But strangely, as I headed down into the subway, my mood was upbeat during the twenty minute ride. Then I braced myself, hunching my shoulders down as I climbed the final steps upwards.

Instantly they saw me and closed in. Four or five homeless beggars, hustling in fast with outstretched hands and pleading faces. They whined and cajoled.

"I haven't eaten, Mr?" They knew I was European. They could see I was white. They were half psychic, from the pain of centuries of crack and hunger and homelessness. A tired-looking woman put on a polite smile. I could see the effort she made to do this. Muttering apologies I let a couple of quarters clatter into her jar. At this, the others rushed at me. One arrived first.

"Mister, Mister, please Sir, you know I just need a break?" I threw my last dime in his fist then backed off, arms raised helplessly.

"Look, I'm just a musician, OK? I'm broke," I said. But my story didn't totally convince them.

One man spat on the sidewalk, then growled

at me, eyes burning suspiciously.

"Yeah but I sleep right here. I got no home. You ain't no lower than me! Please man, just a quarter?" He was advancing on me. I found one last dime and headed off quickly towards where I imagined Leo's place to be. As I left I noticed that one of the homeless was grabbing a fried chicken leg out of a box. They were eating on the job. Why not? You do what you have to do.

Within minutes I was knocking on their door. A tiny child wrestled with the door knob, gaining my entry with a triumphant face. I recognised her to be the trombone player. Then all the family flashed smiles of greeting.

"Aha, it's the British man." Leo's voice rang out in satisfaction as he eyed me.

I looked around. It was a mess, but a joyful one. Kids were racing around. There was a sofa, lots of musical gear, piles of clothes and possessions. The smell of freedom was here.

I caught a glimpse of Maya in the kitchen. She brushed back her long dark hair, and greeted me with a cautious, welcoming smile. Steam wafted from several pans in the kitchen alcove.

It was a serious moment. Leo offered tea. His face was concerned as he asked me if I had found the place OK.

"Lots of beggars at the crossroads," I told him. He laughed at this. We settled down. Pretty soon we were talking. As the kids played around us, the stories rolled out. He told of Russian writers and

Hindu gods. Then we discussed the British and Russian empires.

"My ancestors were Vikings," he announced proudly, drawing himself upwards and facing me.

"I heard that mine were something like that also," I told him.

As I listened to the magical sound of his musical, hypnotic voice, I felt myself being soothed and calmed, and now I was being transported into the past, a world of nobility and honour. It was wonderful to be discussing this together. Never had I relaxed like this since arriving in New York City two years earlier.

The faded, rough old apartment was absolutely comfortable. Once again I was struck by how simple Leo's vision of life and of music could be. My sensation was that time had stopped the moment I had entered Leo's front door.

This was something unusual, because, in New York, everything was normally rushed. Nobody ever had any time for anything. It was a gift and a pleasure if it could ever stop. And yet Leo had done this. It was a kharma moment. Him and his family were gently bringing me back to another time, when things were more gentle, and everything to do with the family was more natural and friendly, and welcoming.

The music never stopped in this house, nor the music talk. It was all so exciting, a story which was about to unfold, how it would be, our future destiny in America.

The kids gathered around with shining eyes. And now Leo was on full form, like a Shakespearean actor. He paced the floor, talking to each of us in turn, bowing, acting, laughing, grimacing and mocking, but within all of this he was promising us the big vision, and even more. Our path ahead was being revealed. I began to imagine things. Was he some kind of wild sorcerer from the Russian mountains? I had no idea. Meanwhile his gruff voice rose and fell, without ever ceasing. It was sheer music to listen to.

At this moment he was describing how things were when the family had originally entered New York.

"It was rough in the beginning," he admitted, hand on chin, eyes following something outside the window.

"But where did you stay?" I wanted to know.

"Maya arrived first, and was with friends for a while," he confirmed. "Then I came, and we were in the shelter. That was tough. We got attacked by seven black guys on the first night." I shuddered. I knew all about the shelters. They were nothing better than the street, bedlam, chaos, with all the dangers and gangsters including hustlers, scam artists, hookers, crack dealers, mafia, junkies, crazies and all the rest.

"But we're better now," Serge suddenly shouted out, defiantly. He had been crawling around behind the sofa, and now emerged with all kinds of paper in his hair.

"Of course we are," Leo replied. "Things

not bad now. Gigs going OK. Pretty soon it will get easier." He went on to explain how he was currently talking to radio, press, TV and many live venues.

I listened with mixed feelings. It was true that this stuff was a big story. Lots of things were happening. There was a buzz about this band. I could smell that they were about to make it. By this time I'd talked to others and all were convinced that Brother Kharma were on a fast path to success.

"But we will never sell out," said Leo. He'd caught my worried look. And he knew that I'd seen enough of the business to know that the big time had a bad side, that basically you would become the slave of a corporation.

"That's it," I said. "I agree. You guys are too intelligent for that. This is not Hollywood bullshit. You're doing the real music, improvisational, like free jazz, yet with rock and blues. But of course you must realize, that there's very little money from this?"

Leo gave me a stern look.

"Wait and see, Max," he said. "No-one else is like us. We don't fit into those neat little boxes. Don't you know that we are free, on the road, like gypsies? Nobody can ever chain us down or make us play bullshit."

"It's true that no-one has ever seen a band like yours," I admitted. "And I think you're on the right path."

By now it was getting darker outside. But here in this warm, friendly apartment, I could forget the chaos and the madness of the streets outside.

He talked on and on, lulling me into a dream world of magical chants and sacred rituals. And now he crashed down hard on America, condemning it, damning and cursing the place forever.

"They worship the dollar," he raved. And what is behind it all? Nothing! And they trick you. Then they want to steal from you! They are lying, all of them. But they will never fool me... I know who they are!"

As he cursed and paced, I lay back and closed my eyes, and now I was seeing America through his eyes, the Mickey Mouse land with everyone in short pants, all talking gibberish, all thieving, hustling and cheating each other, and as he raved on a great sadness welled up inside me, a love for the old world, England and Russia and all the countries in between.

In my mind I was walking in lush green fields, in sunshine and in rain, hearing calm, pleasant voices, and remembering how thoughtful, caring and considerate many of the Europeans had been.

Leo was right. Something had gone terribly, horribly wrong with America, and yet here we now were, trapped and tormented, under the great weight of the madness and confusion of an iron empire that was smashing everything in its past, and eating alive anyone foolish enough to wander inside its dark gates.

Like us. We were being eaten alive. I tossed and turned on the sofa, and desperately tried to cast this vision aside, or it might rock my sanity and leave me gutted and destroyed.

But through all this quagmire the Brother Kharma band forged onwards, smashing a path into the future, continually fascinating to watch, wonderful to hear, and mysterious in every way. Certainly, Irene was extremely attactive and desired by many. This had been established, by all who had seen her.

When it was time to go, Maya walked me to the subway. It was strange and touching how this beautiful, calm woman chose to guard over me in this way, perhaps because only the ones who actually lived at Liberty Avenue knew how very dangerous the streets could be once the sun had gone down.

One day Leo and I arranged to meet at a big music store in town, to look at various pieces of gear together. By now I had discovered a terrible fact about him. He was constantly disciplining the children, sometimes with actual blows. I knew that this was more common in Russia than England, but could not accept it, and was determined to call him out on the matter.

But as soon as I raised the subject, he made a strong defense.

"I am not this monster you talk about," he complained, looking me straight in the face. I have to keep this family together and on track."

"But you beat them!" I pointed out.

"Sometimes, yes. But listen to this. They get beaten with a belt if they do not practice their music. But Irene understands! She agrees with it! She knows that it is the way to make her a truly great musician. Listen to this! Usually I only hit her a tiny bit, like maybe twice, and then she tells me, no Papa, give me three more. You see, she understands. She wants it this way."

This stunned me. I understood it was discipline from Russia, from the old world. However I resolved to talk to the other kids about this too.

We said goodbye. I bought a pack of guitar strings and walked out into the street.

That night I walked outside and strolled a few blocks under the moon. In the lower east side of Manhattan, where we now lived, it was only just safe enough to do this. Back in Flatbush that would be asking for trouble.

There was a sharp wind blowing from the east. I clutched my Nam issue brown leather jacket tighter around my neck and clamped the blue baseball cap tighter down on my head. There was so much trash near the intersection that I had to kick some cardboard boxes out the way. I tightened up the lace of a sneaker, then crossed at the lights. An expensive sedan rocketed out towards the bridge, stereo system blasting a hip-hop groove.

As I walked, images of Russia came to my mind. Why did I have such a soft spot for this family, I asked myself, for the hundredth time? Back in England we had been steadily taught by the media to fear and hate Russians. During my school days the other schoolboys had been quite emphatic about the fact that all Russians were dangerous maniacs and never to be trusted. Yet part of me had always resisted this knee-jerk tide of prejudice and dogma. First of all, how could the idea of equality for all be so wrong? But this was exactly what their revolution had achieved. And then, what about the enormity of talent residing in the Russian artists, the scientists, the writers, the musicians, the dancers and so on? It was impossible not to admire their quiet, calm integrity. Also that particular honesty of the culture, including a sense of old-world innocence. This was something that we in the west were now running short of, perhaps because of a certain cynicism which had infected our own world for so many years.

Yet this cool, youthful spirit was pervading every single thing the Russian family did. Their music jams had a refreshing, natural feeling, as though we were all brothers and sisters together, and that anything could happen, and nothing could be wrong. Then the spirit continued even when the music was not playing. It was there when they welcomed me into their apartment. It was present when Leo talked music, mysticism and politics deep into the night, sometimes jousting good-naturedly with me over certain issues.

For me it was always fascinating the way that he, with his Russian mind, would usually be looking at a situation from an exactly opposite position compared to me, with my British mind, and yet we would nearly always reach some kind of concord on the subject, whatever it might be.

The common thread between us was some

kind of old-world sense of nobility, which I found reassuring.

Could it be true, this incredible accusation of his, that the American system and state actually strove to split up families, the better to use them as slaves of the dollar empire? I thought of all the families I'd seen split up by strange, hidden pressures. And how that in America money was such a crucial issue that it trumped and trashed every other, including friendships and marriage. I had never visited Russia, but if Leo's family were anything to go by, it seemed that very little of this had occurred over there. It appeared that America had a lot to answer for. Over here you could be more lost, and more alone, than anywhere else in the world.

A few cars passed slowly under the moonlight as an old Chinese lady carried her trash bags out into the street.

It was getting late. I headed inside the club and locked up.

By now it was mid-summer. Inside the club it was almost too hot to survive. No air conditioning and no bathroom of any kind. We washed ourselves in the sink inside the tiny toilet, behind the bar. I'd become used to this in Europe, travelling constantly, sometimes with a motorhome.

All I knew was music. I didn't think about how hard the other stuff was getting. Occasionally Marina would attach a rubber hose pipe to the sink and shower herself, and wash her body right there in the toilet, not even caring when the water ran right onto the floor and down into the basement. I tried not to think about where all this was going.

Finally I started playing gigs with Brother Kharma. We began with the New York subway. This was not a gig and yet they were playing it many times. Sometimes they performed to audiences of a hundred or more down there. It might be imagined to be an easy option, compared to working in clubs. Actually it was the reverse. We were soon to discover that to play in the subway required more talent, and more professionalism, than at regular gigs. It occasionally even paid more money too. At 42nd street station, you could usually find a spot in the large underground hall to perform in.

We met at a cafe close by and then carried the gear down the steps, through hundreds of people. I knew the kids were excited, but they kept silent. Pretty soon Leo had marked out a spot. I lay down my guitar and helped set up the sound system. Almost immediately many people stopped walking and started watching. I knew not to look at them. But it was hard to stay concentrated on setting up the gear. When I looked back up again I saw that at least a hundred people were waiting silently.

Irene and Serge worked calmly, not rushing at all. It took twenty minutes to set up, but the audience remained. While preparing my acoustic guitar and amplifier I noticed that the crowd were mainly latinos. It was well known that such folk had a particular love of children, and now here was the proof.

Finally we kicked off. I had never played or sung the blues quite like this before. The voice carries on the subway like nowhere else, it bounces off the cement walls and although you can't really hear much definition, you do pick up the essence. As I sang, I felt partly joyful, yet also slightly desperate, simultaneously. In any case the thing was working. The kids repeatedly smiled at me as we performed.

A singer needs that. We feel vulnerable. That's why singers put on ludicrous stage shows sometimes, to cover up.

But not me. I just sang. It worked out OK. I was not out to prove any big frontman thing. I knew I was basically a jazz piano player, but willing to put on a new style to help out a fantastic bunch of friends. Actually Leo and Brother Kharma were giving me a hell of a huge ride for my money, a big push of faith and confidence. That's why I felt good every time I saw them.

We played and sang twenty minutes of blues, rock and improvised music. There was a full, generous applause at the end of each number. The kids were entirely professional. They had already done hundreds of gigs like this, and were still only ten and eleven years old. As for me, I had worked my way up and down France and Italy several times busking in the street, so nothing about this gig worried me.

I have always loved playing in the street. You feel good and walk tall. There is no boss. No-one to tell you what to do. You feel to be the gypsy hero, and that's exactly what you are. The sensation of freedom is so huge that it can be almost overpowering. Plenty of big name artists have played the street and hidden this fact for years, due to the stigma involved. Agents won't book you and labels won't sign you, since they think the street is some kind of a curse, and that you get tainted or infected, and no-one will trust you after that. But many giant names in music have played the street, and you cannot white-wash the street out of them.

First of all, it's a harder gig than a club. Plenty of club acts are too shy, and soft to play the street. But also, playing the street gives you powers that frighten the conventional music business. You can see round corners. You become psychic. You own reality, and you enter another world, nothing to do with their saccharine, pre-fab world of the conventional music business.

After that first gig on the subway we headed back to their place. Leo filled me in on how the subway gigs were going.

"I know the people were mostly latinos today," he started out, "but pretty often it's mainly black people in the crowd down there."

"Great," I said.

"It's fabulous," he agreed, "and you know what? The police will always eventually come and break up the gig, and then the blacks in the audience will start harassing the police to let us continue!"

"That's really something," I marvelled.

"Isn't it?" he agreed.

THE SPLIT

At this stage Marina and I had a handful of gigs, and needed a bass player. During one of the jams, a drummer friend suggested that we put an ad in the paper.

"Singer with club looks for bass player?" he suggested. "That should bring them in."

A black guy appeared the next day. He looked tough, and spoke in monosyllables. His name was Jay. He played pretty good, with lots of slapping the bass. That was what you needed, if you were trying to combine jazz and funk, the way we were.

Meanwhile Marina and me were hardly talking any more. There had been so many screaming, tearing rows. Sometimes these huge arguments had happened right there in the front room of the cafe, with four or five people listening, and actively laughing all the way through.

I noticed that Marina had stopped sleeping on the stage beside me, and was now bedding down by herself on the other side of the room. This appeared odd, but I didn't mind.

One night she went off with Jay, the new bassist, to buy a car at a police car auction. They returned with a car with a big crashed section on the right wing.

"I didn't see the crashed section when I made the bid," she moaned. I felt sick in my heart. Why had she even gone with Jay, instead of me? After all,

I had been her boyfriend for many years.

Then there came another time when she stayed out all night. In the morning I saw how strange and distant she looked, and confronted her in the basement.

"Just tell me straight," I said, looking her in the eyes. 'You made love with him, didn't you."

She looked at me carefully.

"Yes, I did," she said with an apologetic half-laugh.

"It's OK," I said. "But I'd better move out." She looked grateful that I was not screaming at her. I knew not to do that. We had been in trouble for two years now. There was no point in complaining or denying the change. Why? What to gain? There was nothing left of our romantic relationship any more.

Swiftly I packed a bag and headed out into the street. Where to go? I could not face Flatbush. Where else could it be? I thought of hotels but knew they were far too expensive. And then I remembered Pedro and his squat. The idea filled me with so much horror that my knees buckled. But now I told myself to be strong. What was I scared of? The roaches? The guns? The dealers, the drugs, the AIDS or the other diseases? And then I told myself to grow up. I could handle it.

With a new determination I jumped down the subway steps, paid my fare, and waited until a train roared into the station. In forty-five minutes I was there, knocking on the door. A couple of Chinese guys let me in. The place was worse than ever, but I'd packed a couple of beers and I knew I could handle it. There was no sign of Pedro, but the basket on the top floor was still there, so I bedded down and tried to sleep. Half way through the night I heard screams from a lower floor. Suddenly I knew I couldn't stay longer than one night in this place,

In the morning, as the subway train rattled and roared to Flatbush, my whole body felt cramped and stiff. As I walked the last few blocks back to Jean's house the air was chill on my neck, and all kinds of poetic and tragic thoughts were haunting me. How would I ever live my life without Marina from now on? But I knew I had to let her go. We had been tearing each other apart.

I found Jean in the basement at Flatbush, and made a kind of a joke about how I'd just split up with Marina, and she uttered a wild whoop of joy. This was confusing, but it comforted me too.

"You can sleep on the couch, in my sitting room," she told me. I was grateful. She was like my mother, always looking out for me, checking I was OK.

Later that night Marina phoned.

"Are you OK?" she asked. There was concern in her voice.

"Yeah, I'm alright," I said.

"But what about the band," she wanted to know, sounding even more worried. "Does it go on?"

"The band goes on," I said.

But thirty minutes after, as I lay down to sleep on Jean's sitting room sofa, I felt lower than I'd ever known.

"Thirteen years," I whispered. A few tears came to my eyes. Ragefully I wiped them away and turned round to face the wall.

I had been thirteen years together with a woman who was eleven years older than myself, who had lived the jazz life more than anyone else I knew, and now it was all over. But I still had big feelings for her.

She had saved my life once in a crazy, vicious fight with a heroin dealer in London. Insanely good at lining up deals, and booking gigs, she would even fight with people when that became necessary. And yet the disturbing thing was that she had been consistently abrasive to everyone we'd met, and as a result many could not stand her. I knew that she had been treated badly, even abused, as a child in Rome, and was sorry for her, and this was partially why I had put up with so much trouble from her. All of my family had refused us a place to sleep when we became homeless and desperate. She had given me non-stop mental abuse all of that time, plus I was aware that she often manipulated people and situations to her advantage. So I had eventually become so numb, and beaten up, that I had switched off my own ability to feel, many years previous.

And yet every so often Marina made herself so intensely vulnerable, because of the risks she always took, that you instinctively felt you had to look after her.

Right now, I tried to examine my own emotions. They were a clumsy mess of fear and confusion. New York had never been so lonely, or so hard, as the city appeared to me right now. Marina had always been the one to fight with the club bouncers, and all the other various hustlers we were used to dealing with. From now on, I was on my own. I just felt shell-shocked, numb and vacant at this moment.

I had been loving a crazy b**** of a woman. How to suddenly switch that off? It didn't seem possible.

But for some strange reason I was soon fast asleep.

That night Irene came to me in a dream. She was standing high in a valley, wearing a long black dress. There were thick fir trees all around and many colours and shapes down below, perhaps a city, something wonderful but confusing, and I knew that there were many people there.

Birds were flying down into the valley.

"You can go there too", she said. "Fly with us, like those birds, if you want?"
But a terrible fear was in my heart. It all felt so distant, and foreign. I knew I was lost.

"Don't worry Max", she said, smiling gently. "You're going to be OK. You can make it without Marina. You've got us. We're right beside you."

Then she reached over and kissed me on the centre of my forehead and there was a flash of blinding light and I lost consciousness.

PLEASE MISTER, I HAVEN'T EATEN?

For a few days I settled into life in Flatbush. My emotions were totally confused. Even after being with Marina all these years, I couldn't figure out whether I was losing a manipulative schemer or an artistic and cultural genius. After all, her theatrical CV from Italy in the 60s was astonishing. Not only had she been young and beautiful in her prime, but also her father was a famous actor in Italy, and thus all her friends had always been top level. Like me she had played on radio and tv, toured in many countries and even run her own theatre company.

But what was the value of all of this if she was irritating or mis-hitting with half the people she met? Also she would constantly attack me, complaining I had no balls compared to so-and-so, or that we should immediately start some crazy adventure, like leave immediately for some distant country with no money to survive with.

This very trip to America had been one of her wild ideas.

I knew I had to calm down, get some sanity into my life, hunker down and try to survive at all costs, not give in to this awful feeling of alienation and loneliness that was now flooding my spirit. For Marina had been my engine. She had been fearless at every moment, even when facing down the mafia. Now I understood I would have to carry on alone. New York was a dangerous city. Nobody ever helped you here if you were down. It was just a non-stop, desperate fight for survival. Forget about making it. Simply staying alive was an achievement.

And to survive as an artist was far harder than any normal survival. Artists would be evicted daily. We were s*** on, despised, laughed at and ridiculed constantly. Yet, paradoxically, New Yorkers loved artists and valued musicians more than anyone else.

So it was like a trap, a delicious, enticing honey flower, which beckons you in, then traps you and laughs as you suffocate and die. At times I saw artists damn the very name of art for this reason. Some of us became convinced that we were cursed, or jinxed, by some terrible dark power that could not be seen, yet would eventually crush us to death.

After a few days of worrying and ruminating in this unhealthy way, I got up one morning, walked along the street a few blocks and phoned Leo.

"Hi Max," he said. "What's going on?" I was sweating inside the phone box. The sun was raging down, as it was the hottest part of the day.

"Not much," I said. "Nothing till the weekend anyway. Can I come over?"

"Of course," he replied. "Bring your guitar. We can jam with the kids."

Forty-five minutes later I was climbing up the steps at East New York subway station, bracing myself for the worst area possible. Immediately I stepped out onto the sidewalk, the various homeless vagrants and hustlers picked on me, one by one.

"Some change, Mister?"

"Please Sir, I haven't eaten?"

"Cigarette?"

"Could you spare anything, even a dime?"

"Please Mister?"

Gritting my teeth I crossed over from the intersection and escaped. They had seen my worn, brown leather jacket, patchy jeans and troubled sneakers, and realized I was close to their own condition. Music gigs hardly paid any survival at all, even for the best of us. Not in New York. You had to be made of iron to survive.

Serge was taking the trash out when I arrived. He said hi, dumped the big black bag in the street, and as we climbed up the steps towards the front door he suddenly pointed to a man who was hovering on the sidewalk a few yards away.

"That man said he would give me a hundred dollars if I let him sleep with my sister," he said. Then checked my face as I frowned. We walked inside and he locked the door firmly.

The apartment was a happy, industrious mess. Everybody was doing something, Clothes, guitars and toys clustered every nook and cranny.

Leo was in the corner hunched over some music gear. He half turned, swept the long hair from his cheek and fixed me with a knowing eye. From the kitchen Maya waved as she fussed with rice and vegetables. The small kids were clambering around the sofa like mountain goats, crying out with excitement. Kira was practising her trombone in the hall, concentrating hard as she blew out a low torrent of notes.

The eldest two, Irene and Serge, now bounded up to me with dancing eyes and a hundred questions, breathing fast.

"Max, where have you been?"

"We were waiting for you!" I laughed and made helpless gestures.

"It's good you're here."

"Is that your guitar? Are we going to play?" Now Serge pushed his way to the front.

"We've got stickers!" he exclaimed excitedly. "Can you get us some more stickers?" He showed me some. They were all kinds of attractive colours.

"Wow, they're great," I enthused. "I'll try, OK?"

"And I'm making money," Serge told me proudly. "I sell candies at school. There's a place I know where I can buy them lots at once, and then I make a profit when I sell. Look!" Proudly he held out a fistfull of dollar bills with one hand, and many bags of things that looked like multi-coloured pills with the other.

"My son is the big, tough, dealer man now," Leo chortled from his spot in the corner, taking a huge swig from a soda can, and wiping his beard in glee.

"What's that on your head?" Irene asked me.

"That's my beret," I said.

"I want one," she announced.

"Great to see you all," I told them.

By this time Leo was standing behind them, hands on hips, grinning silently.

"Sit down, Max," he said. "Welcome." I sat down. There was something going on in this vibrant, strange, Russian family that I didn't quite understand, but it felt good. This place felt like a second home for me.

Now the kids were climbing all over my body, continuing their joyful assault.

"Are we going to jam?" Irene asked, deliberately trying to keep her voice as mature as a 12 year old could be.

"I want rock n roll music," shouted Serge, punching my chest.

"Yes, can we jam now?" called Kira, carrying her enormous trombone towards me with great difficulty. I nodded violently.

"Just play anything," Irene suggested. She started to bring out her bass guitar.

"Yes, let's do everything," I agreed, diplomatically. "It always sounds good here, whatever we play. But can I rest a bit first?"

"Let him rest," Maya shouted from the kitchen. "He needs to rest first. Tea, Max?"

"Yes, please," I shouted. "It's so good to be here," I told them.

"Yes, great to see you," Leo agreed, coming out from his corner. "We need to talk. So! Great show we did last Saturday. Plenty of media and press were at the club. It's made a difference." He sat down, chortling with pleasure, but then suddenly turned to me in a serious way.

"It was not really good to fight backstage like

that, but in any case, plenty of doors have opened for us as a result of this gig. The phone never stops ringing."

"Is it right you were featured in a policial program on the radio recently?" I asked.

"Yes," he said. "By the way, I am not a communist. I look for freedom, that's all. But whatever I do turns political, I have no idea why."

"I have noticed that," I said. "Me too, I'm the same."

"I simply want freedom to play my music," he mused. "And freedom is a hard thing to find," he added. "New York is not really free. Too many people trying to sell things too fast, themselves included."

"Well said," I told him.

"Anyway Irene's new modelling career is going well," he announced. "For now, at any rate." Irene looked pleased, in a shy way.

"Great," I said. We locked eyes, both knowing how it might not be easy for her in the future.

"It may not be perfect," he admitted. "But I will be watching her, so let's wait and see how it goes." I agreed.

"And there's more news." he continued. I pricked my ears up. He cleared his throat.

"We've found a new guy, a fantastic, black percussionist. The kids work very well with him, and he likes to be with us. He will be part of the band."

"There's more," he continued. "One of the music papers will do an article on us. The guy says he hasn't seen anything like our music ever before. Next week we will make another video. And now, look over here, have you seen what we have?" He pointed to the corner. "It's a new compact sound system. For gigs. I found it at a great price."

"This is fabulous," I told him. "Things are moving."

"And you haven't heard it all." He leapt up and paced around, flashing his eyes, and playing with his beard. I sat up straight. Now he fondled the new sound system lovingly, lowering his voice to a conspiratorial whisper.

"We may have a booking at the *Bitter End* club, in the West Village!"

"A West Village gig?"

"A West Village gig." Our eyes met. It was a serious moment. We both knew the immensity of this chance.

"My God," I said. "We'll have to rehearse." Then I had a thought. "Am I on this gig? I mean, do you want me to play?"

"Of course," he said. "If you can make it. Because I know you have your own stuff to do also."

"I'll make it if I can," I said. "This is terrific news. I can't believe we're playing the Village!"

"The Village, the Village," screamed the kids, flashing hysterical eyes, twisting my arms and slapping me round the neck. I laughed and rocked on the sofa in ecstacy. We all knew what it meant to be playing the Village.

Maya pushed through with the tea as the kids

continued their shouting rampage.

"Now, back! Down," roared Leo suddenly, raging with his arms. "Let Max be calm and drink tea!" Instantly they folded back down into the corner. The family became quiet. There was silence for a few moments. The dog moaned in his basket and outside, where it was getting dark, I could hear a car engine revving up.

From the bathroom there were the sounds of excited screams. Kira had been playing with her toy boat in the bath and now Maya was shouting out that there was water all over her clothes and even on the floor too.

"But I like my boat," Kira was wailing desperately, "Please let me play more?"

"I don't know what it is with you guys," I said, "but I love coming here." It's totally crazy, I mean, this is East New York, the most dangerous part. How can I be happy like this? But sitting on the subway train, my heart was singing with joy."

"We're free," Leo said.

"It's true," I acknowledged. "But also you're different. I feel refreshed when I come here. Reborn, in a way."

"Thank you," Irene said, giving me a grateful look. Suddenly we became serious. The family had gathered around in a half circle as we drank the Russian tea. Irene was playing her bass silently.

"You deserve it, Max. You're a good guy," Serge said. "And I like how you sing that song about *'I shot my lady down.'*

"What fascinates me is this," I said, speaking slowly. "That you came from communist Russia, to play music here."

"On the street, usually," Irene said.

"In the subway, it's fun," Serge added.

"But what I mean is," I continued, gathering my thoughts gradually, "It's not like you earn a lot of money..."

"We have almost nothing," Leo said. "We're free, I told you."

"And it's not like you live in a big expensive condo in Manhattan..."

"We live in a war-zone," Leo intoned. "They're shooting guns every night here.

"But you're more happy than anyone else I know," I said. "And it's infectious."

"We've got our music," Irene said.

ECHOES

Within days of Marina getting together with Jay, and me moving out, she'd booked our band into a residency, in an Italian restaurant called *Echoes* in the West Village. Bert, the manager, pushed everyone around, cursing non-stop. A huge, aggressive man from Naples, constantly sweating, he immediately picked on Marina and the two of them bickered and squabbled their way through the long evenings. The whole set-up smelled like mafia to me. All eight waiters were illegal aliens. And, most bizarre of all, every evening there would be a line of cops sitting at the bar, eating and drinking for free.

I had a lot on my plate. Firstly, the work consisted of seven sets a night, four nights a week. I'd never played more than three or four sets before. But the main problem was my own sanity. How could I take this? I had to sit and play music with Jay, the big, black guy who was now Marina's official live-in lover, and who was now living at my club with her, and acting like he was the boss of it?

Just hang on, a grim voice inside barked at me. Don't let them win. This is New York. Worse stuff is probably coming. Just survive. Put your head down. Grin and bear it.

By now Marina was arguing and occasionally even raving hysterically, from the unrelenting pressure. Yet strangely, Jay and I had an unspoken arrangement not to fight. Not only this, but musically, he was a great soul and funk player. However he was only starting to play jazz, and this was a jazz residency. It was certainly true that I had some bad and confused feelings about how he had taken my woman. But then Marina's character was far from perfect. So I was fighting internally about whether to get rageful at Jay and make him look stupid, specially since he was floundering around with the jazz tunes. But then we would lose the gig, which was unthinkable. No. So I knew I had to help him along the way, and train him to be the best player possible. It was a crazy, twisted, inferno of a band.

There was a moment at Echoes when Marina had gone out to buy cigarettes. We were on a break, having drinks at the bar. I leaned over and asked Jay how things were going with Marina.

"Goin' OK," he replied laconically.

"You know she has a crazy streak?" I warned.

"I do know that," he replied. "Don't worry, I have plenty of tricks waiting in case she freaks out on me." The look on his face was tough, and it scared me a little. Still, I was right out of the picture now.

Meanwhile neither Marina nor I knew who Jay really was, or where he had come from. He looked tough, and didn't talk much, that's all we could see right now.

One evening we had finished rehearsing at Jazzlands. Jay had gone out for some reason. I had made a coffee, and was looking for sugar in the fridge. I noticed a big brown parcel inside.

"No, don't touch that," Marina said, quickly

pushing it to the back. Suspiciously, I questioned her. Soon I broke her down.

"It's cocaine," she admitted.

"What? That much? That's thousands of dollars! Do you want to get us all locked up?" I was terrified.

"Don't mess with Jay," Marina said, with a scared look on her face. "Just pretend it's not there, that's all."

"Does he have a gun?" I asked. She admitted he did, and then started fussing with dishes, preparing a meal.

"If you go to the store, can you pick up some broccoli for me?" she asked. "He hates it if we run out."

"Oh for christ's sake," I yelled, but she ignored me. I headed back to the subway, totally confused. There was no way I was going out buying broccoli for her mafia stooge.

"One step down," shouted Leo, pointing towards the ground. It was early evening.

There was a man sitting on the front steps outside their apartment. His clothes were dishevelled and he was drinking from a bottle in a brown paper bag. With an effort he slid down a step.

Now Leo could leave the house. He was with Irene, who was holding the Alsatian dog on a leash. Serge had not been allowed to come. He had made a mess in the living room earlier and was being punished.

They walked for a while. A group of hip hop kids passed, in their baggies, baseball caps, and shades.

"When do we go see the new record label?" Irene asked.

"Probably Monday," Leo replied. "I have to confirm tomorrow. Careful, don't let the dog tangle his lead."

They crossed the main street, avoiding a large truck, and headed east. Some guys were stripping out the engine of a green station wagon.

"Do you think Max is OK?" Irene asked suddenly. "He looks sad sometimes."

"Good musician, but dumb guy," Leo said. "That woman, Marina, threw him out and now he's back playing in her band again. He won't listen to me."

"Maybe he needs the money from that restaurant gig," Irene pointed out. "They didn't want me to sit in that night, did they?"

"Don't worry about them," Leo stormed.

"They are bad energy, Marina and Jay," he continued disgustedly. "You know that some people are predators, vampires? They steal your energy." Irene mused on this for half a block. The dog whined excitedly as he passed a white cat, crouching low.

"Is that why we meditate?" Irene asked.

"That's it," he replied, taking her hand. "Meditation, yoga, mantras, chanting. It's all about energy. Our music is very, very powerful in that way. It protects us."

"But is that why we improvise and make it all up?" she wanted to know.

"Exactly so. Originally it was the black slaves who learned to do this, in order to survive. Not to go crazy. To remember who they were. Also, to define who they were. As a protection against the slave masters. To build a wall, like a castle, around themselves."

"Do some people believe that black people are bad?" Irene asked.

"Don't listen to ignorant talk. They are neither good nor bad, Just the same as us. Then he looked at her in a particular way. "Do you know that you are very powerful, Irene?" he asked.

"Because I look good? Mama says I'm pretty." Leo smiled, kicking a pebble into the kerb.

"Partly that, but mainly what you have inside you. Do you remember Russia?"

"Not very well," she told him. "Vague things, some beautiful buildings... palaces, some nice people..."

"Never forget Russia. Always remember who you are. They try to take that away from you here. Never let them do that. Promise me?" He was passionate now.

"I promise," she said.

"Good girl! He picked her up and shook her all around. She giggled delightedly.

"Stop it," she laughed. "Stop it!"

Presently they halted to rest on a bench facing a little church.

Irene picked up a stick from the ground and began to play with it. Then she turned to Leo. Suddenly she was shocked at how tired and drawn he looked. But how wise also. With his long red hair, expansive beard, and questioning, intellectual eyes, there was something priestly, almost sage-like about his fond expression as he gazed back at her.

She put an arm around him, and they were suddenly surrounded by a chatter of birds in the air round them. Now Irene gazed earnestly at the sepia Brooklyn horizon. She squeezed his arm.

"Papa, everyone is chanting in New York. Why?"

"It's what we do," Leo replied with a wry smile. "It keeps the bad spirits away."

"I see them everywhere." Irene continued. "In the street, at the gigs, even in the bank I saw a man chanting. Do you chant?"

"Of course," Leo replied. "We all have to. Especially musicians like us. Otherwise you lose your path. They will take your soul. They are all predators here, leeching away at your mind, your ideas, your soul and of course, your music too."

"But where does all this stuff really come from," she nagged. "All this supernatural, this religious stuff?"

"India," he replied distantly.

"All of it from India?"

"All."

No-one said anything for a while. But Irene suddenly felt a deep love for her father. Not just for him, but for the whole family , and for their music, and also for the strange, charmed musician's life she was living in this wonderfully crazy city. Things always moved so fast that she hardly ever had time to pause and think deeply. It was a moment to treasure and she suddenly felt proud to be who she was, and hopeful about the future too. Sensing this, he gave her a hug.

Now she announced that she was going to the store to buy something, and swiftly skipped off with the dog.

Leo stared at the church silently.

And as he studied the finely carved wooden door, the strangest feeling began to run through his body.

He stood up. Something was happening. At first, he did not totally understand what it might be. Unusual noises in the distance. Now his head was pounding. Strange shapes were before his eyes.

What were those faraway noises? It was almost like the sound of men chanting, and then something like steel clashing on steel. He reeled and staggered, suddenly gripped by an extraordinary emotion, then recovered. There was a bitter taste in his mouth. He closed his eyes, then opened them again. A slight wind fingered his hair.

What had he forgotten? What was that thing, at the back of his mind, crying out to him from the past?

He continued to stare at the church, focussing on every detail of the facade, the stonework, the carved wooden door, the ornate roof. The painted glass window began to spin before his vision. It was becoming a mandala...

And suddenly he was back there, in the old world, crossing Russia as a young man, hitchhiking, playing 'freedom' blues harmonica in the street for money. People were gathering all around him as he performed, clapping their hands delightedly in time with the music, watching him with shining eyes and throwing money into the hat, without any policeman ever coming to complain.

The years spin backwards and now Leo is a young boy, eating supper with his father and mother. She is beautiful and he loves her, and all is calm and quiet and everything is as it should be.

And as time goes by, he eventually grows up and leaves home, and crosses the mountains, and then meets the shamans and learns ancient truths, mystical energies and secrets from them.

In the world of the shamans there are things we can never understand. But in this place of dreams and dark visions he becomes like a bird, travelling far and wide in the Russian sky, beyond the frozen hills and valleys, and also even backwards in time, such that far below him the very earth trembles as Viking hordes surge out from the northern sea, across the hills and the valleys of Asia, while all the time wooden drums are sounding, and the holy men are chanting their mantras.

And now we are at the source, where the an-

*cient, primal forces of mankind are proud and real.
The warriors are rough and hearty, wearing chain
mail and bearing fearsome weapons, and they drink,
laugh and shout with proudly defiant voices, and they
have no fear.*

*As they march across the plains, they fight
monstrous battles, slaying warlords and capturing
beautiful maidens, who quickly adapt to life alongside these powerful, violent chieftains and their kins-
men. This is humankind in its full, primitive glory,
with all the triumph, ceremony and ritual song of the
old world. Choirs are singing and armies marching,
and eagles flying in the sky above, while sacred mys-
tics are uttering prayers and prophecies, and then
comes the final chant, which reverberates across the
centuries, ... one body, one body, one body ...*

Irene returned to find him lying on the ground.
With a gasp of horror she tenderly brought his head
up from the ground, and pulled it to her chest. How
very fragile and vulnerable he seemed to her at that
moment. Frantically she whispered and kissed him
back into consciousness.

He opened his eyes and looked around.

"What happened?" he asked.

Later, they made their way back to the house.
Serge immediately sensed something had happened.
But his angry demands produced nothing. Their
mouths were shut.

LILY

At Jazzlands the flow of customers continued. It was obvious that there were loose women around all over the place. I'd been without a girlfriend for too long and was getting impatient to find somebody. But I didn't want to end up with one of these many women who lived in the street.

One evening something happened that shook me up a bit. I was alone at Jazzlands. Marina and Jay had gone off on some errand. It was raining softly outside and the occasional car splashed its way through the night, outside the glass.

I was changing the strings on a guitar when a girl entered. She was young and pretty, wearing shorts and T-shirt, and she sang gently to herself as she crossed the threshold. Then I saw that she was holding a live crab in one hand. All at once the claws of the crab were in my face, waving wildly. I stepped backwards in alarm.

"Hello?" she said. The short dark hair was brushed back to reveal a mischievous smile, from splodgy red lips. She looked about nineteen.

"Lily! Damn it! Keep that thing out of my face!" Then I became quiet, remembering her mind was almost gone. Half Chinese, an ex GI, she had been raped by ten soldiers before leaving the army.

Right now she was standing close to the basement stairs.

"Come on?" She made as if to pull her T-shirt

up. "Shall we? Shall we ... do it?" she asked. The words were spoken tenderly.

I stared at her for a second. She was young and desirable, and the bright red lipstick smeared around her mouth only increased my sexual tension. Her eyes were inviting me down to the basement. She nodded her head as if to repeat the request. I sighed and looked her straight in the face.

"Lily, we don't need to do this." Her face dropped in disappointment. Inwardly I was seething with sexual frustration, but wasn't going to let this show. I was just so sorry for her.

"You be careful with what you say to people," I told her, as she trailed outside, laughing delightedly at the wind.

That night we jammed at Jazzlands with a bunch of other musicians, playing jazz and funk all mixed up. It was Marina and I, plus three others. Jay had disappeared again. The groove was fairly intense. But suddenly I looked up from my piano to see Marina sliding to the ground, microphone in hand, an agonised look on her face. I jumped off the piano and asked her what was wrong.

"It's my heart," she moaned. By now she was lying on her back. The other musicians had not stopped playing.

"I think I'm having a heart attack. I can't move," she whispered.

"Stop, stop," I shouted out to the band, who were playing loudly.

"Damn you, stop playing," I roared. "Can't you see that Marina's in trouble? She thinks it's a heart attack. I'll take her to hospital right now. Just leave, OK? Stop playing and leave! Do I have to throw you out?"

Slowly and reluctantly the guys packed up and straggled off out the door. I called a cab and got Marina into the car, and I told the cabbie to step on it.

"I cannot break the law'" he argued. "Do you want us all killed now?"

At the hospital I waited a long time, smoking and fretting. Then she appeared, in a slightly more calm mood.

"They said it was not a heart attack," she told me. "It's something complicated. Oh, just forget it, OK?"

"I didn't like that they would not stop playing," I muttered.

"That's New York. What do you expect?" she said.

Every so often I liked to walk along the docks around the Seaport, and stare out into the Atlantic ocean. One night I bought a can of soda and just sat there as the sun went down, trying to forget the stress and fatigue that wracked my mind and body.

All around me a thousand bright lights shone from the skyscrapers.

You could never be alone in New York. The lights from the high-rise windows would keep you company all night long. It was like being surrounded by a wall of precious jewels.

For a while I amused myself by watching people strolling, couples sharing a poetic moment, guys out running for exercise, and then a lot of excited shouting around the hot dog stand. But I could not stop thinking about music, and my new Russian friends, and where we were going together.

It was a wild and exciting path into the unknown, that was for sure.

But behind it all, I had a constant, nagging worry. The brutal reality was that I was still broke. Not only this but also I appeared to be on a downwards path, heading lower every day. Right now I understood that I would have to get a paying gig within days, or the city would destroy me. I'd soon be totally homeless, the way things were going.

It was almost impossible to get money from music in this city, simply because you were competing against the best possible players from every country in the world.

Even with the thousands of gigs that New York offered, there were never enough to go round. Contracts were like gold-dust, always hard to get. Clubs wanted hugely talented acts, who would bring in a stream of paying customers.

Every musician in this town knew what a New York gig meant, how very precious each booking was. After all, this was the city which had spawned huge music careers. Many folk viewed New York as a jazz city, since so many jazz names had made their fortune here. The link with Broadway musicals was a big clue.

'If I make it there, I'll make it anywhere...' The words of the song were true. But there was often a terrible price to pay for the ones who failed.

Also, this was not the only town to make it from. If an act had a strong visual attraction, then LA would be more the place to get to, because of the movie connection.

New York City, although fast, tough and brutal, also remained very intellectual. The jazz legends had created an atmosphere of respect for all improvisational music, rock included. Brother Kharma was now being rocketed right into the centre of this thriving, arty, melee of clubs and international artists.

Suddenly I felt older. Burned out by the city. And I'd only been here a couple of years.

I got up and wandered around, then stopped and gazed at a big ship nestled in beside the quay. A few seagulls landed onto the dock on my right. I threw them a few crumbs of bread from the sandwich I was eating.

Now I cast my memory back, trying to remember how things had been in the 70s.

I'd played a lot of black music, in those days. But then, over the years I'd understood not to scorn or refuse any type of music. I knew I had to learn it all, and perform each style at different times. Music was my bread and butter. I also discovered that you have to learn to read music if you want to earn money.

It was all about survival, and right now I'd noticed that far too many guys were becoming sessioners instead of having their own bands. Having a band was a commitment. It meant giving up some or all of the session work which paid hard cash, and money in New York was always the savage, tearing issue.

Suddenly my thoughts turned to the Russian family. It was obvious that the fact that Brother Kharma stayed together as a unit was due to Leo's parental control, and also his creative vision. Plus the kids were enjoying the music too.

By now the sun had disappeared, and the dark Atlantic ocean looked sinister and disturbing. I shivered as I wrapped my jacket closer, picked myself up and headed for home.

YOU CAN'T CATCH ME

"Max, come here, I'm gonna blow your mind!"

Serge dragged me up and out from my corner, pulling me towards a narrow entrance entirely hidden by a curtain. He was wearing a colourful military jacket from a long gone era.

"You won't believe what's down there!" he cried.

It was later in the month. Brother Kharma had just finished performing at a theatre not far from the Jazzlands. It was a big event with many bands and also variety acts, even circus performers.

They had just ended their set. There had been a reckless, heady atmosphere. The audience had been high on some combination of beer, drugs and sunshine.

As soon as they had left the stage, I'd gone backstage to meet them. They were exhausted but satisfied, doing things with clothes and gear, and talking to journalists and friends.

Now Serge was insisting I come and see something.

"Come on," he repeated, getting impatient now. "Look what I've found!" I was groggy from too much beer, but allowed myself to be lead through.

He pushed through the scarlet, velvet curtain. Instantly we were in a dark, sloping passage. There was a distant smell of camphor, and what looked like a candle burning high on the wall.

Turning to me he grinned, making big eyes. Then began to push on an ancient wooden door on the left. A tiny crack appeared. We both peered through into the half darkness. The room was absolutely silent.

What I saw was something I did not expect. A small orange cat, wearing a light green jacket, standing on a grey wooden table, sipping from a saucer of milk. An unexpected breeze tickled my neck. I wondered if I was dreaming.

"Max, you haven't seen it all," he whispered, easing the door open by another inch. Now I could just make out an old man, wearing a German helmet, sitting in a bamboo rocking chair. And on the left of him, a nun, reading out loud from what appeared to be some kind of religious book, but standing with her face to the wall."

Serge turned to me, deeply satisfied.

"That's only the start of it," he squeaked, closing the door again.

"Who are they?" I demanded. "Circus performers?"

"I don't know," he answered. "But I like it. Come on!"

Now I heard voices down the passageway. Sounds of laughter. We walked on and soon passed several clowns, and also a man in a dinosaur suit. Serge danced around him, giggling, and playfully punched the scaly arm of the monster who issued the obligatory roar from deep within his suit.

I knew that anything could happen now.

We walked on. This place was larger than I had imagined. Now Serge was disappearing down a circular metal staircase. A rock band erupted distantly, the sound booming along the corridor as we descended. All kinds of amplifiers and loudspeakers were stacked up here. Then Serge found a room full of drums.

What happened next really surprised me. Serge picked up some drum sticks, and tried out a rhythm on one drum and then the next, and then the next. Soon he was shouting out words in time as he hit the drum. First it was just nonsense like 'scrambled eggs,' or 'a thousand light years away' or 'what's my name', but then it was different stuff like 'cool guy in the sky', or 'you can't catch me.'

I started to play too, and we shouted at each other for a while. Then we collapsed in a sea of laughter and confusion. He rolled around in ecstasy. Even though I was dull from the alcohol, I knew he should be packing up his gear with the family, and now explained this fact. But he replied that friends were taking care of it all, and that he knew that Leo had to talk business with people here anyway, so that there was no need to worry.

"OK," I said. In this way the magical tour continued. He grabbed my hand again and rushed forward.

"Slow down," I complained, "I'm not your age, you know?"

"Why not, Max?" he argued. "Yes you are!"

We entered yet another box room. He rummaged on a shelf on the right.

"Look," he crowed. "Check this T-shirt with the statue of liberty!"

"Put it down, it's dirty," I told him.

"I don't care. It suits me," he insisted.

Now he measured it carefully against his body.

"It's too big," I told him. "Put it back."

"I don't care, I want it." He slung it across his shoulder.

"You shouldn't do that," I told him. "That's stealing."

"Don't tell me what to do," he snapped. "Nobody wants it. I played my gig here. Now I'm gonna take it. I earned it." At this he turned to me with a serious face.

"Max, I smoke weed sometimes," he said. "Nobody tells me what to do. I do what I like."

"Well I don't think you should," I said. He stuck his tongue out at me. I tried not to laugh.

We moved on to another set of shelves and began rifling through it all. I found a light switch and turned it on.

"So look at this," he said, suddenly struck dumb. It was a Grecian statue of a naked woman, quite large and covered with dust.

"It's Aphrodite," I told him.

"Who's that?"

"She was a Greek goddess."

"So she never existed?"

"No," I admitted. "But she was the goddess of love."

By now we both knew it was time to get back to the band, and soon were out and up the stairs again.

In the final stretch we passed an old man shuffling down the corridor. He had long white hair and a beard and was muttering to himself as he walked, and constantly scanning a sheet of paper in his hand.

"That's my dad, a hundred years old," laughed Serge. He looked down, suddenly serious.

"I don't ever want to get old," he said quietly. "Never." He took my hand once more.

"I am already old," I said.

"No you're not, Max," he shouted defiantly.

We couldn't resist snooping into a few more rooms before finally returning. The next one was packed with crates full of empty bottles.

"Pooh, smelly," he said.

"That stuff will destroy your life," I said.

'We will all die anyway," he pointed out.

"And now I'll bet you've had some of that already," I challenged.

"What, beer? Whisky? Of course. Plenty. Irene's had even more."

"You two should have your heads banged together," I moaned.

He punched me and shouted with laughter, then took my hand again and we walked on.

The next door was slightly open. Inside, Lily was sitting at the mirror, doing her makeup. She was naked from the waist up. Everybody froze. She hardly batted an eyelid, but merely started to put on a pink silk bra, deliberately slowly, watching my eyes as she did so.

"Lily," I gasped, "What are you doing here?"

"I'm getting ready for my gig," she said. "You?" She smiled.

"I'm just part of the audience," I told her. "But what, you're a musician?" I asked.

"Yes I told you! I'm playing with my band," she announced, brushing her hair back proudly. "We're on in about an hour's time," she continued. "I'm playing bongos and maracas." She picked one up and shook it to and fro in the air, laughing at the gravelly sound it made.

Now she noticed Serge for the first time.

"Hey you," she shouted at him. "Fix my bra strap?"

"I'll do that," I told her, stepping forward.

"No, I want him to do it," she pouted. Serge stepped forward and fastened it for her.

'We've got to be back with his band," I said.

"One love," she said, fluttering a few fingers at us, and chewing her gum a few times.

"One body," I replied.

"See you," Serge replied, as we began to leave.

But suddenly she stiffened, staring hard. Then stood up and called us to wait.

"What have you got there," she asked Serge, pointing at the grimy T-shirt hanging from his shoulder. Then she fingered it.

"It's mine," he said. "Get off it." But now she had pulled it off his shoulder and stretched it out in the air.

"Liberty," she shouted, camping it up, making a wildly sarcastic dance on the concrete floor.

"Come on Max," Serge said, grabbing it back. We exited fast.

"Where have you been?" demanded Irene when we returned. She grabbed Serge in an armlock.

"Yes, where?" echoed Kira, whipping my shoulders playfully with an old belt she'd picked up. The two were sharing a slice of pizza.

"None of your business!" shouted Serge joyfully. "Max and I have been exploring. We went on an adventure! There are caverns and magic rooms... and we found a wicked witch!"

At this the girls screamed that they must see it, and Serge lead them through the curtain and they disappeared, still munching pizza.

Now a man swept into the dressing room, handed Leo an envelope full of banknotes, thanked him and departed.

I saw Leo looking at me curiously.

"Kids are so charming at that age," I enthused. "Sometimes I think they see and know things the adults are not aware of."

"It is the third eye.'" Leo said. "They have the gift of extra vision. All children have that. The third eye normally switches off at age six, but I do special exercises with my kids to keep it switched on for them."

"Why does it switch off in the usual case?" I asked.

"It is the society we live in," Leo answered gravely, stroking his beard. "The modern world, and the pressure of conformity."

"That's shocking," I replied. "So what are these exercises?" I asked. His eyes twinkled with satisfaction.

"Many forms of meditation," he replied.

"Could we say that the third eye is a way of keeping the inner child alive?" I asked.

"Of course," he agreed.

One day I jammed with a percussionist from Paris who liked my playing. He told me he knew of a guy called Joe who was looking for a keyboard player. Straight away I called him and he hired me on the phone, just like that. It was to be a bar gig in midtown for the following week.

"Just pass by my place for the charts and cassette'" he told me.

An hour later I walked into a huge loft. Joe was from an Irish family, and looked it, with short red hair, and a tough cut to his chest and neck. Also one eye didn't quite connect with your face. We chatted for a while, and various women flitted in and out, each one of them swiftly getting physically intimate with Joe, a kiss here, a hug there, before flitting out again. I wondered what kind of fairyland I had walked into. Eventually another guy arrived, with a handsome, girlish face, and then disappeared.

By this time Joe had put away quite a few beers.

He turned to me, grinning wickedly at the wall.

"I've always been straight," he pondered. I wondered where this was going. By now another friend had arrived and was listening with interest.

"But that guy just now was damn beautiful," he continued. "You know I'm wondering ... I could almost..." There was a hilarious silence. "Do you think I might ...?"

"That's between you and yourself," the friend retorted, hardly able to contain his mirth. I said good-bye and headed for the street in some confusion.

Yet when we played the the gig, a few days later, it was a savage wall of sound, murderously loud. Joe was totally out of it from the outset. The moment we hit the first number he became a raving, screaming banshee, roaring it out like there was no tomorrow. There had been no rehearsal, but I followed the chord patterns fairly easily. The biggest problem was the river of sweat careening off my face and splashing down onto the keyboard.

Joe had entered another world and hardly seemed to know what was happening. In between numbers he would corner me at the back of the stage.

"What number do we do now," he would ask. There was something pathetically touching about how he had put all his trust in me. I felt honoured.

Then it was over. Our performance had been

a roaring success. The guys were soaked but proud. I didn't care how crowded and hot the place had become. Everyone was out of their heads except me. I knew I had to get the playing right so I had to stay sober.

We played another gig two weeks later at a racetrack slightly north of the city. It was under a marquee with a fair-sized crowd and the sun was shining. The songs were the same, and it was just as intense, except that the intense heat of the afternoon sunshine slowed things down a touch.

Afterwards I felt like a million dollars, heading back across town on the subway lugging my keyboard, stand and amplifier. The money in my pocket was a huge satisfaction. But best of all, in my bag was a scrap of paper with contacts I'd made for future recording work in Memphis.

"Jazz is boring," laughed Leo one night. We had met to talk shop at an Alphabet City hideout he knew. It was a cafe, but unlike any place I had ever seen. Old pieces of redundant computer gear had been fixed to the walls everywhere. I liked this casual conceptual-art take on interior design, that the East Village was so renowned for.

I laughed out loud at his obvious jibe. We enjoyed sparring over these kinds of things. I was a fairly committed jazz player, but not an 'exclusive' like so many jazzers were. Right now I told myself not to get emotional, not to fall into his trap.

"Jazz turns you into a good player," I told

him, but this fell on deaf ears.

"It pays nothing," he added, driving another nail in for good measure.

At this I folded my arms and remained silent, choosing not to argue the point. After all, it was his life and his family, I reasoned. But I felt that he and his kids would pay a heavy price later if they ignored jazz further. However, right now it was true that Irene, Serge and the rest were thriving on the freedom of Leo's musical way to be. They had already been classed as exceptional players.

There was no shortage of musical inspiration in this town. I would grab any chance to tour round the late-night jam sessions, playing and talking with all kinds of people. Non-stop networking was the only way.

Leo was constantly introducing his children to a fabulous array of talented artists. At the Brother Kharma concerts he stunned and amazed audiences with his creative vision and flair for combining styles and sounds. You would see a didgeridoo alongside an electric guitar for example. I liked this imaginative style.

He was consistently original, and New York welcomed uniquely creative characters such as him. Many times I had the strangest feeling that he was much like a painter, creating a vast canvas, and yet his paints were musical notes, but more than this, the paints were his children themselves.

One evening Leo visited me at Jazzlands. Marina had painted the floor of the club room as a giant chequerboard of black and white squares. She frowned and merely continued her work on the phone as he entered.

"It's very timely that you walk in just now," I told him. "Kaspar just called. You know he's been promoted?"

"Yeah, I already spoke to him," Leo said. "But he and WAI always want the same thing now. I told him no."

"What does he want?" I asked.

"For us to advertise their products," Leo said, looking me squarely in the eye. "We will never sell out like that. Plus, you know what happened with Irene, and the modelling deal?"

"What?" I asked.

"Every time she went there, they wanted less and less clothing in the shot and more and more skin. She's twelve! So I cancelled. I am her father and could not allow that."

"Well done," I told him.

"But it's not all over," Leo continued. "Many people saw the show we did, live on air. The record labels are phoning us these days. They have already made offers. Right now I have to go to midtown to talk to a publisher now about a possible contract. You could be useful. Will you come?"

"Of course," I said.

Leo made a quick call, then grinned.

"So let's get over to his office right now? It's

not far." I agreed and hastily packed a bag. It was a short subway ride and then we started to walk blocks. Then he grabbed my arm.

"Hey, look," he said. Through a hole in a tall fence I could see quite clearly through the window of a college building. There were many young men with dreadlocks, sitting at desks, and they were all chanting something together.

"What's going on?" I asked, in some confusion.

"It's the law," he said. "Legal stuff. They learn by chanting it all together." You can see anything in this city," he pointed out, with a quizzical smile.

As we walked onwards I now brought up something that was on my mind.

"Listen, it's about the free, improv music that we both like to do," I began. "This style was big in London in the early 70s, and it's still good today. But to me, there's a good and a bad side to the thing. For example, if Brother Kharma play free music, how will you ever earn money?" He shrugged.

"But seriously, though," I said. "You'll never feed your family with free music." Now he jumped into the attack.

"Forget that," he laughed scornfully. "We do things our way. They will wake up, don't you worry."

"But actually I like it," I continued, flinching to avoid a speeding cyclist. "Of course free music is the best. No programming. No propaganda either. An end to the usual, institutionalized bull****."

Now Leo looked me full in the face.

"You're a good friend, Max," he said. "I like the way you play music with my kids and me. But there's one thing you must understand."

I waited silently, knowing that something interesting was about to come out.

"In India, they had the caste system," he announced, in a very serious tone. "You know about that?" I nodded. I had been there many years before.

"Very simple," he said. "Each caste had their own musician." I nodded again. A limousine drove by. A few sparrows were hopping close to my feet.

"Upper caste is Brahmin," he continued patiently. "They play music to keep demons away." Just at that moment a busker started to play his soprano saxophone at the nearby intersection, accompanied by the wail of a police siren down the block. The sun had gone down by now and every kind of coloured electric sign had lit up, and they glowed vividly against the sepia horizon.

"Lower caste are close to the untouchables," he concluded, stroking his beard, eyes fixed on a distant parking lot. "Lower caste musician makes entertainment, alongside the prostitutes. High or low, it's one or the other. Make your choice."

Gradually Leo was bringing me to understand the power of Hindu religion. It was a little odd to be strolling through the bustling street life of Manhattan while hearing all the details of Rama, the god of truth, Shiva the god of war and Ganesh, the one with the elephant's head, god of success.

Now Leo stopped suddenly beside a street vendor selling silver rings and bracelets. He examined one closely then turned to me with a question. At this moment I felt that he was infinitely far away. His eyes were distant.

"Max, do you think you control your life?" A truck roared by. Heavy rock echoed from a clothes store across the way.

"What a question," I spluttered, taking a few steps back. I reached out to a street lamp to steady myself.

"But I think I know you are going with this," I added.

"You do not control any of it," he said. "It all happens by itself."

There was no possible answer to this. We walked on.

At this time I was discovering that Leo was interpreting the entirety of western culture as a lie, and that western music also was implicated. It was only the rebels that he could tolerate, slave music, the blues, rock, improvisational and so on. To view American culture through a Russian lense like this was refreshing and insightful.

Part of me admired him for his daring, defiant stance. It appeared to be that he had taken on the entire world. I wondered how such a fighting spirit could exist, or more significantly, how long he himself could continue, fighting all the rest in this manner. But actually I welcomed such a rebel spirit. After all, my own parents had been communists for years, railing against the British government. I agreed with him that most governments today were corrupt, and all were in league with the corporations, meaning that they were essentially for sale. Yet another part of me, the survivor part, realized that we would all eventually have to knuckle down, and connect with the system in some way, otherwise become forever alienated and thus finally perish.

Most of all I was concerned how his kids might grow up, having been forged into rebels in this way? How would they fare? Only time would tell.

THE LITTLE GIRL

A little girl is drawing a picture of a palace. She sits silently on the sofa, paper pad in her hand. Outside the streets are full of shadowy figures and relentless, faceless cars. The landlord has not been able to collect the rent for months, due to neverending danger.

Suddenly all the lights all go off. No more electricity. Someone shouts from the kitchen. The little girl ignores all this, knowing that she can continue because the dusky light from the window is still just enough to see by.

Carefully she brings out many pencils, in all the colours of the rainbow. She fills in many details of the palace. There are ornate windows, spires and minarets. With great care she switches from pink to green, and now a rich, deep blue. The palace is in a city, somewhere far away. The city is in a land from the old time, a place of dreams and innocence, and of polite, noble people with elegant, heroic ways.

Irene sucks the pencil thoughtfully, then finishes the drawing, and finally tucks it away into a folder, together with a hundred more sketches, which always depict the same thing.

I went back to taxi-driving. The money was low but I needed every dollar I could get. It was a new office at the junction of Flatbush and Atlantic Avenue. There were about fifteen other drivers, mainly

Arab, and they would kneel down and put their heads on the carpeted floor at sunrise and sunset. This was relentless, hard work, and one time a driver came back covered with blood. A customer had smashed his driving window, indicating that he didn't want to pay. There were long breaks between jobs. I'd arrive back at Flatbush totally exhausted.

Plenty of people would sit in the front of my car with a big brown parcel on their lap. I knew never to ask what was inside. I drove many musicians, and film-makers too. One sunny afternoon I picked up a big Greek guy with staring eyes, who gave me advice on the music career.

"Go to Vegas," he said. "Plenty of gamblers will invest in a band there. Get the film score work! Do you have a showreel or a CV? Try the Brill building! There's money everywhere if you have the song!"

Back at Flatbush I found Jean hobbling around, cooking up some fish and rice in the kitchen. The small black and white TV on the table was switched on, but with the sound turned very low. Her kitchen was crammed with tiny colourful statuettes, postcards, posters, souvenirs, crockery, all mixed up with *gris-gris* and *hoodoo* odds and ends from New Orleans and the Caribbean islands. Beads and amulets hung from hooks and door-knobs.

"Hello, Max," she sang out, in her distinctive *big-mama* wail.

By now she had heard about the live broadcast I had done with Brother Kharma. We began to discuss the band.

"Sounds like you're on to a good number," she added.

In Jean's world, numbers had a special significance. Although she earned her living as a psychiatric nurse, she would sneak out at any possible opportunity to go and 'play the numbers.' This was a form of gambling. However much her family and friends beseeched her to stop, she would not. In the end we had given up in despair. Why judge her so harshly? She earned her money and it was hers to spend. Plus, in many ways, she was like Mama Africa, with all the wisdom of the old continent.

"A very good number," she added. "That Leo, him with his kids, he's already big! And I can see even more coming up." Then she had an idea.

"Max, come with those cards of yours!" I sighed, and went to fetch the Tarot cards from the bag beside my bed.

Together we laid them out on the kitchen table. First she lit up some incense. Then she sprinkled a few dried herbs around the table and some on my head also.

Then we shuffled the cards in a particular way and I laid them out.

Gradually, card by card, a grandiose story was now being revealed, a big voyage, much suffering, then recognition, progress and finally revelations, wisdom, and many achievements.

"I see danger ahead," Jean said quietly. Her

voice was husky as she bent over the cards.

Now she closed her eyes. "I see a golden palace." There was a pause. A few dark birds swept past the window. Outside, a long way down, I could just make out a few figures taking parts out of the engine of a car.

At this point Jean was moaning a little, and rocking to and fro in her chair.

"This Leo?" she asked. "Is he royal? He big powerful man, him." She opened her eyes, large and wild.

"Look, Max! So much swords in this reading," she continued. "Swords everywhere! So much swords! He could be the one we waiting for. I never see cards like that before."

I listened in silence. She was still writhing around, slapping at her neck, pulling at her hair occasionally.

Now she turned and whispered to me.

"Oh lordy! I see him is trapped. Fighting with himself maybe. Something inside him, like terrible stinging bees, that wants to get out, but cannot. Oh lordy lordy!"

"You've got it," I said. "He's being torn apart. But we all are. Do you see what is happening to all of us? The men, I mean?

She moaned a bit more. "Men, and women too," she said. I lit a cigarette.

"Yeah, but the men especially," I insisted. I was in a trance-like state by now.

"He can't move," I whispered. "Blocked on

156

all sides. I feel this too. We cannot breath. No more discipline. No more authority. The women bring up the children. Far too soft. No more morality. Kids in ghetto all gangsters. America finished. It's a decadent world now.

"It's so hard to be a real man, the way things are today," I added, warming to my argument. Then I saw how Jean was flashing her eyes at me in a dangerous way.

"And I do know the women see things the exact other way round," I admitted. Jean suddenly growled like a mother bear, then relaxed.

"But just wait and see," I continued. "Watch out for what's coming. A world we don't want to live in. A place where men are no longer respected." Now I leaned back, took a few breaths and tried to calm down. I was getting too emotional.

There was a huge yelling suddenly down below in the parking lot. Jean opened up the window, put her head out, then sat back down again.

"But you're right about Leo," I added. He is strong like a lion. He may be from some royal family we don't know about. And he is taking on America. That says a lot. Plus he is also fighting a war with himself."

Then I had a thought.

"There's just one problem," I told her. "He's slapping the kids sometimes." Jean stared at me with burning eyes.

"Me, I got whacked every Saturday, back in Trinidad," she shouted. "And I too, I whacked me chilluns every time they got bad. Otherwise they grow up wrong!" Her face was angry and she snorted a bit as she spoke.

"Everybody whack the kids. I ain't gonna bust him for that!" I hardly knew what to reply to this outburst. Then she calmed down.

"They gonna do the big thing," Jean repeated, breaking into a large packet of biscuits. "If they keep it together."

"Keep the family together?" I questioned. "I don't know. The pressure is so huge. It's starting to beat them down. We're in a race against time," I told her. But Jean would only just keep on rocking and repeating the same words, like an endless mantra.

"You mind those Russians," she insisted, "They on a big train to somewhere... maybe Vegas! Maybe California. Maybe big TV. Maybe LA!"

We paused for a while. I cleared up the kitchen a bit. It was dark outside by now. Then I had another thought.

"And what about Russia?" I asked. "Maybe it's time for them to tour, to bring their music back to Russia. Sure, they're here to hone their craft, and get tight, and do deals, but then what about Russia? That's where they're from. No more reason to hold back now. The Berlin wall is finally down!"

But in my heart, I knew this was easier said than done. The fact was that something was happening to all of us, without us truly knowing or understanding it. We were becoming Americanized, with strange new values and feelings. The memory of our past lives was fading every day. The sensation was that you mustn't think about that, you have to let it all be washed out of sight.

But I knew they were special because they were Russian. And Leo was never going to let anyone meddle with that fact. There was a depth, a character, a worthiness, to the family. Something innocent, but with all the good meanings of this word. It was a kind of precious, poetic sadness at life and at the world. However, for Americans, 'sadness' was starting to be a dirty word. Also, anything to do with the past was something they didn't want to know about.

One evening Leo brought Irene to Echoes, the jazz restaurant, so she could sit in with the jazz band. At first Marina refused. I drew her to one side in the break.

"Are you crazy," I hissed. "Why can't she play? She's good enough! It's the tradition here, and you know that. Everybody can play." Now Jay butted in.

"I don't like that Leo," he said. "Putting on airs the way he does. He really thinks he's something, don't he? Why don't they just get the hell out, right now?" A few diners were gazing in our direction. Desperately, I tried to quieten Marina and Jay down.

"It's a public place," I protested. "We don't get the right to say who walks in and out."

"Well I think the sorry mother*****r should just walk right out, the same way that he walked in, and take his sorry-assed scallywag b**** with him," Jay announced, spreading his legs wide defiantly.

"I don't like his style," he carried on. "Who the hell do they think they are? Russians? Weren't we at war with them? I got a good mind to go back and pick up my 38 and give him a good ole roach spray. What's with this Russian crap? Give me a break."

"Look," I said. "None of this is Irene's fault. She's just trying to get some experience.

"Experience my ass! She done trying to take my job away! That's what you mean. Well I won't stand for it. I should just call the cops and declare them as illegal aliens. Get them deported. I don't see why I don't do that right now."

"Well you'll have to deport all nine waiters too," I pointed out.

"No, they can stay. We just remove the ones who make trouble. And those two sorry mother-f*****s are doing just that."

Now something in Jay's tone had made Marina irritable.

"Let her play," she said unexpectedly. "Jay, just lay off, will you?"

The two were too much involved in their argument to realize that Leo and Irene were sitting on bar stools behind them and had heard every word. Now I winked at Irene.

"What do you want to play?" I asked.

"Oh, just anything," she said.

"How about Autumn Leaves?" I suggested. "E minor? She agreed."

At that we sailed into it. There were no problems. She conquered the song like a pro. Her face showed no expression. I admired her disconnected, supercool attitude.

At the bar, Leo and Jay sat side by side, Jay fuming and Leo grinning with pleasure.

NEVER LOSE THE DREAM

Every so often I would grab another chance to visit the family at Liberty Avenue. It was always tough getting from the subway to their apartment. The beggars and hustlers were waiting right outside the subway station.

Over the course of the summer we would sit and talk. Leo usually had exciting news about offers for the family band, recording, gigs, press, and so on. To chat with him made you feel good. This was the American dream, printed out in technicolour letters, glowing in the air. As he talked, the kids were mesmerised. Everybody loved him for this. He knew exactly where he was going, in all of this fantastic labyrinth of New York chaos.

However meanwhile, life for me had become so tough that I was starting to be beaten down. Thankfully the trips to Liberty Avenue helped me survive. The family were like a ray of sunshine on a stormy day.

I had been exhausted by two years of non-stop back-breaking toil, playing seven sets a night sometimes, carrying amps and cabinets on the subway up and down the city, plus constant vicious arguments with Marina. I knew I was pretty much done. But Leo and the family were giving me strength to carry on. He constantly energised the kids with exciting musical projects, keeping them stimulated and motivated in this way.

On top of this, they all liked the way I performed.

"You can play anything, Max," they used to say. I'd never heard it put so plainly before, and was flattered. I told them that if you play jazz, like I did, you pretty much have to cover everything.

I told them the truth, which was that jazz was quite hard, and did not make much money in itself, but that the knowledge would dramatically increase your chances as a session player. However the family didn't totally see eye to eye with me on this, so we agreed to disagree.

In our conversations we soon locked into the issue of Soviet Russia and communism. I was entirely open-minded. I told Leo I'd been brought up by parents who had met at Cambridge university, and who had become communists in the late thirties, and also that half of Cambridge had been this way.

Gradually, I began to make more visits to the family at Liberty Avenue. On one such visit, on a very sunny afternoon, we decided to all venture out and up the hill, into the park, to relax and sunbathe. It was a precious, peaceful moment away from the usual rush and stress.

We found a spot high up on the hill, close to some tall trees and lush flowers. We made a colourful gang. Leo was dressed all in white as was his style, every so often. The kids were wearing cartoon heroes on their sweatshirts. Maya's long dress was blue and white, and she smiled shyly from behind dark glasses, and constantly adjusted her large straw hat.

I felt at home in jeans, mauve silk jacket and NYC sweat-shirt, white baseball cap and shades. Although I had brought my guitar, I now threw it aside and stretched out in the sun for a while instead. Brooklyn seemed very far away right now.

The kids began playing with a kite and then a frisbee, shouting happily. Maya unpacked some food, watched by several hungry squirrels.

It was a precious, peaceful moment, away from the usual rush and stress. But something was on my mind. I propped myself on one elbow, facing the family, and squinted against the sunlight.

"So what was life like under communism?" I asked Leo.

He thought for a second.

"It was not how the west imagined it to be," he said. "Life was culturally very rich and colourful, and with lots of artistic work going on." Then he explained how he had played many big blues gigs, often with one of the biggest groups in Russia.

"It was seen as freedom music," he said. "But when it got too successful, then the KGB started watching us, and stopped things from happening."

I digested this for a while. A helicopter crossed overhead. The heat began to make me sleepy. I opened a can of soft drink, and took a long, delicious pull.

"Fabulous day," I said. "You're lucky to have this park. This is the life." He agreed, warily, as though it were a trick question.

"No, seriously," I said. "Things are good." I

leaned up on one elbow and looked at him. "Do you realise how great they are? For you, I mean? You're doing well. The way I see it, you have everything."

He was not immediately easy with this idea. But I persisted.

"Come on," I insisted. "You're in New York. The band is doing OK. You have gigs. Food, house, all the essentials. Stuff starting to happen in the press and on the radio." He admitted that this was all true.

"What I don't get about this city, is this," I grumbled, incredulously. "People can't even see when they are getting somewhere. This is beyond crazy. It's tragic, and wrong."

"You may have something there," he admitted, stretched and yawning lazily, looking up at the sun.

"Now I see where you are going with this," he continued."People come to this city with big dream. Then city beats them down and gives them little dream. Stuff like run for the money. Do the stupid, lowdown job. Lose the music this way. This is total bull****. I will never be like that."

"Exactly what I was trying to say," I told him. "Never lose the dream. And also, never forget what your dream has already achieved."

"You guys are happy," I added. "It's so obvious. You're free! And moving upwards. Plus, every time I see you, someone is singing or writing a song, or talking about music, or repairing an amplifier. It's nothing but freedom and music."

Now I pointed to the trees, the grassy slopes

and the horizon, and made my final plea.

"Look at us right now! Sun shining, birds all around, little planes in the sky, kids playing. What more do you want? Forget the *making it* thing! This is a whole lot more real than that.

"It's like you've been fighting so long that now you're numb, kind of dead inside, and you can't see that you've won," I raved. "Remember those guys in the war who never stopped fighting?

"You have it all," I repeated, calming down now. "And the kids are playing music. You've done it! Who else ever shared the music thing with their kids? Most families never see eye to eye on what music they like, between the generations. Often they can't even live together any more."

Now Leo sat up.

"Serge, Irene, Kira," he called. "Come over please?"

They came running up. Kira brushed some leaves off Serge's jeans.

"Sit down, please," he said. "I want you to hear what Max is saying."

They sat down.

I began to talk. They listened quietly and seriously, never interrupting. I explained what I had just said, and more. I told them they were lucky to have a father like Leo. I said that I wished I had had parents who had taken me round the world playing music like that. I told them that most kids had lives that were just boxes within boxes, everything safe, planned and controlled, with nothing real, exciting or inventive ever allowed. I didn't talk too long, and was pleased to see that they nodded and accepted what I was saying. Then they ran off again.

"Thank you," Leo said. Then I lay back on the grass in the sunshine, closed my eyes, and was lost in my own world of thoughts for a while.

One night I was at Echoes, the jazz restaurant, on a break, smoking a cigarette on the pavement outside.

Then I noticed Bert arguing with a yellow cab driver, an Indian guy, who was sitting in his car at the kerb, with his door wide open. There was some kind of an argument over money going on. Their voices got louder and louder. Suddenly Bert slammed the door on the driver. I heard a muffled scream from the driver and now he was re-opening the door and staggering out of the car. Blood was running from one eye, and from his left hand too. Bert backed off a few steps, but then stood his ground. The Indian started to chase Bert in slow circles, around the sidewalk. They were swearing, grunting and glaring at each other. Bert kept on stepping backwards, looking around as he did so. A small crowd had gathered by now. Bert caught my eye. He was looking very uncomfortable. I sidled up to him.

"You disappear," I hissed. "I'll handle him."

"I know," Bert gulped, and slid back into the restaurant.

There was nothing more that the taxi driver could do. He got back into the car and drove away, leaving circles of bright red blood everywhere on the pavement.

I'd finally turned into a mafia stooge.

I stubbed out my cigarette, and headed back inside to the piano. Then I handed a chart to the Japanese bass player. It was 'Satin Doll.'

"Not too fast," I said.

Marcello was heading down to Bleecker Street to tackle a difficult customer. One of the restaurants that his uncle owned was run by a big guy, called Bert, from Naples. The rent was hardly ever paid on time, and never without some kind of an ugly scene. But he knew that this was his job, to collect that money. So he hardened up and marched forward, pulling down his hat to protect his neck from the slight mist of rain that had begun to fall.

As he rounded the corner, what he saw slowed him down. Outside a Chinese take-away store he hovered, taking in the scene. Two men were walking in slow circles, facing off. There was blood everywhere, all over the face of the smaller man, and his shirt too, and then in a circle around the sidewalk.

Now Marcello understood that the bigger man was Bert. He did not look angry. His face merely wore a careful, almost a scientific expression. Then Marcello recognised Max whispering in Bert's ear, and saw Bert slip back inside. It was hard to know what Max was mixed up with here, but finally he understood it was not a good day to ask Bert for rent money. He turned swiftly on his heel and slipped back the way he had come.

Italy - 1988

It's many years earlier. I am a young man, striking it out in the world. I have a van, a girlfriend, a guitar and a dog, and we're driving across southern Italy in the late summertime.

It's brutally hot. But the only time it's truly unbearable is waking up in the morning. The van is an inferno at that moment.

I have almost no money but I don't care. I know we can survive with our music alone. It's a relief to have broken out of England and all of that cloying, suburban self-satisfaction.

At night we sleep on cliffs above the sea, or in deserted lots at the edge of some village.

One afternoon we stop the van in a small town close to the sea. Park the van. Find a water tap. Fill the water bottles. Then bring out the guitar. Marina has her shaker too.

As far as the eye can see people are selling things, laid out on tables on the main street. There's an Arab man selling carpets close by. He sees us start to sing.

"Play 'America' for me," he shouts. We start the song. He's clapping and cheering you along.

Day by day we work your way south. The busking doesn't always work. But when it works it's very powerful. One night we lead five hundred people in a huge crocodile up and down the piazza at midnight under the moon. They're all singing along.

I play pop, rock, Brazilian and the occasional blues number.

The busking is always a test. Some days we arrive in a village in the late afternoon, and have to sing a sleazy, thirties, American ballad to two or three old men in a deserted cafe. We don't get your brioche and cappuccino until they are satisfied. They grin and chat excitedly, showing all kinds of mis-shapen teeth.

I know that I am doing something unique, establishing my value as a musician, proving my manhood, actually becoming a man.

It's an endless trail of sweat, heat, sand, surf, cappuccino, songs, sleeping by day, and singing and driving through the night.

One evening we park the camper in a back-street of a little seaside village not far from Tropea. We'd done a decent night's work the previous evening, playing to three restaurants. In the final place there we had performed to a riotously happy table of fifteen, a local plumber with all his family. After a couple of Brazilian songs they had asked many kinds of questions about who we were, and did we really always survive on the road like this? Marina had told them a few secrets about the artist life before handing out percussion instruments so they could sing and play along, which they then did, with a power and a gusto that only Italians have.

Brazilian samba had a magical ability to seduce and please like no other music in Italy. It was not always delicate or refined, like bossa nova. It often had to be played rough and tough, with everyone in the place shouting and shrieking along, much like the chanting at a football match. I would smash and rip into my guitar strings with all my strength. We were doing samba like it was heavy rock, and it worked. In fact, it was the only thing they could take.

Right now I clamber out of the vehicle and take the dog for a walk. There is something very lonely about the endless, dry, sandy streets and the sun-drenched, white bungalows and villas. And suddenly I know I am more lost than I have ever before. But the feeling is good. My whole body is charged with excitement. I have become a tiny dot in the world, surrounded by waves of oblivion. None of my family and friends know where I am any more, or who or what I am now turning into. For the first time I am understanding that to be lost can be a wonderful thing.

Back in the camper, Marina has prepared a feast. There is pasta with all the trimmings, prosciutto, parmesan, local olives and ultra-fresh mozzarella.

And now the conversation goes all over the place. Are we going to make it in music? Have we already perhaps made it, without knowing? Who she was going to kick the ass of, back in Rome. Who had already kicked our asses, and what we were going to do about it. How she was going to kick her father's ass, and her sisters too. What gigs we were gonna play, and how she was gonna book them. What news-

paper journalists she was gonna attack, for yet more press. Which top sessioners she was gonna grab.

And there is more.

Which radio stations she knows we could get some exposure in, or even our own show. Which labels are signing acts like us. Which contacts of her father's she is going to hit into next.

And how we finally have a major label within our grasp. How the master recording has gone well. Our song for the Roman Carnival. How with major promotion, we are gonna be sitting pretty once we get back to Rome. It will be first class treatment.

I love it when Marina is in this kind of mood. I occasionally mention a few extra people, or media outfits, and she then gives me the lowdown on each.

"He's a mofo, or he's OK. This one's a traitor. That one, he f***ed with me 20 years ago and I'm gonna f*** him up back. That one - she's a pushover. They're tough. They're real evil mofos. He's a laugh. They don't exist. I can handle him. He messed me around. I knocked him out. They knocked me down. He thinks he's won but I know how to f*** him up."

I lean back on my seat, amazed and entranced by this symphony of curses, praises and revelations. Without looking at me she continues her rant, 'all in one piece' as the Italians say, totally animated, still eating in a wild and hungry fashion, but driven, like an automaton, doing what she has been put in this world to do, stomping on the global music business, winning her place in the final scheme of things.

"Marina, have some more olives? Relax!

Shall I make coffee?" I demand. She ignores this, but makes some vague motion with one hand.

Now she is back to the music again. She needs a shit-hot slapper bass player, she insists. Then she starts laying into me, telling me I cannot play jazz, not the real jazz, not like the jazz she knows about.

At this point she glares at me and lights up a cigarette.

"And your blues is not the real blues, Max, you know that, don't you?"

This angers me but I know to bottle it up. We've had a great couple of days. Why mess it all up with an argument? Diplomatically I swerve the conversation back to other things, conspiracy theories and suchlike. Yes, the authorities are evil and insane. No, the Americans have no morality whatsoever.

"I should have stayed with my anarchist friends," she now declares, baleful dark eyes fixed on the horizon outside the camper window. This makes me sit up. I am well aware that for years she had been carrying a gun, agitating in the streets with the anarchists at various political demonstrations.

"Delicious mozzarella," I point out, intent on calming her down.

"You can thank the Unita party for that," she agrees. "I loaded up with everything half price earlier today."

I nod my head in agreement. It is true that the Unita, communist street parties are much loved by everyone. They make sure that desperate folk like us will never go too hungry.

At this moment I hear a piteous whine from under the table. The dog is begging, so with a gentle platitude she tosses him a scrap.

Now, as the sun descends and the sleepy Italian village makes ready for bed, we feel temporarily satisfied about who we were, and what we've done, and the combination of a good meal, coffee and cigarettes adds a luxurious, sophisticated touch to things.

At this stage our talk will veer violently and erratically through an astonishing and heady checklist, every topic under the sun, including cosmology, philosophy, blues, yoga, comedians, my mother, the Roman empire, modal jazz, New York and quantum theory, before we are finally done. Groggily we put out our cigarettes, and curl up in the high bed above the cab, under the stars.

Nothing moves in the lonely moonlight outside except a lizard.

And in this way we are touching the very inside of the world, feeling its Italian heart, and discovering how quaint and erratic real life is. Nothing is ever the same, from one moment to the next, as we freewheel up and down the sparkling Italian coastline.

Back in Rome, the topsy turvy world continues. It's hard to stay well balanced and objective when one college gig is followed by begging in the street a few days later. In the midst of the chaos we are offered a RAI TV live broadcast, which goes well. After four months of living in the motorhome we fi-

nally rent a store in Trastevere to live in.

All of this is punctuated by violent, screaming arguments between Marina and I, and also within her family. The romantic notion of being an artist in Rome is soon destroyed. It's just dog-eat-dog, every man for himself, and f*** the rest of them. Italians are very often child-like, I now discover, to my astonishment. And there's more.

Every business deal goes wrong or turns mafia. There is no solidity to anything. We try anything and everything to stay alive.

We start a percussion school, then a dance school, but I end up on the ground fighting physically with one of the Brazilian dance teachers. Marina gets a job translating an American TV program, but then one Saturday morning our vehicle is petrol bombed by some rivals. The smoke and flames are visible for hundreds of yards down the street.

We host a radio show at a communist radio station and organise the Carnival of Rome, restoring it after it had been banned for a hundred and ten years. We are offered a TV show, but the producer has been living dangerously, and he now shoots himself. Marina and I are evicted from three apartments, one by one. It's back to the street again. We make it up to Milan and find a manager but then he machine guns the wheels off the tour bus of a band because they didn't show up to play his concert. Realising the danger of this man, we cut the communications and head back to Rome.

We end up begging around the Vatican, and

after many weeks of starvation, miraculously get hired as actors in a Verdi opera, dressed as Roman soldiers. Finally we get a really good band into shape, and play some decent-sized gigs, do a radio and TV tour, play the Palladium, and then head for America.

New York City - 1995

Leo's negative comments about jazz had un-settled me. One day I phoned him, and after much yelling and pleading, finally got him to admit that the kids would benefit from a few jazz lessons. He promised that he would get them to study at a Manhattan jazz college, two sessions a week.

"But I cannot understand one thing," Maya confided, one late rain-swept evening, as she and Leo walked the dog together outside in the street.

"Serge is acting very strange sometimes," she added. "It's usually just after he has come home after one of these jazz lessons. Are you sure it's just jazz they teach at that place? He is so full of himself. So confident, but in a weird way. Something feels wrong."

"You may have a point," Leo admitted. "Also, Irene spends hours on her makeup now. That's never good. She is so pretty anyway. What does she want to do to all the young boys, kill them? I will have to keep an extra sharp eye on her."

"There's another thing," Maya added. "Serge talks into the mirror now."

"Talks to the mirror? What about?"

"I don't know," she moaned. "It's not normal. I worry about him."

"I will watch him also," Leo confirmed. "There shall be no more of that in my house. I will bring him into line, whatever it takes." He laughed roughly, however the sound of his laugh made Maya even more nervous than before.

"Let's go back," he told her. "I want to know what mischief my young lions are up to. They turned and headed back through neon lights and pouring rain.

More time passed. Jean finally let me know that I would have to move out. This was the second time I had been thrown downstairs to the evil conditions in the basement down below.

"But there's a small room, slightly better, at the other end of the basement," she consoled. "The super will probably let you have it. Just talk to him?"

With death in my heart I searched him out. He came to the door of his apartment wearing nothing but boxer shorts, and a can of beer in his hand.

"You want the other basement room? Sure. I'll get you the key. You have my fifty dollars?"

Downstairs, in the new place, I had never seen so many roaches. It was far worse than the previous basement room. Plus, what little space around the bed was jam-packed with supermarket trolleys containing dollar store items. A friend of Jean's was storing his stuff here. I had to climb over all kinds of items, radios, clocks, toys and make-up gear, just to get in and out of bed.

After a few days, a black man from Columbia moved into the room opposite from mine. He looked tough.

"Watch out for him," the super advised. "He always flies into New York, deals drugs, gets busted and deported, then immediately flies back in again. It's been like that three times. And by the way, he carries a gun."

One night there was a knock at my door quite late. The man stood there.

"Can you help me?" he asked.

"Someone in my room. Bad spirit, I think. Can you come look?" I felt in two minds about helping this person. What the hell was he playing at?

Anyway, it seemed best that I check out his room. As I started to walk out I cursed myself for being a fool. Surely he was just going to rob, maybe kill me?

I poked my head round the door of his room. There was just blackness there. But then I saw two bright eyes staring out. As my eyes became used to the darkness I saw it was a black cat, sitting silently motionless.

"It's a cat," I said.

"Just a cat?"

"Yes, a cat. That's all."

"No bad spirit?"

"None that I know of. Just an ordinary black cat." He looked relieved. Then he turned and faced me.

"Could I sleep in your room?" he asked.

"Sorry, no-one ever sleeps in my room," I told him. Plus, there's no space inside anyway. I can hardly get in myself. Look, it was only a cat. You'll be OK."

We said good night.

Another day arrived, and things started badly. There was a cold wind off the sea, and sinister clouds on the horizon.

We were having trouble at Jazzlands. Several kids had been trying to break in through the back door of the club. They knew we were inside, and didn't even care. We could hear them trying to force the lock. Every so often I shouted at them to quit, threatening them with the cops. This worked for an hour or so, but then they always returned.

Around noon I understood they were gone for a while. I opened up the back and started cleaning up plastic bags of shit, thrown by a Chinese mental defective from the third floor. He'd been at us all year, trying to stop our music, but there was no way we were going to give in.

At around 2pm, Marlene from the theatre next door knocked to complain once again. I knew that she was a driven woman, tough and determined.

Now she faced me defiantly, her face hard and set, one hand on her hip.

"Your music was too loud last night," she told me. "We couldn't hear to rehearse our theatre play. Can we make a deal? Like you rehearse one evening then us the next?" At this Jay broke through from the rear room. I could tell he was in a sullen mood.

"We ain't making no deals", he rapped. "We wuz here first. If you don't like it, then you can skidaddle. Marlene stood her ground, but her face flushed slightly.

"We have every right to be here, and you're breaking the law by playing so loud. We're doing Shakespeare," she continued.

"I don't care what sorry-assed English bull**** you think you can do," he growled. "If you know what's good for you, you'll clear out." Without a word Marlene disappeared back into her storefront.

Later that afternoon, I was sweeping a mountain of trash from the front steps. Just over the road, Marlene's actors were rehearsing in the parking lot.

The words of the actors were clearly audible up and down the street.

"O, never shall sun that morrow see!
Your face, my thane, is as a book where men
May read strange matters," shouted one stocky, blond man in tights and jerkin, with an Elizabethan ruff round his neck.

Chortling to myself, I swept on.

Now a big black car arrived and entered the car-park slowly, sidling right up to the actors. I realized it was Jay, returning after having gone to borrow his uncle's car.

I put down my broom and screwed up my eyes against the sun. At this moment Marlene had raced over to Jay's car.

180

"You can't park here," she shouted. Jay wound down his window and stuck an elbow out.

"I park where I like," he retorted. "You guys shouldn't be here. It's for cars, not dumb-ass bull**** like what you clowns are up to."

Another actor had sidled up to the other side of the car.

"The devil damn thee black, thou cream-faced loon!

Where got'st thou that goose look?" he shouted, cleverly.

"Who you calling cream-face?" Jay shot back. "Get the hell out of my window. If I say I'm parking, I'm parking and that's final."

By this time I was crying with laughter. A small crowd had gathered, including several tramps. Lily was giggling and dancing beside them on the sidewalk, licking an ice-cream cone.

"I'm calling the police," Marlene snapped, waving an angry finger at him.

"You won't," Jay said. "Cos you know you shouldn't be here, that's why. So you can get your sorry ass the hell out."

Another actor had danced up. She was in a long blonde wig and a kirtle and bodice.

*"You taught me language, and my profit on 't.
Is I know how to curse,"* she yelped.

The crowd were convulsed with mirth.

"Irene! Where did your mama buy that dress of yours? Down the pawn store? Ha ha!"

Marcie Taylor spat on the ground, smirking at her. Instantly Serge came running up.

"Leave my sister alone," he menaced. "At least she's prettier than you and your dumb-ass brother." The Taylor twins glared back. It was a chilly lunch break in the schoolyard with a slight hail storm beginning to fall.

"Come on Serge, let's get back to class," Irene warned quietly. But he would have none of it and continued to stand his ground, even while remembering that the Taylor brother and sister were the toughest, blackest outfit the school had.

"Yeah little guy, take your *ho* back to teacher," Matt Taylor jibed. All in one second the two boys were at each other's throats, while the girls circled each other, lunging and scratching wildly. Then it was over. A female teacher had raced in and separated the four of them, sending them all home instantly with double homework as punishments.

"What's this?" Maya wailed, back at the apartment, as she saw so many bleeding elbows and knees at once.

"Matt Taylor called Irene a *ho*," Serge explained sullenly, fixing a glass of tap water for himself. "But is there any orange juice?" he wanted to know.

"What's a *ho?*" Kira asked. Everyone ignored her.

"No, the orange juice got finished last night," Maya explained.

"They started the fight," Irene said. "Serge tried to defend me."

"I'm proud of what I did," Serge yelled. "I'd do it again." He punched the air madly, spinning on his heels. Irene's face was a poem.

On the sofa, Leo was exploding with paroxysms of silent mirth. Maya shot him a worried look

"I'm not sure this is good," she said.

"Nonsense," he retorted, coming to his senses. When you are raising young lions, this will happen. Get over it."

"Daddy, are we really like lions?" Irene asked.

"Of course," Leo said. "Our entire family are lions. Come and see my teeth. Stroke my mane." She put her arm around him affectionately.

"So you think we should be fighting people?" she asked.

"If it's necessary," he replied. "Actually we come from Viking people originally. Never forget that. Life is a fight. It's better that you figure that out early."

The next day the Taylor twins stayed on the south side of the playground, and the Russians in the north. The territory had been staked out. Both sides knew that to cross it meant death. However there was a certain amount of ritual scowling and vulgar signs.

Many other children became involved and chose one or the other as their gang to join. The Russians had the whites, the Asians and various others, the Taylors had the blacks of which there were many. The latinos were mainly on the Russian side also.

As the lunch break progressed the kids in the Russian gang began to question Irene and Serge on what was going on with their music band.

"Is it true you've played a real gig, and with your ma and pa?" This from a Chinese boy with a squint.

"Do you get paid a lot?" another kid hustled.

"Is it scary?" a third demanded.

"How do you know what to play?" a small girl questioned, fighting to get the words out past a badly shaped dental brace. The questions became a flood as Irene and Serge were surrounded by gaping mouths, and persistent stares.

"Do you ever play a wrong note? Do you sing? Have you been on TV? Are you gonna make it? Will you remember me when you've made a million? Will you live in LA when you're a big star? How did you learn to play drums? How did she learn to sing? Does she have a boyfriend? Can I be your girlfriend? Can you teach me music? Can I join your band? When's the next gig? Can I come?"

In the end the two consented to write out autographs onto scraps of exercise book paper, promising to bring cassettes of their latest recording to school the next day.

When they arrived home that night, Serge

went to the kitchen crying for supper. He was hungry. His lunch had been stolen, he said. Maya was shocked.

'Only a sandwich now, that's all," Leo shouted. "We have to rehearse the band. Don't forget, Friday, it's a big gig and we've got to be good. This is a chance to earn proper money, and right now even food is short. There's nothing in the fridge." He glowered at them across the living room, beard twitching with expectation.

"Perhaps they should rest first," Maya suggested timidly.

"Nonsense," Leo shouted, eyes blazing.

"Let's have the young lions on stage, and rehearsing this minute. Come on! The drums are set up, and the PA is switched on. Irene, get out your bass. Kira, bring your trombone."

"OK," Irene replied. Serge wolfed down his ham sandwich, and slid grudgingly down onto the drum stool. Then deliberately crashed hard on the cymbals exactly as Leo had bent down close to them, to make a delicate adjustment to the sound system controls.

That earned him a swift slap round the face. He howled and ran off. Leo stomped after him, caught him by the ear, and lead him back to the music area. Irene and Maya watched with grave faces. Now Serge stopped crying, and climbed back on the drum stool once more.

For the next half an hour the music progressed as it should. Yet something was missing. It sounded heavy and without spirit.

Time was moving on, and was evening was getting late. Serge sat silently at his kit, playing his drums in a wooden, robotic way, staring at the wall. Irene shot him worried glances now and then.

"Leo, I think they are tired?" queried Maya. He stiffened. Then levelled with her once more, speaking in a calm, clinical manner. His voice was like honey, yet with a touch of acid.

"Do you want to be out on the street, in the shelter again?" he asked. "Because that's exactly what you are suggesting. How many times do I have to say this? I am tired of repeating it. No rehearsal means no gig done well. No gig means no pay. No money means eviction. Am I making myself understood? We do this for ourselves, to survive. There is no other way. You all think I am monster. Is not the case. To me you are monsters. You threaten security of my house, my family. Get it?"

There was a troubled silence. Then suddenly all hell broke loose. The drums were knocked over as a tiny figure sped out from the rehearsal area, knocking things over as he ran. It was Serge. He had already tipped over an entire table of plates, cups and food by the time Leo caught him near the front door. The family winced as they heard cries of pain from both of them, the sound of a frantic struggle followed by a long drawn out howl of agony from Serge. Finally he was lead back and made to rehearse more.

As soon as Leo and Maya were asleep that

night, Irene and Serge hastily and silently packed their bags and slipped out into the street. They headed for the subway, avoiding shadowy figures in their path.

An hour later they found me at the door of Jazzlands. It was 1am. I was just leaving for Flatbush, after a late rehearsal.

"Irene," I called, suddenly concerned. "It's so late. What are you two doing out here?"

"Dad beat Serge up," Irene said. "I thought to call the police but then Serge said no, let's come here."

"Oh no," I muttered. "Come in then. Are you OK? Is Serge badly hurt?"

"It's nothing," Serge said. "All I want to do is sleep," he yawned.

"Me too," Irene agreed, rubbing her eyes.

"Crash on my floor at Flatbush?" I offered. "It's awful, but better than being outside." They nodded glumly.

By this time Marina and Jay had appeared, and demanded to know the entire story. Jay was joyful at the news.

"That old rascal. I knew it," he crowed. "Didn't I say that old piece of trash was gonna crack? Now it's jail for him. Holy crap! It's enough to turn a guy religious, when the world looks this good. I don't see why I don't crack open that new crate of beer I was holding back for some special occasion. I reckon this is it."

"But it's serious," Marina protested, with a

disapproving eye. These kids can't be on the street. Too dangerous." Jay stamped with irritation.

"Hey, that pixie ragamuffin b**** gonna haul ass like everybody else," he growled. "She gonna learn that life is all about hard work. I don't see why she don't start washing our dishes, for starters. Plus we've got all kinds of heavy trash in the basement which needs lifting and throwing out. I need my bass amp cleaned. Why, she could prove real useful."

He strolled towards Irene.

"Come here," he ordered. "Can you sew and cook, and do all the proper things that a woman should do? Can you get down on your knees and scrub? Hey? 'Cos you in trouble. You're just lucky that I may be able to help your sorry ass out, if you're good, that is. I know your papa ain't no good but maybe you're better than him. Hey, I'm giving you the benefit of the doubt." He glowered at her with much satisfaction.

"Hold on Jay," Marina protested.

"We're going with Max," Serge said. "Come on Irene." He grabbed her hand. I made a wry face and opened my arms helplessly.

"It looks like they're coming with me," I said.

One hour later we were entering the Flatbush basement, under a pale moon. Mercifully the side door worked. The kids were amazed when they saw all the shoddy dollar store items piled high in my tiny room.

"What's all this?" Irene asked. I sighed with exasperation.

"It all belongs to a friend of Jean," I told her.

188

"He was given all of this stuff. Someone had been hiring him at a dollar store and they could not afford to pay him, so he accepted it all as an alternative."

"But why is it in your room?" she asked.

"He had been renting the place earlier," I said. "Actually, as of now, he still is. The super collects rent from two people at once."

"That's impossible," Serge protested.

"Oh yeah? This is New York," I said.

"Anyway, does anyone want food or tea?" I asked.

"Where is it?" Serge wanted to know. "Over there," I pointed.

"All I see is lampshades and socks," he said.

"Underneath. Can you help me dig out the eating area?"

In a few minutes a space had been cleared. We hunkered down and I proceeded to fry some sausages for them, on an electric ring on the floor, and then I made toast, and finally boiled the kettle. There were only 18 inches of space between the bed and the wall in which to do all this, in beween two tottering walls of dollar store curios.

"Where will you two sleep?" I asked. "I mean, we have to dig your areas out."

"I'll bed down in the cosmetics area, near the window," Irene announced.

"I like the toys," Serge said. Pretty soon they were all dug out.

"Now, the clothes ration," I said. "You each get a couple of jackets and pairs of pants to sleep on.

No cushions or blankets, I'm afraid. I have no use for them. You can fold up a T-shirt and stuff it full of underwear or socks to make a pretty good cushion though. Oh, and I have to have the TV and the radio on, all night."

"All night?" asked Irene.

"Yes, all night. It masks out the neighbourhood noise. This they understood.

We lay down and I lit a candle, telling them that it would relax us. Then I switched off the light. All was calm for a while. Now suddenly I heard the crackle and pop of dollar store plastic packets. Serge had started moving around again.

"Max, what's this?"

"What's what?" I called out drowsily.

"This paper on the wall. Something about banks like churches?"

"Oh that? It's a poem I wrote."

"It's a bit hard to read your handwriting," he complained. But then he started to read it out loud.

AMERICA.

Banks like churches.
Churches like theatre stages.
Songs written by computer programmers.
Musicians wearing army fatigues. Food made of powder, served by actresses.
Politicians pumped by dollar corporations.
Stars sliced by surgeons.
Surgeons sued by lawyers.

City streets sued by people who fall.
Children know all.
Old men nothing at all.
I jump the subway turnstile, and fly 200 blocks,
laughing ...

"Max, when did you write all that?"
"I don't remember," I grunted.
"And why?"
"Look, can we sleep now please?"

"Sergeant Tilson?"
"Yes?"
"There's a situation. Two kids gone AWOL at Liberty Avenue. Can you put a search out?"
"Will do. Details?"
"Eleven year old girl, named Irene, white. Ten year old boy, named Serge, white. Russian family. Last seen Liberty Avenue, late night, 11pm."
"Got it. I'll get on with it."

In the morning the kids woke up complaining about the cold.
"We're hungry," they wailed, in chorus.
"OK, I hear you," I yelled back, shifting mounds of clutter to clear a space to work. Then I cooked more sausages, with eggs this time, and plenty of toast.
"Do you think we should go back home now?" Irene asked, dipping a fragment of toast into her coffee.

"Yes, but no rush," I told her. "First we need to talk to Jean upstairs. She's very wise about things like this."

At Liberty Avenue, the phone never stopped ringing. A man and a lady from the social services had visited, demanding to know every possible detail of the kids. Leo had been repeatedly interrogated and cross-examined. The local news had been alerted.

Maya was sitting on the bed, crying silently. At 2pm the police phoned, requesting that a statement be made at the police station. The younger children were wandering around, alternately wailing and stealing food from the fridge.

The details of the missing children were now on the police computer network. Cops on patrol in all the relevant areas had been notified. A statement had been made on community TV and radio in the tristate area. Up in the skies above Brooklyn, police helicopters scanned the area, looking for not only Irene and Serge, but countless other missing kids, and also criminals on the run.

After breakfast we rode the freight elevator up to Jean's apartment. Fortunately it worked at the first attempt. Jean's apartment door was unbolted, as always, so we strode inside.

"Oh lordy my, what is all this?" Jean crowed, from her place at the TV table, in the kitchen.

"Visitors," I announced. "This is Irene and Serge. They are the children of Leo. You know, the

Russian family who I play gigs with."

"Well look at that," she cried. "Come on in. I was just finishing up my breakfast. Do you chilluns need any? I can put on more porridge, and we have cereal too?" They consented to eat cereal.

"But why are you all here?" she wanted to know.

"They slept the night with me," I said. "They're on the run. Leo disciplined Serge because he wouldn't rehearse enough. There were a few slaps."

"That's terrible," Jean said, eyeing Serge carefully. "Are you with bruises?"

"I'm OK," he said. "But we had to get out."

Now Jean had more words to say about this.

"You know, we do have to rehearse," she said. "I've been hearing all kinds of good things about you and your family band. You're all on the road to something big. That's very exciting. Now it ain't gonna be easy, I have to tell you. You will have to work very, very hard. And rehearsal is all part of it."

"Yes, but we were tired," Irene broke in.

"I do know all about that," she answered. "I've been tired all my life. Do you think I don't know what tiredness is?"

"We'd done a whole day's school and I was sleepy, and he beat me up but I couldn't even play. My eyes were closing," Serge complained.

'Well you do what you have to do to keep those eyes open," she said. "Listen to me, nobody gonna pay for you when you're older. It's everyone for themselves. There ain't no free lunches out there. That's why we all have to work real hard."

"Now come and sit down with me for a second,"she told them. "Listen closely." We gathered around.

"You're gonna need a song," she said. "Do you have your song?"

"We play songs," Irene answered.

"They do play songs," I echoed.

"Yes, but there are songs and songs. Do you have a real song, a proper, big song? It's all about the song," she insisted.

"Yes we do have a proper, big song," Serge said.

The kids ate their cereal while Jean and I moved through to the living room. Then I discussed with her the question of what to do with them.

"You could take them to your club in Manhattan," she suggested. "There are musical instruments there. Get them to play a little bit and be happy! And then take them back to their parents." I immediately saw the wisdom of this advice. The children were still traumatised by recent events. They loved music and this idea would probably help them relax and feel better. So, after they had finished eating, we got on the train.

After a few stops, at Atlantic Avenue, a man got on. Incredibly, he hauled a large armchair right into the subway car, sat down and brought out a newspaper and scanned it. I had seen some wild things in New York, but never this.

"Why is he doing that?" Serge wanted to know.

"I suppose he likes an easy ride," I told him

"The club is closed," Marina shouted, shutting the door on us firmly. I knocked again.

"Marina," I said. "Come on now! I still pay a third of the rent here, remember?"

"You and those clowns ain't wanted here," Jay announced. I took a deep breath.

"Well maybe you can enter," said Marina.

"But the rest can haul butt right back to where they comin' from," added Jay. Irene looked troubled by this remark.

"Look, we're coming in," I shouted, and pushed the door open. Once inside the dog licked my hand.

"Hell, I'm goin' downstairs to clean my gun," Jay said disgustedly. "I ain't even woken up yet. Don't need no sorry loser pixie bass slappers in my club. I was lookin' to put my feet up and have some broccoli pie. But now it's all messed up, hell I ain't hangin around in this pigsty. You can do all the foolin' around you want, I'm outta here. Just nobody touch my bass, OK. Specially that pygmy KGB gnome. She gives me the shivers. Lay off it, understand? She thinks her pa is trouble? She don't know me, that's for sure. This n***** don't take no mess. OK?" He stomped off down the steps, still mumbling and cursing.

"And stay down, *Broccoli boy*," Marina shouted. "And can you chill out? It's too hot for you to mouth off like that." Then suddenly she turned to me and lowered her voice.

"I suppose you want coffee. But the children must pay to enter the club." At this she splayed out her legs, blocking our way inside the door.

"Marina!" I said, testily. "The young boy has been assaulted. The police are probably out searching for him right now."

"Forget it," she snapped. "There's plenty more than that for the cops to worry about. The kids will get home soon enough. But first I have an idea. I will give them a music lesson."

"Why?" I asked. "Why now?"

"Because they are young and starting off in the difficult world of music. New York is very hard. I mean to teach them some scales, and some free-jazz singing."

The phone rang. Marina talked for a few minutes and then returned, very excited. Her eyes were shining.

"No music lesson today. Max, take the children back. Then meet me in town. There's a record label that wants to talk. Now hurry. This could be a big break for us." Silently, the kids packed their bags.

An hour later I walked the children up the subway steps at Liberty Avenue, and then stopped suddenly.

"I'm not going any further," I stated. "You will be fine, don't worry. They must be half-dead with worry by now. I'm proud of you both. Go on to your apartment now. I'm heading back home."

Irene turned to me gratefully.

"Thanks for taking us in like that," she said. "We were desperate. I thought we were going to have to sleep out on the street last night."

"But you would have been OK," I reasoned. "You're a rock musician. Plus, you're Russian. That means you're tough enough for anything! Anyway, you've got Serge to look after you."

"Thanks, Max," he said, and gave me a hug.

Suddenly I looked up and Leo was standing in front of us. He flashed his eyes at us, looking very angry.

"So, you finally come home," he said to the kids, with some sarcasm. "Go back to the house right now. Maya is very worried." They disappeared.

"Have they been with you all this time?" he wanted to know.

"I had to persuade them to come back here," I told him. "Why did they leave," I demanded. "Did you hit them?"

"No", he said.

"I'm sorry, but I think you did," I told him sullenly, folding my arms and spreading my feet apart. His face became dark suddenly.

All at once we were wrestling on the ground. He was tough and wiry and knew all kinds of Russian fighting moves that confused me. Quickly, I was forced right down to the ground, and trapped in an armlock, on my front. My head was pressed against the hard Brooklyn asphalt. Then suddenly he started laughing and released me.

"I'm sorry, but I can't carry on," he exploded, eyes flashing with glee. "It's just too funny, the way you fight, so British! You are a man from two centuries ago."

I sat up and brushed dirt off my clothes.

"That's as maybe," I grunted suspiciously. Then a slow smile crossed my face.

"OK, you're right," I said. "Why are we fighting? You're my best friend. We've been through so much together. Can you see how crazy this is?" My shirt had torn and now I tucked it into my jeans as he helped me to my feet.

"Max, you are such a gentleman," he said, still chortling. "The classic British. Hey, it was easy to bring you down. How did you guys make such an empire? Big mystery!" Right now I chose to ignore this provocation.

"Can I say you are the classic Russian? I never ever know what you are thinking," I answered. "Come on, give me a hug."

We embraced.

"Brits cannot be real friends until we've fought," I told him. He made no reply to this.

"I'll be back in a few days," I said, and headed back down the subway steps.

It took me a while to calm down. My clothes were all dirty and a shirt sleeve was torn.

Later I found Marina leaning against the wall outside the record company.

"Max, your face," she shouted, in alarm. "What have you been up to?"

"Leo attacked me," I told her sullenly. "It's OK. We made it up afterwards."

"What, are you crazy? He's a hard guy! And Russian! Never fight with a Russian!" she squawked. I soothed her feelings.

An ambulance screeched round the corner, and disappeared, heading uptown.

"There's no harm done," I told her. "Here, what's happening with this appointment?"

"I blew him out," she said.

"What?" I gaped at her.

"He was lousy with me," she insisted. "Told me to make more demos then talk to him again. Who the hell does he think he is to talk to me that way?"

We headed for a diner where it took me several hours to calm her.

"This is a tough business," I told her. "Who is this guy anyway? Don't let anyone put you down, OK? You are who you are." She looked at me gratefully.

"Thanks Max," she said. "You always cheer me up. Hey, let's go check out the live acts along Bleecker Street!"

"Why not?" I said.

MY DOLLAR STORE PRISON

One morning I woke up to find another side of my tiny cell had been deluged with yet more dollar store items, six foot high in places, almost blocking the door.

This time it was umbrellas, winter socks, gardening items, dolls and all kinds of phones including plastic imitations. There were also boxes of fake flowers and plastic birds.

I cursed and waded waist-deep through gadgets to the tiny fridge. It was buried under clocks, calculators and novelty wigs. I slapped a couple of roaches off my legs.

Outside in the corridor, the Columbian drug dealer was pacing and talking in a high, soft latin voice, on the phone, loading his handgun as he did so. He ignored me as I cautiously headed for the bathroom.

Once inside a nightmarish vision met my eyes. The super hadn't cleaned up for months. There were mounds of human waste all over the floor. I had to step carefully to get to the toilet. It was a relief to finally get out again and jump back to my office, relock the door and dig out a space to work in, phone a few contacts, make a fried egg with beans, smoke a cigar, then start practising scales on the keyboard. Pretty soon I checked my watch and saw that it was time to head on out.

I prowled out to the elevator, then glimpsed

a mountain of brand new clothes that had been trashed down here last night. Joyfully, I rummaged through the lot. There were fashion jackets and shirts, luxury brand names, and the best designer jeans, plus good, solid cowboy boots. I raced back to my hide-out with at least eight complete armfulls of loot. Some areas of my room were now packed with clutter almost all the way to the ceiling. A few essential bags had unfortunately been buried under yards of kitchenware and toiletry items. As I threw stuff around I cursed the man who was doing all this to me. I knew it was the previous tenant who had done some crooked deal with the super, giving him the continual right to store stuff, even though I was now paying for the room. In other words, the super had rented the same exact space out, twice, to two totally different individuals.

I cursed some more, ran my fingers through my hair, packed a bag, locked up the huge padlock into its chain around the door handle, and finally headed for the elevator. I pressed the button. Nothing happened. I pressed it again, harder. Still nothing. Yet I could hear the freight elevator whizzing up and down, transporting other residents. Those were the ones who lived in the real world, who paid proper rent, who had status, and the right to exist. I didn't have any of those things. Damn!

Wearily I made for the side door and checked it. It was locked. I realised I couldn't get out until someone upstairs heard me yelling and who then finally woke up the super who was probably with a hooker by now, stoned on beer and coke, lost from the world.

I hunkered down on the damp stone floor and started to yell, at regular intervals.

"Hello! Hey there! HELLO! Can you hear me? Please? Somebody, HELLO!"

It was going to be a long morning.

"Liars, all liars," shouted Leo. We were back at the apartment after a day of rehearsing, hustling and so on. He was back on the same old topic.

"OK, I get it, you hate America, it sucks," I told him, trying to pacify him gently. He turned and glared at me, hair and beard wild and crazy, and eyes full of emotion.

"They are all in short pants," he growled, striding up and down the room. The dog barked suddenly. Irene ran to him and stroked him. I tried to make rational sense of the situation.

"OK, I'm on your side. I'm not keen on America either," I told him. Then I grinned suddenly. "But why are we here? There must be something good?" He sat down wearily, putting a hand through his hair, and staring at me, searching for comprehension.

Kira stomped up, holding a steaming cup for me in her tiny hands.

"I've brought you your tea, Max," she said, with a big-eyed grin, then disappeared. There was a quick smile between Leo and me.

"Plenty wrong with America," I conceded.

"They kill millions, in wars, like Vietnam. The food is junk. They constantly lie, just to get money out of you. The poor are in a horrible state. They have ghettos. We're in one right now. It's like living in a warzone. People are shooting each other all the time. It goes on and on. There is no integrity here. No art and no culture. It's a disaster area. This country is totally decadent, and going off the rails. And the worst of it is that we, the British, started them off!" He roared with laughter.

Now he stared at me intensely, picked an old cardboard box out of the trash, then ripped it up dramatically

"Families break up here, all over the place," he growled.

"They're not breaking us up," shouted Irene, smiling mischievously from the kitchen, where she was helping Maya with the meal.

We laughed. But then I acknowledged Leo's point.

"Yet it is very true that families often do break up here," I admitted. "So why is that? Because I have noticed that even if they don't split by accident, due to arguments, they will split by design. What I mean is that at a certain age a kid will just relocate to college, somewhere often at least 2000 miles away, and many times he'll never come back."

"It goes deeper than that," Leo said.

"I know it does," I agreed. "I don't think love can exist here. There's too much paranoia."

"Listen to me," he continued. "Over here,

you become a slave of the dollar. Have you noticed that? The dollar is the state. The dollar-state constantly needs slaves, people without minds, people without a family, which is the same thing. The family gives us strength, gives us the power to fight back. But the dollar-state needs to constantly expand, to be invading new countries. It needs faceless soldiers, without brains. America has almost no morality at all. That was something only of the old world. Nothing is casual here. This is the reason we are losing our memory, forgetting who we are, running for the dollar like little rats..."

"Daddy I need money for chewing gum," Serge shouted suddenly from the other side of the room.

"You see?" Leo said.

"Well come on?" I argued.

"No, it starts like that. Everything is for sale here. And not just for sale. The products are screaming in your face. It's all about status. They want to reduce you to the level of an ant, if you don't buy their product, if you don't become a dollar slave, a zombie of the dollar state."

I digested this for a while.

"I suppose that, for you, back in Soviet Russia, there was none of this, I imagine," I started out.

"Of course not," he said. "We were actually OK. I agree they would censor the most extreme opinions, that is true. But mainly, we could think straight. Here, nobody can. Just look at this newspaper!"

He hurled one to the ground in disgust.

"No news. Just lies. Look at the TV. No, please don't watch TV. It's all sugar, sweet lies, all corruption, totally false. Just like sticky honey to catch the little flies!"

"I see what you mean," I said. We paused for a moment.

And then, unexpectedly, he started to defend America, but in a bizarre way.

"It's a country based on slaves," he said. "And the slaves created music. The blues. And that's the one great thing they did. And that's why I'm here. That's why Brother Kharma are here."

"Me too." I nodded sharply. "This is what brought me also. The incredible black music. The way it happens right here in New York, and all over America too. For me, it's blues and jazz, mainly. It's the powerful, liberating feeling you get when you listen to it it, or when you play it here. It's not just something inside the musicians, it's inside the audiences too. Music is a living thing, or should be. Do you know, at the jazz restaurant where I play, we've had them dancing on the tables sometimes? And it wasn't even the hippest, most modern, fusion jazz, it was old time jazz, like New Orleans, Dixieland jazz? That's the dream for me. This is what nourishes my soul, and so that's why I'm here."

I paused to reconsider for a moment.

"Americans are different from Europeans," I said. "It's not something in them, it's something that's not in them," I added. "They're not getting shy, and switching off every second, the way they do back home." He agreed.

"And you've brought your family here, to play to these audiences," I marvelled. "That will change and shape them. They are lucky to have a father like you. What would I have given for my father to bring me to America to play music in New York, to the audiences they have here!"

"Thank you," he said.

It was 2am. Marina, Jay and myself were eating a plate of pasta after playing the usual seven, forty-five minute sets, at Echoes.

Jay stared at the miserable food in disbelief.

"Is that all Bert can give?" he grumbled. "After seven sets? Seven hours we been working? That ain't right. I should walk right out.

"What about some meat or cheese?" he grouched. "I can't do nothing with that. Nobody can take this Italian garbage. I ain't even hungry when I look at it. There ain't nothing there. What, they call this sauce? It ain't nothing but a drip of some slimy stuff."

"It's called pesto," Marina explained. "We get the musicians' menu."

"That's what I'm talkin' about," Jay exploded. "We get low class food, nothing like what these stuck up clowns get. Anyway, I don't want that Russian *Rasputin* guy prowling around my hideout no more," he growled. "His sorry ass was there yesterday, and I'm telling you, I can't stand it no more. I'm done with him. He gives me the shivers. All that long red hair and crazy looking eyes. I should waste the mofo. Give him some roach spray.

"And you know what?" he continued. "He even tried to tell me how to play my bass guitar. Told me that little pixie b**** of his could play bass proper and I should listen to her. Well I ain't gonna listen to no pixie ragamuffin b****. She can get the hell out of my hideout too. I ain't runnin' no club for no sorry mofos like this KGB gang. We've already suffered the cold war way too long. I hope this new president rips off a few nukes to really wipe those commie clowns out altogether."

He was well into his thing now, talking louder and waving a fork around.

"Look at all this dancing and squatting these Russians do. I seen 'em on TV. That ain't dancing! And I've heard they get all sweated up in log cabins, pack full of vodka and then beat each other up with logs in the snow. Well they can get the hell back to Russia and sweat and flay all they like, I ain't having none of it."

"Leo says he may have a deal with a major label," I murmured, delicately picking out the last of my pesto sauce with a spoon.

"He's lying," Marina laughed.

"Yeah I wouldn't trust one word that old slave-trader says," Jay declared. Look at him with those kids of his. They ain't nothin' but slaves. I've heard he lashed 'em with a flail one time. I'll bet he even has a white hood and a flamin' cross back at that roach motel he done gone landed up in.

"Now listen up," he continued, warming to his story.

"I overheard him giving them a KGB pep-talk yesterday. We're all gonna make it," he said. "Listen to what a wild pack of lies he's dreamed up. First he said he was gonna knock our band out, for starters! Get a load of that! Now he's telling them about this luxury villa in Bel Air he says he gonna buy with their first million dollar advance. Haw haw haw! He ain't gonna have no advance. This time next year he'll be in some swamp in Florida, playing to a shack full of child molesters and alligators, you mark my words."

"Come on, now," I protested. "Leo's not that bad. And I think he does have some serious interest from the powers that be."

"Powers? What powers? He ain't got more power than a dead roach. Well I'm sick of him anyway. And I don't want him in my club. I'll kick his ass next time he appears."

My club? I wondered whether to remind him who's cash had set up the place, whose relative had signed the lease, and whose girlfriend had organised everything. Ah, but now she was Jay's woman. So I clammed up.

Now, for some odd reason, Marina shifted to Leo's side.

She glared at Jay, thyroid eyes burning with irritation.

"Can it, *Broccoli boy*," she shouted.

"I know why he talks big," she said. "If you go for the top, you get a little, but if you go for a little, you get nothing." She gestured towards the ceiling, then to the floor, to illustrate her point.

Suddenly I saw Bill clambering in out of the night, slapping the rain off the arms of his big brown leather jacket.

"Bill," I shouted.

"Hello, my old mates," he called.

"Oh no," I groaned, "The gig's over. You could have sat in."

"Maybe next time," he smiled. I showed him to a chair. It was inevitable that we soon start talking about Brother Kharma.

"Yes, they're kind of weird," he started out.

"Goddamn freaks," grumbled Jay. Bill ignored this.

"Nobody can really figure out who they are, or how they get that sound," he continued. An Indian waiter appeared.

"I'm sorry sir, you're too late, the kitchen's closed," he confessed regretfully. But Bill glanced at him in a sly way.

"Just an apple-pie, hot with cream? And a coffee?"

"OK, we can probably arrange that," the waiter admitted, scuttling out of sight. Then Bill got back to Brother Kharma.

"We don't know where they're going, or where they've come from," he marvelled. "But they're real. Loads of energy. They do the business and please the crowd. I know I like it, that's all."

Jay shifted around in his chair, grumbling away.

"It's their conviction that I like," I told him. "They believe in what they're doing. More than anybody else. They've gambled everything on this."

The man with red hair is walking outside the house. He meets the super. They talk a little. It's getting late. The sun is just going down.

Suddenly they notice an elderly black man, walking as fast as he can, coming back from the store where people change money and so on. There are two younger men following his footsteps. Quickly they gain on him, take him to the ground and put a gun to his head. All in a flash the elderly man has reached for his shoe and pulled out a roll of bills. The thieves head off and are instantly gone.

THE RUNAWAYS

That winter the city was lashed by sixteen falls of snow, which often immobilised the traffic entirely. It became bitterly cold, and life was tougher than I had ever known. Why go through hell and back in this way? What kept me going? Many days I asked myself this question, but could conjure up no real answer.

Except the music. This was the key. I knew this to be a unique moment for my career, and that there would never be another chance.

Jean's son now arrived from Chicago, to stay 24 hours. Jean had explained that I would have to be at the club with Marina and Jay, purely for this one night, since her son would be sleeping on the living room sofa, where I normally slept. I gave her my okay, but then with a heavy heart I found myself trudging out into the street just as the light began to fail. It was true that I had told Jean that I was heading for the club, but now I finally knew that I could not stand to sleep under the same roof as Marina and her lover. Where to head for? I had no idea, but for sure I had to find somewhere, and fast, as it was getting darker and colder every second.

With a new determination I jumped down the subway steps, paid my fare, and waited until a train roared into the station. The doors opened and instantly I was staring into the faces of Irene and Serge. They were just getting off, so I decided to miss the train and to find out what was going on. It was a shock to see the two young kids out alone like this.

"Irene, where are you going," I asked her. Where is Leo? What's going on? Where is the family?"

"We ran off," Irene said, with a guilty giggle. "They are arguing so hard. It was at this studio. We're not going back, I've made up my mind. Not tonight anyway. I'm old enough to look after myself."

"You're twelve," I exclaimed.

"Well we're doing it anyway. Do you know where we can sleep? Just for a night or two?" she asked.

"I was about to ask you the same thing. Marina and me have split up just recently. She's with Jay now."

"I'm sorry," Irene said. "Does it hurt?" I laughed bitterly. The train disappeared into the tunnel.

"Don't be sorry," I said. "It's true we were a long time together, but she has a very difficult side. Actually she can be really tough at times."

"Is she a b****?" Serge asked, grinning wickedly. "I think she is," he decided. "Don't worry Max, you're gonna be alright. Stick with us."

"Thanks," I said. "But listen. "I don't have any place to sleep either, even for myself." I explained about Jean's son sleeping on her sofa tonight.

"So where are we going to go?" I asked.

An overweight woman blundered past us carrying an enormous bag.

"Not our house," said Irene.

"And not Marina's club," I replied. "I don't want to be there." We stared at each other.

"You said you were in a squat one time," Irene added.

"That's where I was about to suggest," I told her.

"What is this place?" Serge asked. "I'll take anywhere, I don't care."

"We know how to defend ourselves," added Irene.

"I'll defend you both, if there's any defending to do," I told them, sticking my jaw forward defiantly.

"Me too," shouted Serge. "I'll defend us too!" Suddenly we were all laughing.

"It's not this train," I told them. "Actually, we can get there on foot. Come on."

We walked and walked. It was getting dark, and the neon signs of the restaurants and bars were bright against the evening sky. I took the kids' hands, one on each side.

"This is boring," I said. "Let's sing."

Now the kids started to sing some rock anthem together. I joined in for a few choruses.

"But what kind of song do you want to sing now?" Serge asked me. I wracked my brains for a moment.

"Well, it could be a blues, or just a regular song?" I suggested.

In the end we started making up nonsense songs as we walked. This was fun for a while and then Irene almost tripped over a cracked paving stone and we all stopped to check she was OK.

"Feet, feet," I reminded her. "Never forget the feet. Stay grounded." She threw me a peculiar look.

"I don't want to walk any more," sang Serge, moaning out the words a bit.

"'I'm so tired I wanna die," echoed Irene with lots of mournful sass to her words.

"How about an old English sea shanty, or maybe a folk song?" I ventured. Serge gave me a puzzled look. So I began to croon.

'*Long years ago when I was born, the flowers they bloomed and the birds they sang...*'

This gave them a chuckle for a few more blocks.

Just as night fell we arrived at the squat.

"Oh no," whispered Irene, as she saw the horrific barricade around the door. She tensed up, and suddenly I felt very protective about her.

"I know this place," she said distantly. "I think I was here with my family a few years ago."

"I know this place too," echoed Serge. "And I remember the guy, too." He looked down at the ground.

"Just stay alert," I warned. "We"ll get through this. Look tough. Put on the New York mouth, you know, the fish face?" The two immediately made fish faces so hard that I burst out laughing.

Now we banged on the door. Nothing.

"Looks like we gotta wait," I admitted. "Come on, let's sit down on the kerb. Don't worry, we'll get in eventually. I've been here before, with Marina, one time, long years ago."

"So have we," said Irene.

"*Long years ago, when I was young*," sang Serge, sarcastically.

I could not tell them my worst fears, which were that the heroin dealers would be arguing, and possibly fighting around us all night.

The kids had gone to sleep when someone finally arrived and let us in an hour later. I woke them up and we shuffled inside. The place was exactly the same, grim, deserted and filthy as ever. We began to climb. On the second floor a door was open and I saw a desolate figure hunched over, writing something at a table. On the back of his yellow workman's jacket were written the words 'AIDS - MEDICAL WASTE'. It stunned me that a guy could have AIDS and then laugh about it in this manner. I hurried the kids onwards.

Wearily we continued and finally reached the top landing. It was dark and dingy up there, but I was amazed to see the cradle still in its place, in the middle of the floor.

"Nothing ever changes in this place," I said. Now I realised I had to get tough and take control.

"OK, let's be like the army now," I said. "There's the bathroom on the left if you need it. You two, jump in the basket, right now. I'll sleep on the floor beside you. 7am we're out of here. The street is better than this place once it's daytime."

As I lay down in the darkness my heart was full of emotion. Talking to the kids about losing Marina had set off a big emotion. Right now I understood she had been everything to me. She was the original wild child, the tomboy rebel, packed with energy and culture, and all the magic and beauty of Italy. But she had betrayed me. And yet I could not think badly of Jay. I knew that she had started this romance, more than him. I could not hate a black person after dedicating my life to playing black music. They had been slaves. What mattered a tussle over a woman, in the face of three hundred years of slavery? And deep down I knew that you cannot fight to restore love that has gone. It was over, and I would have to deal with it, and survive.

Just then Serge let out a huge snore. Irene had her arms wrapped around him, and she shook him a little, and then he mumbled something and was asleep again instantly.

And now in my heart I blessed the kids for being beside me in my desperate moment of need. With them there, I knew I would be OK. I marveled at the strange chance of fate that had brought us together today. Pretty soon I sank into some kind of shallow slumber.

In the night I dreamed Marina was a huge lioness, and that she had finally arrived home to Africa and found a male lion to be with. I woke up around 3am crying. I had lost her forever, and the pain had only just begun. Then I remembered where I was and saw the kids fast asleep, hugging each other, and all at once I knew that life was a fight, and that by some strange twist of fate I was now looking after them for a while. This calmed me.

I was just going back to sleep when I saw two shadowy figures emerge from the staircase. One was limping.

"Pedro?" I called, softly, through the blackness.

"Who is it?" He was instantly alert, and now there was a gun in his hand.

"It's Max. Remember me?"

"No, I don't. Who the hell are you?" His voice was full of menace.

At that I sat up. He saw the kids and softened a little.

"What, a whole family here tonight? Yes, your face is familiar now. You were with Marina that time?"

"Yes, but actually we just split up earlier today." He calmed a little more, putting the gun away carefully.

"These are your kids?"

"No, but I'm protecting them. They've run away for a while." He gave a curt little laugh.

"Now I remember you, Max. You stayed in the fire-eater's room."

"That's right."

"You two were musicians."

"Yes, and these kids are musicians too.

They're from a Russian family."

"Russian?" He looked thoughtful for a second. Then his face brightened up.

"Look, Max, I need to sleep now, but I have an idea. Come with me tomorrow morning to WAI studios? All of you? There's a big guy there, a friend of mine. He's looking for Russian kids who play music. They can earn money."

"Are you serious? That's fantastic!"

"Yes, let's do this," muttered Irene, still half asleep. She had been listening. Serge let out another huge snore, and she wrapped her arms around him again.

"This is great, Pedro, we're ready," I told him.

"Bye," he said, and disappeared. Then he popped his head out again.

"If Klaus appears in the night, just ignore him. He's a bit mental. He thinks he lives up here, but just chuck him downstairs if he tries to take their basket."

He shut the door. The darkness was total. By now I was totally on edge. Who was this Klaus?

At 4am I found out.

A great hulk of a man arrived and slumped into a corner, then immediately fell asleep. But at this stage the kids and I were awake. There was deadly silence in the pitch black. Just the sound of a water drip somewhere. Now Klaus moaned and gurgled a bit, then crawled into a ball and all we could hear was a long slow sound of breathing. Every so often there would be a tiny piteous little cry from him, and then silence. Gradually the kids and I relaxed, and eventually I fell into a troubled sleep.

In the morning we grabbed a quick breakfast in the diner opposite. Serge buried his head in a plate of egg and beans, then emerged with a sudden thought.

"Is WAI a big studio?" he wanted to know.

"Big? It's massive," I told him.

"What is it, a music company?" asked Irene.

"It's everything," I told her excitedly. "News, entertainment, music, advertising, films, the lot. WAI is international. This is big time. It's crazy that Pedro has somehow wriggled in with these guys. I never would have believed it.

"They have an enormous building at Rockefeller Plaza," I gushed. "You probably know it already. Plus, I've heard they have big basements too. A whole underground city, I'm told."

Serge choked on his beans. Irene slapped his back.

"I can't wait," he chortled. "Me, live on WAI! Is it going out to the whole world?"

"Quite a bit of it," I told him.

Now Pedro appeared, wearing a satisfied smile. There were two others with him. They sat down at another table.

"Marcello?" I said. "What a surprise."

"Good to see you again, Max," he said. "And the little guys are here! Hi, Irene. Hello, Serge. You lot played fantastic at CBGBs."

"They very good. They the best. Gonna be big," the third man spluttered.

"Now Klaus," calm down, Pedro said sharply.

I looked Klaus up and down. He was dressed in an old, trampish overcoat, and his trilby hat had a couple of holes in it.

"Marcello and Klaus are coming too," Pedro said. At this I quickly ushered him to one side.

"Is that wise that he comes?" I whispered. "You yourself said he's mental!"

"He's essential," Pedro replied. "They love him there."

"Where?"

"Where we're going."

"And where are we going?"

"To play on the sidewalk outside WAI studios."

"And where's the music gear?"

"Don't worry, it's all arranged," he announced. I shrugged. Now I saw that Pedro and Serge were talking like old friends.

"What, you two know each other," I asked, fairly mystified. Serge began to stammer about something. Pedro laughed brutally.

"We met a few times. At his gigs." I relaxed on hearing this. But Serge had an uncomfortable look and wouldn't meet my eye.

"Come on, drink up your coffee," Pedro rapped. We have an early appointment." I looked round at the kids.

"OK, now who needs the small room?" I asked.

"Do you mean the ladies room?" Irene asked sweetly.

"Who needs the can?" Klaus roared. Serge giggled.

"I think I do," he said.

"You think, or you know?" Klaus thundered. I saw that one front tooth was missing, and he was chomping down with his mouth. Chronically unshaven, too.

"Now, leave the boy be," I demanded. "He's a good kid. Hurry, Serge, we have a schedule."

"Do they have two or one?" Irene asked. "Because I know I have to go too."

"Five," said Klaus. Everyone ignored him. The kids hopped off into the corner.

Soon we were on the subway. I sat beside Marcello. The noise of the train was overpowering, so I knew I could talk to him without being heard.

"Pedro is in with the big guys at WAI?" I asked incredulously.

"Yeah, I know it looks nuts," Marcello replied with a wry grin. "He makes a ton of money delivering the stuff to them, but look where he lives. It's a total dump, when he could afford a penthouse loft. Why? I'll tell you why. In that place he's in, they can't even find him. He's invisible." I chewed on this for a while.

"Well my thing is this," I replied. "All I know

is that he gave me and my woman a place to sleep when we were totally desperate. And then again, last night, he kind of guarded over us."

"He's the right guy for that," Marcello muttered. "But watch out. Don't ever cross him. He can be deadly if he turns against you."

Right across the aisle Pedro and Serge were making baby faces at each other, and then Pedro started to tickle him, chortling with glee.

"He's like a big Daddy right now," I said.

"That's my Pedro," said Marcello. "He's one of my team. You know, he saved my life twice a few years back."

"And what about Klaus?" I asked. "He looks like a sure deadbeat to me. Do we really need him with us? He's just a homeless derelict, isn't he?"

"That one is a wild card," Marcello admitted. "I've only just met him and I'm still trying to figure him out. Pedro says he's cool, though."

Just now I was horrified to notice that Klaus, sitting opposite, had taken out some loose bullets, and was counting them. A few people looked alarmed, and one woman got up and walked away, with one hand over her mouth.

"Klaus!" Pedro shouted. "Put them away. You don't do that in public. Get them out of sight."

A couple of hoodlums sniggered down the aisle. An old lady looked like she was about to cry. Tension was rising fast in the subway car.

I felt an enormous laugh rising up inside me, but shut it down immediately.

Klaus shuffled the bullets into a pocket with a suppressed roar of frustration, then leaned back with a totally blank face. Irene giggled. Even Marcello had a little smile.

"I guess I have him a little more figured out now," he said.

Now Klaus began to pick at his teeth with a rusty nail. A couple of women looked away, totally sickened. The train crashed onwards.

Finally we arrived and headed up into the street.

"Damn, we got off one stop too late," snarled Pedro. "OK, let's walk. It's only four or five blocks."

"Why not a cab?" Marcello protested in some disgust.

"I need to think and plan," said Pedro.

"But I thought we were late?"

"No, we're right on time." He strode ahead, along the sidewalk.

All we could do was follow him, muscling through the crowd.

"Stop," roared Klaus suddenly. He disappeared into a store and then returned, handing out sweets to the kids. He was eating an ice-cream cone and had strawberry and chocolate everywhere in his beard, and was grinning with triumph.

"Klaus," exclaimed Pedro, very shocked. Then he turned to us. "He steals," he confessed. "I've tried arguing with him about it, but Klaus is Klaus. What can a man say?"

Meanwhile Marcello was choking with

laughter.

"You," he spluttered! "I will never understand latinos. I know what you are up to. I know what you sell. I know where you sell it. And now you preach to poor Klaus. Oh man, you are such a comedian, *stronzo, merde*, you are a funny man!" Now it was my turn to be shocked.

"So that's why we are here," I said to Pedro. "OK, I get it. I'll pretend I never heard."

"You bet," he said, and for the first time I saw something sinister in his face. Then he switched back to friendly mode.

"Come on guys," he urged. "Two blocks more."

The storefronts on the right flashed by, with sunlight dancing off bright colours. Thousands of cans of spaghetti, then soup, then metal kitchenware. Now a gun shop with fearsome weapons on full view. Then film stars and album covers, and now a display wall packed with monkey-wrenches and drills. Finally a thousand bags of every possible brand name, size and colour.

Soul music blasted from a bargain mall. We walked on, past a shoe-shine stall with a couple of beggars leering and holding out cans to us. Then a latino barber-shop quartet on the corner of the sidewalk who instantly broke out into a wall of falsetto harmonies. Their smiles from behind greased-back hairdos and round sunglasses added the correctly nostalgic touch.

All of a sudden two cute little Japanese girl

teens appeared. They had spiky blue hair, and were on skateboards, and were hustling the kids. Irene seemed to know them.

"It's Yoshi and Rika," she said, turning to me incredulously. "Friends. They come to our gigs sometimes. Can they come with us? Please? They want to come." I opened my arms helplessly.

"OK by me," I said. Pedro grunted his assent, and marched on, staring at the horizon.

"I'm tired," moaned Serge.

"Jump on my board?" offered Rika. "It's big enough for two. Just for this block?"

"I'm really tired," he repeated, but could not resist the challenge. The two of them sailed off.

"Now hold on," I shouted, at the next stoplight. "Serge, hold my hand." We ended up in a line, all holding hands, Yoshi, Serge, Rika, Irene and me. Passersby winked at us as we sailed on down. Pedro and Klaus marched behind.

Then we turned the corner into Rockefeller Plaza and Irene gasped.

"It's all set up!" she screamed. "Are we gonna play now?"

"Yes we are," said Leo.

I swerved on my heel to face him.

"What the hell is going on?" I asked.

"It's on the news," Leo said, with a grim smile. "Brother Kharma live performance on the street outside the WAI news building. The whole city knows about it. Well done. How did you do it? Maya switched on the radio, and we heard. Then Marcello phoned too. and I came straight down. Big time deal, guys. You are learning fast. But exactly how did you swing this deal?"

"I did it," said Pedro. "Just one phone call to the right guy, that's all." Swiftly I explained who Pedro was, how he had put us up, and even how I had moved out from Jazzlands.

"Of course Marcello was part of this," he added.

"Me too," said Klaus. "I helped."

The three launched into a swift checklist of what had been going on. It appeared that Pedro and Marcello had the contacts to make this happen. There was lots of complex stuff to do with camera details, production companies, news agencies and an international project, but Pedro suddenly shouted for all to be quiet. Just at that moment Irene pointed to two figures hustling down the sidewalk, one big and one small. The small one was holding very tightly onto a trombone that was longer than she was.

"Mama," screamed Irene. "And Kira!"

"Sorry we are late," gasped Maya as she arrived. Sofia was breathless and excited.

"Good work, guys," said Leo proudly.

Now Marcello took over control.

"It starts right now," he said. "They are waiting for you. The deal is that you will be live on air even as you start to walk down the block. They know about you, all about how your family band is well-known for playing on the street, and they love that. This is an exciting pitch because it's so different from what happens with bands normally. That's why you are going out on the news right now. Do you get it? They want this thing to be live and real and totally authentic. Are you ready?" Leo took out his harp and grinned.

"Just say the word."

"Max," are you ready?" Pedro grunted.

"Me? Am I part of this?" I was amazed.

"Yes, he is," said Leo.

"So I am ready," I said.

"Irene and Serge, ready?"

"Ready."

"Klaus, ready?"

"Him," Leo asked, suddenly taken aback. "No, he's not ready. He's not even in the band."

"You don't understand," Pedro said. "They want a guy to be a heckler, you know, to trouble the band with a kind of rough street stuff. He's gonna laugh at the band, make stupid comments and things, generally cause confusion and trouble." At this there were a lot of blank faces. People started to grumble and complain. Marcello immediately took over.

"Now wait," he said. "This is the kicker. At a certain point he will get on the congas, and hey, he can actually play." I started to giggle a bit.

"Man, I am the greatest. I can kick some serious ass," said Klaus proudly, grinning and revealing a horrific miscarriage of dental work.

"Did you know you smell a bit?" Serge asked him.

"Did you know I could have you as a hamburger after the show?" Klaus asked, with a wicked smacking of his chops.

"OK, just cool it now," Serge said, putting on a brave front.

"Ready guys?" Pedro shouted. "Now walk!"

We walked. For a couple of minutes nothing happened. Then as I got closer I saw cameramen huddled around enormous machines, men wearing body-cams, other men on lighting gantries and a troupe of crewmen clustering around audio mixing gear. There was no stage. Just a shining set of drums, a bass with an amplifier, an acoustic guitar plus another amplifier, congas and a few extra mics on stands. And then the name Brother Kharma on a banner, rippling in the fresh afternoon breeze at the back, against a low concrete wall. And in front of it all, a hat with a couple of dollar bills already in there.

Cars rolled past, and taxis honked on their klaxons. A few police straggled the nearby intersection. An ambulance passed. I wondered if we would be heard. And then I looked round and saw the sound system. It was a big one, many yards from the stage area, a column on each side.

"Let's do this, guys," Leo said.

He lead the way, walking slowly and calmly, as the kids followed him excitedly. Serge sat down at his kit and immediately began making adjustments to the drumset. Irene put on her bass, after examining it with interest. I picked up the guitar, put the strap round my neck, and tested the strings. The action was just about right for some hard street-style strumming. Leo was blowing through a couple of harps, off mic, warming them up. Now the sun suddenly burst through the clouds. It was three o'clock, I noticed. Not that it mattered.

"Play a blues, Max," Serge said. I started one up. It sounded loud. A few people began to gather on the sidewalk. Their faces were interested. Irene looked happy. Serge laid down a huge, solid beat. Now Leo began.

It was an onslaught. He attacked that thing with everything he had. Irene grinned mischievously. I responded to the power of his delivery and whacked up my volume and intensity a few notches. It was going well. We were delivering. We picked up a modest applause at the end of the first number.

I had just broken into the second song when I saw a ragged figure causing a disturbance on my left. It was Klaus, beginning his bantering act. He danced around cursing near Serge and then tried to grab a drumstick. Leo made an ugly gesture with his hand, telling him to get out. The audience had swollen to a few hundred by now, and many had become fascinated by this crazy tramp, wondering what he would do next. At the end of the number there was an argument between Klaus and Leo.

"I can play better than all of you losers put together," Klaus roared. A few hip hop kids yelled with mirth at this, slapping each others' hands.

The crowd was loving it. Leo glared. And now Klaus had run behind the congas and was beating out an intensive salvo. The kids shrugged to each other and joined in. Finally Leo and me also.

In the air above us two camera operators were swerving ever lower, grinding their steel cranes closer to the action. One wore a crazed expression, the other was smoking on the job, disconnected and bored.

Sometimes a gig can become total madness. I don't understand how a performance can turn out like that. But this was one of those gigs. From then on it was nothing but a wild drunken ride through every possible crazy, wonderful and impossible situation. For me, all I knew was that I was hearing a mass of incoherent sound, and seeing a blur. I ended up blindly yelling out song after song, with the kids prompting me to start a new number every time I stopped.

Before we knew it the crowd were singing along, and a few homeboys were following Klaus, and mimicking his wild antics. Then the kids reduced their backline groove to a lowdown, swamp-funk pocket. This was a professional touch that made me proud.

Now Leo moved in on his microphone.

"Thanks very much," he said. "You have been a great audience," he told them. "Please give a big hand to the band. They instantly applauded. We finished with a blinding bass solo from Irene and then finally ended with a huge percussion battle between Serge and Klaus. At this point it was over.

I was pouring with sweat and almost unconscious. Serge looked at me, a huge laugh in his eyes. No-one knew quite what to do. For a moment we hovered there, stunned by the intensity of it all, and completely full of love for the music, and for each other. The crowd knew this and warmed to our success. By now they had figured out that this was a carefully scripted big-time event, not just a bunch of unknown buskers, and they watched us with interest, knowing that something was going on here.

A man in a jogging suit, baseball cap and a headset appeared and swiftly congratulated us, before hustling us inside the huge glass entrance of the WAI news building. We packed into the elevator and he pressed a button to go down.

Once inside the basement we walked along a long corridor. The man was talking closely with Marcello. Then Kaspar appeared.

"Hi Max," he said. "Hello Leo. Nice gig, guys."

"What are you doing here?" I asked. "Yeah, great to see you."

"I work here," he said. "There's a lot going on. We're about to walk across sound-stages and you'll see a load of film equipment." The gang looked pleased. But at this point, not much could surprise me.

I grabbed his arm and got him to one side.

"Kaspar, did you arrange all this?" I asked.

"Yeah, it was me," he said.

"But Pedro and Marcello say it was them."

"Bull****", he laughed. "OK, they had their part. But I'm in charge of this project. Don't bother arguing with them about who did this. Leave them be." Stunned, I staggered onwards, still groggy from the show. Maya looked at me curiously.

"Are you OK, Max?" she asked.

"Do you know your voice sounds funny?" asked Serge.

"He's hoarse from singing," Irene told him.

Suddenly we walked into the biggest room I had ever seen. To the left, big film cameras everywhere, mounted on dollies and trackways. Dry ice and fog in the air. An entire production set with numerous separate sound stages and a system of gantries, ramps and platforms all the way to the roof. Hundreds of camera crew and also sound and video engineers were clustered around control stations and master editing suites on the right.

'Come on,' Kaspar said, "There's a man I want you to meet." He lead us down a ramp and through a series of entrances. Now we were entering a long corridor with openings on every side. I caught glimpses of business meetings, executives thrashing out contracts, technical areas, make-up rooms, cafes, rest areas, recreation areas and broadcasting rooms.

Now we were escorted through a labyrinth of halls, foyers, up and down stairs and elevators, and then along a conveyor belt.

Finally we reached a door on the left. Kaspar knocked.

"Come in," a deep voice called. We entered.

"This is them," Kaspar said proudly, pointing to the kids. A big man with shaved head and dark glasses climbed to his feet, buttoning up his heavy business suit as he scanned us curiously.

"So you are the musical kids? I'm Manfred Schmitt," he boomed. "You ready to play music anywhere and everywhere? That's what Kaspar tells me. You wanna earn some money?"

"Yes, they do," Kaspar broke in.

"OK, so this is the pitch. We like the show you did for us just now. It went out live on Russian TV, you know that?" The was a chorus of satisfied grunts.

"Next week we're gonna have you come back and do exactly the same thing. To play your music in the street right outside the WAI building all over again. This will become part of a series of pilot commercials, testing out what works in the Russian markets which are just opening up right now. Soap, whisky, cars, shoes, perfume, you name it, anything that sells. Listen, this is how it will go. You kids will play your music. We will be shooting you as a series of commercials, outside in the street. You guys are Russian, right? Now here's the thing. You will get paid hard cash for this, and get to wear some great clothes, and play with good music gear. It's your lucky day! Occasionally we will have you speak a few words about the products, in Russian. but very casually. The point is that for the average Russian watching this in Moscow or wherever, he won't know it's a commercial. They will just believe this is a focus on music in the streets in NYC. The whole piece will be slicked up and packaged to look like the news. Nobody except us will know it's a commercial try-out, the latest run to see what works with Russia. Cool? Got it?"

"Contracts?" Kaspar asked.

"Screw the contracts," Manfred thundered. "Cash in hand only."

"You know how young they are?" Kaspar asked.

"I don't want to know. It doesn't matter. I'm making you famous, right? Just hang on to that."

"When do we do this?"

"Next week. OK, here's something for what you did just now."

He handed over a wad of bills to Leo.

"While we're talking money," Pedro began...

"Yes, I know, I have your money also," Manfred told him. "Do you have my package? You do? So come into the other room with me for a moment." The two disappeared and closed the door. I noticed that Serge had sneaked in behind them. After five minutes they all returned.

Now Manfred faced us.

"Right, one last thing," he began. "We need to set up an interview right now. One of our anchors will be asking you questions about how life in America compares to Russia, just routine stuff, culture only, no politics. Make it simple, we don't want any cold war starting here. This is to set up the scene for the Russian viewers. They need to know a bit about you over there."

"They know me over there," Leo started to say, but Manfred had already turned away and was talking to Kaspar. Pedro urgently reached up to Leo's ear.

"They want to believe that they have discovered you," he hissed.

Now Manfred was exiting, and beckoning us all to follow.

He lead us out through another tangle of corridors and elevators. Then he gathered us together and pointed to a door.

"You're gonna love this," he said. "Follow me."

Passing through the door we entered another huge room where a childrens' TV show was being prepared. A giant lizard approached. He stopped and the head unzipped itself and a bald man in glasses, covered in sweat, shouted for water. A woman in a tight black mini-skirt raced up with a bottle and a glass. Then a giant ape appeared. All kinds of other characters were walking up and down. Some were surrealist, a bar of soap on legs, and a walking computer following it. Lights were flashing and dimming, and various commands could be heard coming from a distant loudspeaker. There was a little cafe on the left and everyone gathered around it. Kaspar ordered cups of coffee, with soft drinks for the kids.

By now the lizard man had stepped out of his suit. The ape strode closer, bow-legged as they are, and then he stepped out of his suit also.

"I want to try that thing on," shouted Serge to the monkey man. The exhausted actor nodded vaguely and collapsed onto a couch. Seeing what Serge was up to, Irene demanded to try on the lizard man's suit. Within a few minutes the pair were gambolling around and had soon whisked out of sight.

The rest of us had been deep in drinks and talk. Just by chance I looked round and saw the kids were gone.

"Oh no," moaned Kaspar. "Please god don't let them blunder onto a live set?"

"They will, if I know my kids," observed Leo, in a rather dry voice.

Half an hour later they were back, pouring out their story excitedly. They had done exactly that. After becoming completely lost they had panicked and blundered inside the live-to-Japan WAI news broadcast, and created havoc. Fortunately, being children, they had merely received a very serious warning and told to get the hell out.

"But we were seen by the Japanese," added Irene, implying that some kind of victory had been achieved.

Now Pedro took control of the situation.

"Guys, it's time for the interview," he pointed out. "Kids, out of your suits. Let's go."

We followed him.

Finally we entered the interview room. Once again the cameras were ready and the lights bright.

"Hello there, you must be the adorable Russian family," a lady in a sequined gown called from a pool of shadow. "I am Nancy Armstrong, your host. Absolutely delighted to meet you!" She was blonde and smart in a pink, Italian, three-piece business suit. The kids goggled at her dramatic blue eye-shadow and how each finger nail was a different colour.

Then she showed us to our chairs. There was a small audience of about fifty already watching with interest. Swiftly it was explained that interviews were carried out round the clock here, and that the crowd knew all about the band already, and were excited to be there.

An aide offered glasses of water to all of us. Meanwhile Nancy explained that this was a new experiment, a cultural interchange between America and Russia.

"We have been waiting for years for something like this," she said, clasping her hands together in a froth of anticipation.

"Is this live TV?" Kaspar wanted to know, asking from where he stood offstage, alongside Marcello and Klaus.

"No, this will be recorded, and then parts will

be used," Nancy explained. It's not a live broadcast."

"OK, silence in the studio. Now... hold on! OK, now... what is it dude? Don't f*** with my head, OK? Now... SILENCE! Everyone ready? OK, now ... ACTION," came the frenzied shouts from the director, invisible at the back of the room.

Instantly the host began.

"Hello, and welcome. I am Nancy Armstrong and this is 'Good Morning Russia.' Right now we are inside the WAI studio in New York City, talking with a most wonderful group of Russian musicians, a family band," Nancy enthused, laughing and gesturing with delight.

"First of all, Irene and Serge, please come here, as I have something to give you," she announced.

They walked over expectantly. She held up two enormous floppy bundles.

"These are for you," she declared.

"My gorilla suit!" screamed Serge.

"And my lizard," whispered Irene.

"They are a present to the two of you from WAI," she added.

"You can take them home." And she held out the two animal costumes to the pair. Silently the kids reached out and clasped them.

"Say thank you to the lady," said Maya, from her chair ten feet away.

"Thank you," said Irene.

"Can we put them on right now?" asked Serge, starting to unzip it.

"No," said Leo sharply.

"Yes, of course you can," said Nancy. "Just leave your heads out so we can do this interview, OK?" In the corner Klaus burbled with delight at this quaint little notion.

Now Nancy gestured at the little one.

"And little Kira, you play the most wonderful trombone!" Nancy continued. "Maya, what an astonishing family you have! It must be hard work cooking for so many children?"

"Yes, they get very hungry," Maya admitted.

"And you all work so hard! Playing in the street like that. Does it ever get dangerous?" she probed.

"I keep an eye on them," Leo replied, with a broad smile.

"And I hear that things are going well, lots of offers for contracts, even TV and radio now?"

"Ask them what communism was like," demanded Klaus, from his corner. The audience froze. Nancy simpered at this. Then she became professional and relaxed.

"Sure, I know what you mean. But look, if we go into politics then they won't broadcast this in Russia." Everyone relaxed at this idea.

"I like America," Irene said. "I think women get a better deal." Hearing this, all the cameramen started focussing on her.

"She's pretty, that kid's gonna do well in America. She's a star," shouted Klaus.

"Yes, Manfred tells me he has an WAI film

contract for you all to sign, and a special modelling deal for Irene also," Nancy said proudly.

"Yeah, but he won't sign it," argued Klaus. "It's not enough money." Nancy giggled.

"Well, I'm sure something will be sorted out."

At the back of the room the director, covered in sweat, was issuing orders to remove Klaus from the room immediately.

"Just get him out! Get him out now, any way you can! Remove him!" he whispered hysterically.

Everyone on the stage were now shifting in their chairs, shooting worried glances at each other. The audience had become tense with anticipation. For a few seconds you could hear a pin drop.

"They grew up under communism," insisted Klaus, with a big grin.

"Is that right?" asked Nancy, looking a little confused.

"Ask them what it was like," Klaus prompted.

"It was nothing bad," said Maya.

"Mum says it was better than here," shouted Serge suddenly.

"Serge, you don't know anything," barked Leo. "But it's true that the Western press have made it sound far worse than it was," he admitted.

"Leo doesn't like America," Klaus suddenly shouted. "Tell them, Leo. I know what you think. You always say it's the land of Mickey Mouse. Marcello told me." Klaus was animated now, walking up and down impatiently, swinging his arms around, at the side of the stage.

"He's a communist!" he raved. "They all are. They're a bunch of commie reds! Plus, Leo's dad was with the KGB. Everybody knows it! They shouldn't even be here! Grab them! Lock 'em all up! Deport them!"

THE FIGHT

Now all hell broke loose. A physical tussle broke out between Leo and Klaus. In alarm, Nancy got up and stepped out of the way, and then her microphone wires became tangled such that she could not move any more.

In the master control room the program producer could not believe what he was seeing. His jaw dropped. He made a sudden lunge at the mixing board and confronted the four nervous audio engineers.

"What? You've got live action and you're not broadcasting?" he roared. "Patch them in. Go to live! It's all configured for that. Go, buddy go! Do it now! This will whack the ratings up, goddammit. Patch them in! Patch them to live!" The technicians began fighting with knobs and sliders.

"We're there. We're live now, sir," the first tech gasped, in a scared but triumphant voice.

Now the director turned and roared at the other three.

"Are you all patched in? Are you live? Give me live! Stay on this!" Then he had a thought.

"Are you live to the tri-state area?"

"We are live, actually going out to the nation, sir," one whispered.

"And Russia too?"

"Russia too, sir."

Just at this moment Marina and Jay were lying down, eating bananas and biscuits, after having just made love. The bed at Jazzlands was merely a thin mattress on the stage. Marina was playing with her walkman and a pile of cassettes on one side, and on the other side, Jay had his gun out, and was oiling the mechanism. The dog, the cat and the pigeon were all close by, sitting in a line, begging for crumbs. A small black and white TV was perched unsteadily on a chair, flickering.

The news was on but nobody was watching.

For a while nothing happened and then some kind of special WAI release began. Jay looked once, then went back to his banana. But something made him look back. He rapped on Marina's arm. His face was incredulous.

"Can you believe where that sorry loser has ended up right now," Jay started out, talking slowly, yet dropping his biscuit and banana which were swiftly grabbed by dog and bird.

"He's done gone on TV!"

"Who," asked Marina sleepily.

"That clown!"

"Who?" She peered at the screen.

"It's that Leo."

"No, it cannot be," asserted Marina. "That Russian family are just tryers. They are not professional and have no talent. Trust me. I know who people are, and where they are going.

"Anyway," she continued. "It cannot be him. This is the national news."

"It is him," Jay announced irritably. "If I say it's him, it's him. And it is him. Stop saying it ain't!" He whacked her shoulder with the back of his hand. She winced and stared at the screen as the camera shifted to another figure.

"That's Max," Marina said. Her jaw dropped.

"It's the whole sorry gang of those commie clowns," Jay spat in disgust. "I don't see why I don't switch that damn thing off." He hurled a bedroom slipper at the screen but missed.

"No, Jay, leave it be. Let it run. I have to see this."

"They may be on national TV but these clowns are wrecking their own show," Jay pronounced with some satisfaction. "Don't these losers know how to act when you're on TV? I told you they were a bunch of good-for-nothing deadbeats."

Russia - 1995

Somewhere in Russia, a few men were chatting in a bar. They were watching the news on a TV mounted high on the wall.

"And now for a special report," the program anchor announced. "This is a new initiative. We bring you an international, cultural exchange, a Russian family band playing their gypsy music, live, from the streets of New York, in the United States." The camera loomed in on Leo.

"I don't believe it," the first man said. "That's Leo. Remember my old friend? The red haired devil? Well now he's in New York City! How did he get there? And look, Maya is there too! And I guess those must be their kids, all in a music band together! They've been busy!"

In St Petersburg, Olga Marovich looked up from her dishwashing.

"Is that Leo? My lover from all those years ago? It doesn't seem possible. Not Leo? How can it be? What's he doing in New York? But he's looking good and playing well! Good for Leo!"

In Moscow, inside the office of one of the leading record labels, Ivan Medanski, the boss, watched the show with interest. He needed a band like this, one who had first conquered Russia, and was now starting to take on America. He made a memo to get the international office to make some inquiries.

Inside the enormous concrete headquarters of the KGB, a phone call was made.

"Remember the red-haired devil?" one deep voice said to another. "He's on the move again. In America now. We plan to watch this man. He has balls, and could possibly be the one to put Russia back onto the international stage, in a cultural way. The name of Russia has been insulted by the western media, in recent years, for no good reason. But right now our friend the red-haired devil has created an international situation, and it just might work in our favour.

"But first we'll have to talk to him, and get him to understand what we need him to do. Do you notice how he works? Wherever he goes he creates confusion. It's his way to make a smokescreen. And then it ends up with the agenda going his way. That's his technique. He is a clever man. We need more Russians like him. I will put forces at work to bring him back to Moscow."

"OK, I get it," the other said. "Leave it to me. We"ll bring this guy home."

New York City - 1995

Back in the WAI news studio, the party was full on by now. An operative heard wild sounds and opened the door from the outside passage. He could not believe what he saw, a huge lizard and gorilla were fighting over the refreshment trolley, shouting 'Yes comrade', or 'No comrade' to each other. A huge, wild old tramp had grabbed a red-haired man and had immobilised him. The lizard and gorilla were rushing to grab money out of the red-haired man's pockets and then further torturing the poor guy who was now wild with rage, shouting out expletives in Russian. All of this was being filmed at close range by a frenzied, bearded director in a hoody and kha-ki shorts. As three giant cameras loomed in and out, a tired, patient, dark-haired woman was sitting on a chair on the stage playing what appeared to be free jazz trumpet with a tiny child who was blowing into an enormous trombone beside her. A few other men

246

had strayed off the stage to make desperate, helpless gestures to the small studio audience, some of whom appeared paralysed with incomprehension. The interview host had become trapped in microphone cables and other wires, and an operative was frantically attempting to free her. Half of the audience were running for the exits with scared looks on their faces.

"Don't go in buddy," one warned. It's out of control in there."

One of the ceiling sprinkers began to drench the far end of the studio.

"Esmeralda, just look at my hairdo, it's completely ruined," squawked an old lady to her friend in the back row. "And I only just had it done!'

"Cut," shouted the director, already drenched. "Save the gear. Get everything under cover. Don't let any cameras get wet! Cut, cut! Get out, guys, get out of here!"

It was the end of a long day. There was a lot of explaining to do. The chaos had gradually ended. We found ourselves, wet and exhausted, in a rough circle in the passageway outside. Manfred Schmitt finally appeared, clucking like a chicken, doing his best to calm everyone down.

"I've just left the program producer's office," he said. "They are arguing about you in there. Looks like you've started something." Then he became serious.

"Listen to me now." He scanned our faces for a second.

"I'm all for a good story and a gutsy confrontation," he added.

"But it's not cool that you triggered the sprinklers," he continued. "Come on, get real guys! These cameras cost a lot of money! Yes, I know you didn't mean it.

"But great interview anyway, guys. Well done, Klaus! It's all about dissent and freedom of speech. You have just cracked open one big story. Up till now our producers said not to touch this issue for political reasons, but hey, you just kicked the door open and it had to come out some time. These are big topics and you had the nerve to debate them live on air. You guys rocked this place, and totally kicked ass, and almost got me fired, by the way! But well done.

"Like I said, it's all about freedom of speech. There will be more about this later, don't worry. And meanwhile you're performing again, right here, next week, remember?"

"With products too?" Serge asked.

"Exactly like that. Russia is a brand new market for us. Let's do this. Sorry, gotta run. I have to stop the directors from killing each other! All caused by you lot. But don't worry, you're beautiful, I love you! And I'm gonna make them love you too, even if I have to stick a gun to their heads. Only joking! Hey, the way out is down that passage, then follow the signs. Did you get paid?"

"Not enough," growled Klaus.

"OK, I remember now, I paid you myself. He

glared at Klaus.

"Klaus, mind your own business if you wanna stay on the payroll," he barked. At that he limbered off down the corridor.

We were left standing in a circle, shivering.

"I'm wet," said Serge.

"Me also," added Irene.

"Me too," said Kira and started to cry. Maya picked her up and soothed her.

"Well, get out of your wet animal costumes for a start," Maya suggested. "It's probably nice and warm outside in the street. We'll be dry soon."

"Let's go home," Leo said. "I'm not that happy about what you did, twisting my arms like that," he muttered to Klaus. Then he reconsidered.

"Ah, what the hell. We did the gig, and then gave them one hell of an interview," he said. "Come on guys, let's move. I'm hungry. And now give me back the money you stole, please?"

Silently the kids handed over a few banknotes.

In a fairly dazed condition we now managed to thread our way out through the complex system of alleyways and halls, until finally reaching the street once more. The sun was just going down. I looked up and down Rockefeller Plaza, and then at the family, and sighed with relief. I didn't want to forget this moment.

"It's been fun," I told the family.

"You were great, Max," Serge said, grinning up at me.

"He's the real thing," Klaus said.

"No, you are the real thing, Klaus," Irene said, staring at his enormous girth with some amusement.

"Come on guys," Leo said. "Job well done. Let's get home." He indicated with his hand in a military way.

"Are you all sorted out now?" Pedro asked, looking at me. "You don't need to crash in my crib again?" I told him no. I knew where I was heading now.

"Thanks for being there for us when we needed you," I told him.

Kaspar and Marcello had stayed behind inside the building.

We all hit the subway together, then climbed on different trains.

Later, back at Liberty Avenue, a real physical fight broke out, but it was with a lot of screaming and laughter this time. In the end Maya had to calm everyone, and eventually bribe them with cream cake and chocolate biscuits, special treats bought with the WAI money. The kids went to bed excited, still talking about the day.

After Leo and Maya had cleaned up, they talked a little.

"So Pedro is a drug dealer for those big guys?" Maya said in some wonder.

"Try not to think about it," Leo advised her. "This is America."

Once I was on my own on the subway, all kinds of strange thoughts crossed my mind. There was no possible logic or sanity in any of this. The idea of a tramp being in with the big TV guys in this way made no sense to me. And Pedro, a dealer in the gang too? This also was completely weird and unimaginable.

The train rattled and roared to Flatbush. Back in the street, I walked the last few blocks back to Jean's house. The night air was chill on my neck and all kinds of poetic and tragic thoughts were haunting me. How would I ever live my life without Marina from now on? But I knew I had to let her go. We had been tearing each other apart.

I waited a few hours before telling Jean what had happened, meeting the kids on the subway, sleeping at Pedro's place, and then the astonishing WAI story. She was amazed and overjoyed.

"I told you," she crowed triumphantly, jumping up and down. "They got the *hoodoo*! They gonna be OK! You stick with them, Max, I never seen anything like that family before. And it's only just begun!"

I had to admit she was right.

THE SHAMAN

Leo was a shaman. I'd figured this out by now. All the signs were there. The chanting, the rituals, and the way he could play games with reality. His music was all about reincarnation. He knew many secrets from the shamans of the Russian mountains. He also understood that there were many hostile, predator spirits here in New York, and he was able to offer protection from these.

Others felt this way too. Many people were attracted by the mysterious movements of Brother Kharma. Maya was constantly busy cooking welcome dishes for visiting friends, back in the East New York apartment. It appeared that the family had some kind of an answer to the various troubles we all suffered from. They were healers, for sure, perhaps without knowing this. It was in their slow, measured speech, and calm reflection and easy conversation. You felt they had no ulterior motive, that they were not using you, or playing some game, whereas many folk one met were doing exactly that. In this paranoid city, trust was hard to win, and Brother Kharma was all about sincerity and integrity. They were reassuring and a little addictive, and I valued and treasured my visits to their place.

By this time Brother Kharma had a huge underground following. They had figured out how phoney the major labels and their contracts were. I'd seen musicians commit career suicide by signing these things. We knew about a better scene, a subculture with integrity, where people were more intelligent, and artists had soul, and there was plenty of give and take, plus caring, supportive audiences. "Making it', for us, was no longer the goal. Why strive to be successful in the commercial world which was rotten to the core?

Yet Brother Kharma were certainly making something. Exactly what, we were about to find out.

People flocked around the band. They were becoming a cult. Audiences were getting bigger every concert.

A video crew had begged to move into the family apartment and cameras were rolling 24 hours, capturing every possible event.

Russia had finally heard about the band, and an article appeared in a national magazine, selling 170 thousand copies instantly.

Finally the world understood that now had arrived a unique band who were prepared to sing and talk about real issues, reincarnation, spirituality, corruption and so on. And most of all, this band were prepared to defy America, and all that it stood for, and to do it from within the very heart of the machine.

Brother Kharma had become a story now, and editors began publishing many articles about every aspect of the band, and their visionary take on life. A rumour spread that Irene was a child goddess, a reincarnation of *Parvati*, and for a while Hindu priests could be seen in the audience at gigs.

A freak street performance at Times Square was filmed by syndicated TV, and thus the band went out live, worldwide, all over again. I was playing with another outfit that day and felt bad not to be with them. But the performance was electric. The kids played like crazy, and Leo went wild, jumping around, even lying for a brief moment on the sidewalk right over the grill where the thundering roar of the subway train combined with his harp to create sounds never heard before.

All this time the family continued living at Liberty Avenue, which merely became more dangerous every day, as if to reinforce the very impossibility of what was taking place.

A stray bullet shot in through the living room window one morning, burying itself in the sofa inches below where one of the children slept. Tramps, hookers and crack-dealers continued to prowl. One homeless derelict was living permanently on the front steps.

In my section of Brooklyn the streets remained as tough as ever. One afternoon I got held up in Flatbush Avenue. A big tough kid pulled a stale old trick by pretending to bump into me and dropping his paper bag. There was a crash, and a brownish liquid leaked out onto the sidewalk.

"Oh no," he wailed. "That was the last money my pa gave me for that bottle of vodka. He's gonna beat me. Now you gotta pay for it. Gimme ten dollars."

I tensed up and scowled. Then slowly, I took off my glasses and faced him. Seeing this he swiftly backed down.

"OK, OK, mister," he hustled. "Forget it." As he disappeared I breathed a sigh of relief.

"Your original WAI musical performance was top notch," Kaspar announced one day, after arriving suddenly at Liberty Avenue.

"However the interview has caused chaos," he continued, crashing into an armchair wearily.

"The State Department has given us a warning. Several operatives have been fired. My job may be threatened also. WAI now view you as a wild card, and possibly a serious risk."

"Why?" Leo asked. "It was Klaus, not us. I hardly know this man," he complained irritably. Kaspar sighed.

"You have to understand how sensitive broadcasting is, and also the international situation. The word 'communist' is a huge *no no*. When our program director patched your interview to live, half way through, it went out to many countries causing seismic shockwaves everywhere. We have been banned from certain areas now. Our directors have been traumatised and two have resigned. One even had a stroke. Yes, it's bad. I don't think you know what you are playing with here.

"And it gets worse," he continued grimly.

"Sensitive regions such as Kosovo, Chechnya, the Spanish Basque country and Cuba, have been badly inflamed and destabilised. It may not be in the papers yet, but our sources tell us that underground forces are at work, de-stabilising the US and our allies.

"Good," said Leo, and laughed heartily. Kaspar scowled.

"Yes, I know all about your anarchist leanings. It's so fashionable. You are very cute." Leo made a bad face at this.

"But meanwhile, let's get real," he rumbled. "You guys need money. I want to help. Look at this s***hole of a place you are living in."

"We like it," Kira chirped, indignantly. "Mama says she's very happy here."

"Your mama is a very long-suffering and wonderful lady," Kaspar soothed. He turned to the others.

"Now listen up. There are many things we can do. It's not so easy to get you on a live WAI news broadcast again, but we can have the kids doing advertisements. It pays well, you know?"

"Never," growled Leo. "Kids not for sale, ever. We don't need your dirty money." At this Kaspar became electrified.

"Come on, dude! Do you want to survive, or not? You're drowning here. Do you think it doesn't hurt me to see that?"

"Talk about music, and I listen," Leo said. "Mention advertisements, and I say goodbye. We are artists. We don't need your dirty commercialism. We are not for sale." His face was carved rock as he stuck his jaw out and turned away, humming to himself.

"But Pa?" Serge whined. "I'd like to do that."

"Keep quiet and shut up," Leo barked savagely. "Only speak when you're spoken to." He rapped Serge's knuckles, hard, and the boy started crying. At this Irene turned pale, and Maya looked worried, and hugged her daughter protectively.

"Leo, I don't think it would really harm them..." Maya started out.

"Never!" Now Leo stared at Kaspar with cold eyes. "I believe our meeting for today is over. Thank you. I have other matters to attend to."

At that he marched off to another side of the apartment and started fixing some music gear. Maya went into the kitchen, still looking worried.

Kaspar got up and headed for the door. The family clustered around him. There was much whispering, and people pointed to the giant lizard and gorilla outfits occasionally. Kaspar scribbled a phone number down and handed it to Irene. Then she let him out as they exchanged secret smiles.

Many nights I would be out touring the jam sessions. New York had many such to offer. They came in a multitude of flavours, blues, cajun, zydeco, rock, soul, funk, R&B, country, folk, bluegrass, latin, rock n roll, unplugged, spoken word, electronic, punk, and then stuff I had never heard of. Plus, when guys talked about what style to play, you could hear some wild and crazy names, almost like a whole language of its own.

One evening I was playing onstage inside a small, dark club, just north of Houston Street around Second Avenue. I knew that any kind of music was OK here. We had just finished rocking out to a twelve bar blues, and now a sturdy black guitarist with a Mohican stepped up.

"How about a skanking groove?" he asked us. "Reggae, dub, old school?"

"Or maybe some Jewish funk," suggested the Chinese bassist, scowling with concentration. "Something I can slap too?"

"Yo, that would be totally sick," growled the German dwarf of a drummer, from behind his kit. He had giant mirror shades on, so I could not tell if he was smiling. "Hit me one time, babe. I'm cool with that."

I stepped from foot to foot, testing out sounds and riffs on the club keyboard.

"What you wanna play, Max," the bassist demanded. "Can you start something?"

"A righteous kind of thing?" I asked. "Or a crazy outside riff?" The eyes of the guitarist glazed over on hearing this idea. Hastily I shifted tactics and turned to the bass player.

"No, listen, how about I just lay down a New Orleans shuffle pocket? Or maybe we could all trip out to an *M-Base* kind of riff together? And then build on to that with some chromatic chord changes from this thing? You know, like a pad? But you would have to anchor it and stay locked down on one root? Sounds cool?"

Everybody agreed except the guitarist.

"OK, I can dig that," he said. "But I'll just add my skanking thing anyway, OK?"

The gang nodded. I started the riff. In my head I had decided to start very abstract, with some free form sounds, then a wash of Brazilian colour chords, and just hold the tension and the poetry of it till breaking point, and then finally release the funk medicine.

Within a few minutes I knew it had worked.

The musicians were cooking like hell. People started dancing. All the guys were tight, and laid back, only playing the essential notes. There was none of that verbose over-playing which happens in amateur jam sessions.

Now we stripped it right down, so all you could hear were the bare bones of the jam. Here the dreadlock guitarist went to town, building up the atmosphere, using a cry baby pedal to good effect. Him and the German drummer, and now the bassist, had all locked together. It was more than tight. You could feel the tension, and the sweat and blood, and also the urgency and intention of this music.

Finally we brought it back up, and I sounded out a gospel groove, and then together with the bassist, morphed it out into a hoe-down figure. By now we were throwing rich, colourful, modal chords at each other, together with smouldering riffs, chock full of honey and sunshine. The room became saturated with a feeling of celebration, and also hope and revelation. Sweat was pouring down onto my keyboard. Guys were shouting out with joy. Then suddenly it was over, and I knew I had to leave the stage and let another keyboard player on. The musicians punched fists with laughs and winks, as I headed outside into the darkness.

It was a cold night and as I walked a gust of steam funnelled up out from the subway, venting out of the pavement. Before I had exited the block I heard something I liked coming from an entrance on the left. I pulled my jacket a little tighter around my neck and hustled inside, following the sounds. Now it became clear. A couple of horn players were playing free

jazz. I stumbled down a dark flight of steps. Breaking into the light I entered the club to witness musicians just finishing off their set.

Now I recognised two guys who used to come to Jazzlands and play all night. It was Gabriel and Karim.

"Hey Max," Gabriel called from the stage. "My communist friend!" I winced a bit and looked around. Nobody had taken any notice. I knew Gabriel by now. He loved to shock the crowd in this way. It was almost part of the act. Except that he was being real.

"Come and sit down with us?" I did so.

Gabriel was tall, black and intellectual in a way that pleased me. He had an elegant way to talk, and an enormous command of the English language. Plus a sense of fun, even in tough times.

"Hey Christo", he shouted. A tall Greek man

with dark hair and olive skin strolled up.

"What's going on," he asked. "Finished already?"

"This is Christo," Gabriel told me. "Owner of Trojan records. He's a useful man to know." He winked at me.

"Oh it's just a little thing I have fun with," Christo muttered in a dismissive manner. "Mind if I sit down?" He did so.

"Your label 'aint so small," Karim said, brushing his long dreadlocks back. "You distribute with a major, isn't that so?" Christo admitted it with a sly smile. Now Gabriel turned back to me.

"How is Marina doing?" he asked.

"She's with Jay now."

"What, like together? Like a couple?" I saw how much he was trying not to laugh, and swallowed any feelings I might have had. Karim sat down. Both men were wearing enormous saxophones which they toyed with occasionally.

By now I was beginning to relax. We dived straight into a big talk about communism, exactly like the old days at Jazzlands. I told him how the Russian family were doing, and what had been happening with WAI news.

"So Leo is broadcasting to Russia from a US news station," he laughed. "That's priceless."

"He's thriving on it," I said. "I don't think he knows which side he supports, America or Russia, but he's creating controversy for sure."

"He probably doesn't want to know," Gabriel

added. Then he continued.

"You say this Klaus guy called him a communist, half way through a live interview broadcast from America to Russia?"

"Yeah, and they wound up fighting on air," I added moodily.

"So what the hell did the Russians make of that?" Gabriel asked.

"We're waiting to find out," I said. "But you know, Leo was famous over there already, even before coming to America. He played some big blues gigs there which helped to trigger the perestroika." Gabriel's eyes widened.

"Who is this guy?" he asked in wonderment.

"He's known as the 'Red Devil' in Russia," I said.

"What?" Now Gabriel could hardly control himself.

"Is that just a casual name? Or does it mean what I think it means?"

"I think it does," I said. "Red means communist."

"Yet he's the communist who helped bring communism down?"

We stared at each other.

"I guess we'll never really know," I said. "I mean, he's a regular guy basically. A good friend. I trust him. He just wants to get on, and get his music happening, like all of us. To be honest, I've heard him talk against both systems, Russia and America. Look, ultimately he's a musician, first and foremost.

A great blues harp player. He's like me in that we both love black music. We live for that. It's freedom music. Freedom for the slaves. Freedom from Soviet oppression. Freedom from capitalism. We all know the story, but it happens to be true, even if no-one wants to hear. Today we are all slaves, black and white together. We are all n*****s.

"Right on, brother," said Gabriel. "But personally, I chose to defend communism," he continued. "It's the dream of a shared world. The media has gone totally ape-shit right now. All hard right wing."

"Let me tell you a story," he continued.

"The Berlin wall came down and Russia has entered the free market. We know this. But now just as that happened, guess what? The American media started to lock down and censor stuff. OK they always did that anyway. But listen to this.

"Do you know, Max, that when Russia opened up to the west, a few years back, that a survey was made. They watched as various cinemas in all the towns across Russia started showing American films for the first time. Well they monitored the murder rate around those towns and found that when the American films began, the murder rate increased in that area. It's because America makes so many films that depict people dying in a horrible way.

"What does that tell you?" he asked.

I saw his point.

"And they call this freedom, and our country the land of the free. And then invade country after country, causing an enormous amount of bloodshed, and then they call that democracy and freedom. I don't buy it."

"Yeah, and I'll bet that no-one in the west will even cover that story," I muttered. We sat in thought for a while. Karim blew a few experimental notes through his horn.

"Enough preaching politics," Gabriel laughed as he got up. "Time for me to do another kind of preaching. With my saxophone!" I laughed at that.

"Good talking to you, Gabriel," I said.

There was a knock.

The man with red hair slowly opened up his door. Instantly a large, silver handgun was aimed directly at his head.

"F***ing noise! Quit with that f***ing row, you bastard! Shut up the noise!" It was the neighbour, a large, brutal Haitian guy..

The red-haired man didn't move an inch.

"I'm gonna waste you, you f--ing roach!" the Haitian roared. "Just shut that f***ing row, you hear me?"

The guy raved on.

"Very nice gun you have," the man with red hair commented.

This unnerved the Haitian. He moved from foot to foot. After a few more seconds he turned away and shuffled off, glaring and cursing.

THE MUSIC LESSON

It was a rainy Saturday afternoon. Leo had finally agreed that Marina should give the kids a music lesson.

Just five minutes before, Maya had dropped them off at Jazzlands, and departed with a friendly wave. They had arrived looking rather forlorn, running in through the rain, and I was now trying to cheer them up. We were in the club room, at the back. I told them to hang their wet coats up and then Irene began to experiment with chords on the piano.

"Do we have to do this?" asked Serge, looking glum, and walking up and down uncertainly. The dog nuzzled his hand, as if to encourage him.

"Look, it's better if you do," I whispered to the children after Marina had gone off to prepare a coffee. You don't know how she is when she gets upset."

"Is she a witch?" Irene asked, turning to me with interest. I kneeled down beside her, lowering my voice.

"Probably," I told her. "She's capable of putting a bad spirit into you. She's done it to me so many times that I think I'm immune now. But it's not pleasant. So do what she says."

The back door to the yard was open. It had stopped raining and the sun was shining once more.

Serge pricked up his ears and pointed to the yard.

"What's that?" he asked. We could hear voices coming from the back.

'In the caldron boil and bake;
Eye of newt and toe of frog'

"It's only the theatre company, in their back yard," I told him

"Sounds like witches over there too," said Irene warily.

"Just a bit of Shakespeare," I soothed.

The actors continued. We could hear them shrieking with laughter now.

"For a charm of powerful trouble,
Like a hell-broth boil and bubble."

"I don't like it," said Serge. "Things are weird here. You guys are into bad stuff. I think I wanna go home." Just at that moment Marina arrived with mugs of coffee.

"Irene, sit on the stool next to me," she commanded. Serge found himself a chair and I sat down wearily on the stage. The phone was ringing in the next room but we all ignored it. Serge looked up and down at the various pictures of jazz musicians on the wall.

"Now do you know that you are a very pretty little girl?" Marina asked her, staring at her in a very fixed manner.

"What if I am?" asked Irene, cringing a little.

"You've got makeup on, haven't you," Marina whispered incredulously. "At thirteen! You should be ashamed." She grasped Irene's chin and rotated it in order to get a better look. At this Irene swiftly extracted herself with some irritation.

"Why not?" she asked. Marina fixed her with an angry eye, then threw her arms up in exasperation, turning to me for moral support. Finally she gave up.

"What the hell," she exclaimed. "This is New York. I understand it is different here." Then another thought occurred to her, and she sat down on the piano stool next to Irene.

"You know all the men are very bad, don't you?" Marina warned, pointing vaguely towards Jay, Serge and myself. "Be careful!"

"I've heard that, sometimes," Irene agreed patiently, wondering where all this could possibly be going.

"It feels good to be young, doesn't it? Do you know you have a big chance in music here?" Marina asked.

"Maybe, I don't really know," said Irene.

"America loves young girls," Marina added. "But you need the right song. Did you find your song yet?" she asked, lighting a cigarette, and looking thoughtful.

"Yes we have," Serge shouted.

"Can you get me a tape?" Marina asked. "I want to hear it."

"No," shouted Serge suddenly. "It's secret."

"You are a very wicked little boy," Marina said, suddenly reaching out and slapping his wrist with a ruler. He ignored this but gave her a savage look.

Through the open back door I could hear the

sound of a plane passing overhead. The afternoon was moving along. A slight breeze gusted in through the door.

"I'm going out to buy a soda," Irene sang out suddenly.

"We have some here," I told her.

"Not the kind I like," she retorted, slipping out through the front with a hasty smile.

It wasn't good to see a little girl head out alone into the street like that. After five minutes I went out looking for her. But she had disappeared. Then I spied her a little further on, slightly inside a store entrance, talking to two men. I walked closer. As I moved nearer I was astonished to see it was Pedro and Manfred.

"Hello? I said.

"Max?" Pedro exclaimed. 'What a surprise! How are you doing?"

"I'm the one surprised," I retorted.

"Good afternoon Max," said Manfred.

"But what are you all doing here?" I asked. There was an embarrassed pause. Manfred moved from foot to foot.

"It's confidential, but if I must reveal it to you, then I guess it's OK. You are one of the band, after all."

"I am responsible for the children," I said. "We are in the middle of a music lesson right now, but sure, come inside my club and we'll talk."

"You have a club?" he asked. "Very convenient." We strolled back.

Once we had entered, Marina, Jay and Serge all gathered round. I showed the visitors to chairs in the back room. Manfred lit a small cigar, and studied me intently. He played with the cigar smoke for a moment, then began.

"This very intelligent young lady, Irene, phoned me earlier. We have a business deal," Manfred informed us, glancing at us shrewdly, one by one. "It's supposed to be highly confidential, but as I can see, you are looking after the children today, and need to know what's going on."

"That's right," I said, fairly curious by now.

"Well, it's like this. Irene and Serge are starring in a series of advertisements which are airing in many countries," Manfred continued. "The children are very lucky to have been offered this. Unfortunately, Leo would not agree to this extremely lucrative and privileged series of contracts, so we took matters into our own hands. We are planning to adjust the legal status of the children such that they can be employed, and went ahead with the production schedule without informing the parents.

"But you can't do that," I broke in, openmouthed.

"Unfortunately we can do it, and we have done it," Manfred replied.

"And that's only the start of it," said Pedro smugly. "They are on a rollercoaster now. Cash is pouring into their accounts."

"They have bank accounts?" I asked.

"Yes and there are plans to buy property too,

I'm afraid," Manfred informed me gently, as though he were dealing with a mentally defective child who was unable to understand.

"And Serge even gets extra payments from me, running errands, delivering stuff," Pedro boasted proudly, with a gleam in his eye.

"So, Irene, you seized the moment during our music lesson to go and do all this?" Marina asked. "Without even telling us?" It was obvious she was getting upset. I shrank. Marina could be exactly like a volcano, and when she blew out, you had better not be in sight.

Right now I could see she was getting ready to erupt.

"Shut your trap," grunted Jay irritably. "I say let the kids get on. They have their shit to do, and I ain't gonna stand in their way. Walk that golden highway in the sky, that's what I say. I had it rough, and I don't see why they have to stay in the s*** for one second longer."

"Yes, this is all very well," commented Marina tartly. She brushed back her collar and shoulders smartly, in the manner of a military nurse.

"But I think it is my duty to tell their parents," she intoned blandly.

"Now quit, sister, if you know what's good for you," Jay roared. He marched over and rapped her on the arm, hard.

Now I saw Marina wilt and collapse exactly like a delicate, faded flower.

"Yes, but nothing should stand in the way of

"If you lived here, it would be easier because then Leo would not be able to know where you are all the time," she whispered. "I suggest you move right in. Come round tomorrow, around midnight?"

This was too much for Serge to take.

"No we won't," he announced. "You're jealous, aren't you?" he asserted. "I think you just want to make commercials like we do," he continued bluntly. Marina's face went through various colours but she remained calm, but with some difficulty.

"You see, you and Jay are just tryers, but we are the real thing," Serge added. It was astonishing to hear these words from a ten year old boy. Somehow Marina managed to control herself. Ignoring his words, she sidled up beside them.

"Run away", Marina whispered into Irene's ear. "Stay here with us. We will treat you well. Lots more food and nice things? And I do know how your father beats you."

"No, I won't," protested Irene angrily, wriggling away from her. "And he's not that bad."

"Maybe he isn't,'" Marina acknowledged sweetly. "But I'll tell you what he is."

"We all think he's a shaman, a kind of holy man," said Irene.

"Yes, he may be that, and more," Marina conceded. "But do you understand what that means?" She stared at Irene forcefully. "He will not rest until you are all homeless." There was a pregnant pause.

"But all the same, he has a fantastic, terrible power," she conceded, turning away and staring out the window.

"You are scaring me now," Irene said.

"But I'm proud," Serge cut in. "He's my pa."

"He lives for the spirit," Marina said. "He puts everything into the music. The rest of it, all the material things, he has no need for them. So he lets them just drop away. Like I said before, I have something of this in me too. Leo and I are similar in the sense that we cannot accept any authority, including working for any boss. So we end up in trouble, even homeless on the streets.

"But you know what? Your father is just the tip of the iceberg. There are millions upon millions of people such as him, all over the world, artists and rebels and healers, standing up against the system, determined to live for what they believe in, defying authority, and harnessing ancient, psychic forces to establish a new way, an unknown world, something no-one has ever seen or even imagined ever before.

"Leo is more than strange. He is a total outsider," she continued. "Just look at him! See that big beard waving around! Hear his proud, arrogant laugh! And then the staring eyes! I'm sorry, but it's too much. He is a wild, primitive, fearless man. A complete loner, constantly up against the authorities, but at the same time I admit that there are many who are this way, and part of me wants them to win, because the people who run this world are very sick now."

The children gathered round, fascinated by this description of their father. There was a mixture of distrust and admiration on their faces.

"He is quite a paradox," she added. "Intelligent and with lots of knowledge, for sure, but he is also rock-hard, aggressive and even violent sometimes. It is a clash. These things don't go together easily. He is a unique man, I admit that. But personally, I don't get along with him. He's too rough for me," she added, shaking her head in disapproval.

"I don't like that you talk about my Pa like that," Serge butted in. "He says that it's you who are bad. Who are you to say all this? I don't believe any of it, and I can't see why we have to stay here at all. I want to go home. Let me go home!" But Irene immediately clasped his arm and put one finger to her lips to make him quiet. Then she turned back to Marina who was fretting, fussing with her hair nervously.

"I don't mind that you are telling us this," said Irene. 'But we're not moving in with you."

"Have it your own way," said Marina haughtily, stroking the grey cat who had nestled up beside her.

"Let's get back to the lesson," she insisted.

I had remained silent most of this time but now felt I had to say something.

"Hold on," I demanded. "There's more to say about Leo.

"He lives for the family," I asserted. "Plus, he does not like capitalism. Did you know that he actually hates America?"

"Then why is he here?" she demanded.

"You know why," I told her. "Music, music and music. They left Russia when things were in turmoil. They are doing well now. But he says he doesn't want to make it in music here because the system in America is so corrupt, so why be part of that? You have to understand the Russian mind."

"Are we so different, to be Russian?" asked Irene, looking at me with her sad, beautiful eyes.

"You're so much better," I told her with a smile.

"But I feel like an American," she said uncertainly.

"Yet Leo has told me that you sit there at home, constantly drawing pictures of Russian palaces," I said gently.

"Well, I would like to go back there one day," she admitted.

"Take me with you," I begged. "Let's tour!"

"No you don't," barked Marina. "You're my keyboard player! How dare you talk about touring Russia! You're grounded! Now, back to the music lesson!" She glared at Irene ragefully.

"Not so fast," I argued. "There is more. Leo is a holy man. Yes, I know he looks like a tramp. But he is channeling the divine spirit."

"No, he's far too aggressive," Marina complained, snorting with laughter at the very idea. I looked at her carefully.

"His god is a Viking god," I told her gently. "He is bringing us back to the beginning, when things were more honest, and more simple. And part of me believes that he is right."

"What, hitting the children?" Marina exclaimed.

"It is the Russian way," I pointed out. "He insists that he does this because he loves them. He calls it the whip of love." The children were silent all this time. Irene had a troubled expression.

"For sure he does discipline his family," I added. "And can you see that the western world has nothing like this discipline any more? Only decadence. We are in big trouble here. Our time is over. But Russia and Asia have only just begun.

"I cannot believe you are defending a man who hits his children," Marina growled. "Get real, Max! He'll only wind up in jail, you know that."

"When I'm big I'm gonna hit him back," Serge whined.

"But do you prefer that the anger gets stifled and then returns as knives and guns, or even nuclear weapons instead?" I asked. "The modern world trains us to suppress all this rage. But it only comes out in another form, far worse."

"My dad don't have any nuclear bombs!" Serge shouted. We all laughed. The two began to play a game with their hands as we talked. But I had not finished.

"Leo is Russian. In the west we do not understand Russia. But they are the people who share things the most. That's what communism was all about. Yes, I know they say that millions were killed. But it was all at the time of revolution. People died for what they believed in. The point is that Russians have their mind set on higher ideals than us in the west. And Leo is part of that.

"On top of this he is channeling energy from the ancient Scandinavian gods," I added. "I am talking about the Vikings of course. By the way, he and I both descend from those people.

"Yes, he is angry. But it is honest anger. It is the way of sincerity and truth. In the modern world, we have made all that taboo. But our society is sick now. We can no longer bear to look at what is real. I have to defend my friend, and the thing that he and I believe in. For some, it looks like Leo is all alone right now, just him against America. But it's not the case. Like I said before, there are many like him, all rebelling from the madness. I recognised who he truly was, right from the first moment we met, and once again I am proud to call him my friend. Yes, I do know that his way to be will eventually take him down to the streets, and to homelessness, along with all the Indian holy men, the fakirs. It is his kharma. Let him be who he is."

"Hey, what a speech about my Pa," Serge said gleefully. Marina sat herself down with a look of disgust on her face. Irene stood near the back door, repeatedly combing her long hair, a faint look of amusement on her face.

"I like him the way he is," Serge added.

"So do I," added Irene.

"Well I don't," said Jay, who had been listening in as usual.

"He ain't no fakir!" he shouted. "He's a faker, that's what he is. Haw haw! He ain't no fakir!"

THE BLESSING

A little later, Marina made the kids a meal. I lay down in the basement and immediately fell asleep. Then I began to dream.

We were crossing America in a wagon train, all together. After fighting our way through a range of mountains, then fording many rivers, we entered a long stretch of dry plains. It was a rough, weary trek into the very heart of the west, but finally we arrived into a golden valley where the land was fertile, and now we halted.

Many trees were felled and after several months a basic but homely wooden shack had been completed. Now the entire party set to work to make the land good for planting crops.

We worked side by side, one big, happy gang of survivors. All of the Russian family were there, and so were Kaspar, Marina and Jay, and then Jean and Klaus also, plus a few others too.

Every day the family tended the land, the work went well, the sun shone and sometimes the rain fell, and Klaus was wearing ripped old dungarees, as ragged as ever, and enjoying his newfound freedom very much.

And in my dream I felt the cool wind, and smelled the thick, long grass, and all the animals were there, the black dog, the grey cat and the pigeon too, all dressed in their jackets, working on the farm, and even complaining too.

And in the evenings we gathered round the fire in the dusk, and the cat's eyes gleamed as the animals sang songs, while I played guitar and Leo blew on his harp. And the animals sang of the old days, all about Vikings and wanderers, and minstrels and tramps, and then tales of glorious battles and kings and princesses, and also dynasties, and empires rising and falling across the ages.

As I listened I thought I could hear snatches of the old communist songs of the revolution, but no, something was very odd, the words were not only that, they were also about America, all about the slaves, and the blues, mixed in with Vikings and Russia, and even the British empire too, and now Jean and Jay were adding in stuff about chitlins and soul food, and working on the canal, and then I would stare through the flames and the fire-flies into the awful darkness of the night, and watch the bats hovering around our wooden shack, and know that something in my soul was being healed, some terrible conflict that had always troubled me. And now I understood that we were home at last, and had almost come to the end of our story.

And as I stared out through the flames it seemed to me that all the African slaves were there, standing in a great circle at the edge of the firelight, and I felt sure that they knew who we were, and what we had done, to play their music for so many years, such that they never ever be forgotten, and that they were satisfied with this, and were blessing us, and were allowing us to finally rest in peace.

And just as they began to chant, I fell into a deeper sleep than before.

At the WAI marketing division main office, Manfred and Kaspar were arguing.

"The kids are worn down," Kaspar complained. "Did you see Serge last session? And remember Irene fainted last week?"

"Nonsense," Manfred replied. "They're making good money. No reason to stop. And Irene's face is selling a lot of hairspray in India. Have you seen the figures? We can't afford to slow down now."

"Yeah, but I don't like it," replied Kaspar.

"You've burnt out child actors before. It destroys their life and then you lose the income too."

"OK, enough," snapped Manfred testily. His face was a mask. "I give the orders here. Just do your job and quit yapping, OK?"

Meanwhile back at Jazzlands I was talking to Jay in the front room, behind the counter. I was trying not to notice the fact that he was wearing one of my shirts and had even ripped the sleeve of it slightly.

At the back of my mind it was dawning on me that the kids must be returned fairly soon. But now Erica appeared at the door. She was a tough black girl from the local *hood*. Very pretty, also.

I had made the mistake to invite her out on a date once. We had walked around the Italian street carnival for an hour and all she'd ever said to me was, *'hey, pass me a five-bill'* or *'hey y'all that shit is fat'* or *'do you have a ten bill'* or *' that n***** is a corn-pone'*. At the end of the excursion my wallet was empty, and I'd hastily told her goodnight.

Right now she scanned us all.

"Hey y'all," she shouted, swaggering and posing, as she minced into the club.

"Hi there," Jay said. "Looking for something?"

"I need work. Money," she said.

"To pay for what?" he demanded.

"Well, are you hiring, yes or no?" she yelled.

"I ain't gonna hire no *scallywag ho* who shout at me, that's for sure," he chortled.

"I ain't shouting. I said, are you hiring?" she repeated.

"You wanna wash up?"

"I guess."

"So go wash up then," he commanded.

"She went to the sink and began washing dishes. He scanned her slim elegant form, up and down, from behind her. She craned her head back to find him.

"What you staring at, n*****?" she demanded.

"Don't n***** me, I ain't no n*****, you sorry ass b****," he barked. "You wash on and less bad-mouthing, OK?"

"I hear you," she said.

Now the dog and the cat appeared, both

wearing little jackets. Marina had dressed them up to please the children. The cat sat on a chair while the dog put his paws up against the front window glass, and surveyed a group of people who were walking their dogs outside in the street.

The sun suddenly burst through the clouds.

In the club room, Marina had the kids sitting in a circle around her on the checker-board floor. She was well into her philosophy lesson by now, pleased to have such a captive audience.

"Nothing is casual," she said. "Nothing is random. It all happens for a reason. Everything is all connected."

"Even the wind?" Irene asked.

"Of course," Marina replied. Do you know your own power?" she asked the children. "Do you know what God is? He is in you. But actually I believe we are fighting with God. What do you think life is about? Do you want to make it in music? Do you want to earn a lot of money?"

"Yes," Serge said.

"Money is nothing," Marina replied. "Money is no protection against the world. And here's another thing. Are you living forwards or backwards? Some people are living backwards. And whose time are you on? Everyone is on a different time. We are musicians and we have to know what time we are in. For example, is it jazz-time, blues-time, rock-time or what-time?"

"I think it's leaving time," Serge said, getting

up. "And I'm hungry."

"What is this jackass crazy-time stuff she spouting now," Jay asked, rolling his eyes upwards in exasperation as he chewed on a strip of beef jerky. He had crept in once more, fascinated by so much insanity in his own house.

"Shut up, Broccolli boy," Marina spat.

"I don't like jazz," Serge said. Marina gasped with horror.

"You are a very ignorant little boy," she said. "How dare you talk about jazz like that?

"Of course I realise that you are far too young to be familiar with these kind of adult ideas," she continued, in a rather patronising tone. "But one day you will understand that jazz is everything. It is life itself. Jazz is why we exist. Do you slap your bass, Irene?"

"No. I don't like slapping," she said.

"Is that because your father slaps you?"

"He's never really slapped me," Irene replied indignantly. "Anyway this is all nonsense."

"I say he has slapped you," Jay broke in, grinning smugly.

"He has not," Irene argued back.

"*Zita!*" Marina screamed, face purple with rage. "*Silencio!* Shut up! Or I will slap you myself. Now, I am not going to say it again. I repeat. You should slap, and you must slap your bass." Irene shook her head silently.

"Your makeup's all messed up," Jay snorted at Marina, weeping with laughter. It was true. Not only this, but she had put on so much that she looked rather like a racoon.

Undeterred, however, she ploughed on with a further probe.

"How are you going to play the real, happening funk without slapping that bass?" she demanded.

"I don't want this lousy band. They suck. They are not commercial. I don't know why you have driven to see me today. I am not interested. The Brother Kharma band are no good," said Marcello, slamming his hand against the wall. "Do I make myself clear?"

The two men glowered at each other. There was total silence in the expensive living room of Marcello's uncle's mansion.

"WAI have a strong interest in this band's success," Kaspar replied blandly. He lounged on the sofa, crossed his legs, and sipped at a shot of gin, while staring at the swans in the distance.

"Tell me why?" Marcello shot the words out. "And what the hell is this to do with me, anyway? OK I admit we filmed their documentary, but the thing turned into a disaster. The LA ratings were terrible. Plus, I think that you know that this father of the family band, Leo, is a total clown."

"He is a dangerous man, actually. A very dangerous clown," Kaspar sniggered. "I would not mess with him, if I were you. Anyway, I admit we have a special relationship with him. The KGB are involved. Don't worry, it's top secret stuff."

"KGB?" Marcello's jaw dropped. "What the f--- are you talking about?"

"This is America. Wake up, Marcello." Kaspar's words were cold and precise. "There's been a lot happening since the iron curtain and the Berlin wall came down. It's a new world now. Many strange and unusual liasons, not just ours. So if you cause us any more trouble, or make any more difficulties regarding promotion of Brother Kharma, you will regret it."

Now it was Marcello's turn to laugh.

"Oh boy, now I have heard it all," he chortled. "Do you understand who you are threatening? You know perfectly well who I am, and how powerful my uncle is. You are aware of which areas of Manhattan we control, and exactly which businesses. And anyway, the KGB have no jurisdiction here. This is America."

"Except that both FBI and CIA are with them."

"Oh, is that so?" The two men glared at each other once more. Now the phone rang. Marcello walked into the adjoining room, failing to close the door.

Kaspar heard him pick up the phone.

"Yes, uncle." Kaspar pricked up his ears. "What, you are out? You left the country? Where did you say? Bogota? Why? Because it's where you can be invisible? I guess it makes sense. Look, uncle, I have dumped Brother Kharma." Now there was a long pause. Then when Marcello started to speak again, he sounded scared.

"Get them back? Yes, of course, uncle. Yes, I'll do it. Sorry, uncle. No, I didn't mean to make you angry. Yes I'll get them back, I promise."

Then Kaspar heard the phone being put down. When Marcello returned, he was looking apologetic.

"Sorry, Kaspar, you're right," he said. "It's on. We will promote Brother Kharma together. Don't worry about a thing. I've made up my mind."

At Jazzlands, Erica was entering the club room.

"What's this, a cat, a dog and a pigeon?" she asked. "My oh my. Are they gonna fight?" she wanted to know.

"No," said Marina, glaring. "I've trained them to be good."

"You've trained them? But everybody knows a cat and a dog are gonna fight?"

"Mine don't," said Marina firmly. "I've taught them not to."

"My dad doesn't like jazz," said Serge.

"He's a loser," said Marina. "So it's good you're here. Now you can jam with us.'

"I don't like jazz either," said Serge.

By now Erica was sweeping around the piano.

"So this here is a music club?" she asked. "Say, I can sing? Can I sing here? D'you wanna hear what I can do?"

"No," said Marina, bluntly.

There was a chorus or protests from me, Jay and the children at this.

"OK, but just a little," said Marina. "But no amplifier."

"Well I need a pianist. Who can play with me?" Erica wanted to know.

"We have no pianist here," Marina said.

"Max plays the piano very well," piped up Serge, winking at Irene excitedly.

"I'll do it," I said.

"No, Max only plays with me," Marina said, getting angry now. I noticed she was sweating and a vein in her neck was bulging.

"Can it, *thyroid lady*, let the girl sing," roared Jay. "Let her sing if she wants to sing!"

"Come on," I said. "She only wants to play a song. It's not long is it?"

"No it ain't long," she said.

I sat down at the piano and set up the piece. It was a slow, smoky R & B tune. Her voice was lovely but untrained. At the end the kids clapped.

"She done good," said Jay. "Hey sister, come on over here. You wanna beer?"

"Leave it," shouted Marina, getting wild with jealousy now. Jay stormed off disgustedly.

"I think we'd better be going home now," Irene said, getting up suddenly.

"Nonsense," shouted Marina. "Sit down!"

Later, after Erica had left, Serge asked me

how she sang so well. I countered with a question.

"So why do you think black music is called soul music?" I asked him.

"Do you mean R&B?" asked Serge.

"Because it's all about soul?" Irene asked, ignoring her brother.

"Exactly," Marina broke in. "It's all about life and death," she added. "Everything comes from gospel music. All dance music comes from that. It's all about religion. Listen, when the slaves came from Africa, religion was pretty important. It was their final, last defence against the brutality of the slave masters. Today many people tend to laugh about, and dismiss religion. But if your life is on the line, the way it was with them, then you care about religion a lot more.

"Now when a guy is playing music, and he's righteous, it's totally different," I continued. "You hear lots of spaces between the notes. He's holding back, playing just the notes that matter, playing for the singer and the band, and for the song, rather than just playing for himself.

"There are way too many musicians who play too loud, too busy and don't really feel what's happening with the band," I added. "I can't take that."

"Am I too busy when I play?" Serge asked.

"Sometimes," I said. "We all are, every so often. It's so easy to put back a few drinks, have a laugh, turn up and blast. But that creates lousy music."

"I want to be righteous," Irene said. I smiled.

"I think you are, already," I told her. Now I glanced at my watch. It was already mid-afternoon.

"I'm hungry," moaned Serge.

"Let's go back to Liberty Avenue," I said. "You kids have been out long enough."

"Hold on, not so fast," said Marina. "Before you leave, we all pray together. It's the rule of the house. Now, everyone, down on our knees."

Only Irene consented to do this. Serge was becoming more rebellious every second. Jay had his hands over his eyes in despair.

Finally Marina had us all kneeling down, eyes closed, hands in the praying position, palms together. Now she began to whisper, in feverish incantation...

"Our father, who art in Jazzlands..."

A few minutes later Klaus arrived. Our club had become a regular stop for him ever since he had discovered that Marina made really good Italian pasta meals. In return he would leak out all the latest information from inside the corridors of WAI.

"Klaus!" Serge shouted. "When do you ever change your pants?" Klaus grinned and snorted amiably. For some reason he was wearing a pair of ancient, khaki, riding jodhpurs and an antiquated sun helmet.

"Pasta," he growled, hanging his coat up, "I'm hungry."

"Now Klaus, what's going on at WAI?" Marina hustled. "Sit down. Relax! You'll get your pasta later." Klaus stared at her in disbelief, then howled in agony at being thwarted in this way.

"There's nothing much to tell," he snorted, slumping down on a bar stool. "Except that Kaspar has been promoted to global production manager and his office is bigger. He shouts more now, mainly at me." He looked at the kids glumly. "The soundstage where you were interviewed is completely different now, with better lighting too. And the Russian section has expanded."

"Can it with this Russian stuff," said Jay irritably. "I've had just as much as I can take. Hell, I don't care, I'm heading out anyway."

"Where are you going?" called Marina. She sounded terrified.

"None of your business," he barked, slamming the door.

There was a figure behind the glass door. It opened slowly and Bill strolled in. The kids were delighted to see him. Immediately they were all over him, hustling him to come back through into the club room, and get on the drum kit.

"Play, play," shouted Serge, pushing him physically in the small of his back. "I love your playing!" Without a word, but grinning amiably, he sat down at the kit, and broke into a mean, smoking New York funk groove.

Marina had prowled after him. She was obsessive about drummers, specially good ones. Bill started with a few rolls, and then began to lay down a solid, burning rhythm.

"Oh wow," chanted Marina in a fit of ecstasy.

I was fascinated. By this time Irene had jumped on the bass and locked in, with an impossibly clever, lithe figure that satisfied the soul, and made us click our fingers and slide around in our chairs.

Now Marina began to dance, with a delighted face. She had always been a great mover, and all at once I began dancing too. For a few minutes the club was alive with magic. Then it all ended.

Klaus had come into the room and was holding his head in his hands with an agonised expression.

"Stop, stop," he shouted. "Stop!" Reluctantly we all ground to a halt.

"What the hell has got into you?" demanded Bill, in some amazement.

"Nobody ever understands," moaned Klaus. "The noise rocks my balance so I can't think. It's making me crazy!"

"Calm down," said Irene. "It's OK. You are with friends." She looked at him carefully. "Can I get you a glass of water?" she offered.

"You are very kind," muttered Klaus, sitting down and looking around at everyone in despair. There was a short pause.

"You see, I was exactly like you," he continued. "I was a musician too. Everything happened so fast. I became famous. The big money arrived. Also lots of women. Everything you could wish for. Sex, drugs, you name it."

I stared at him curiously, not knowing how much to believe of this strange story.

"I was selling records. Life was a dream," he burbled, in a half-demented tone.

Irene handed him a glass of water carefully. He swigged and slushed at it, and some drops poured onto his shirt.

"Are you sure this is all true?" Irene asked.

"It's a fact, I promise you," Klaus moaned. He held his head in his hands once more. "I loved being a musician so much," he continued. "We lived for that. And then suddenly it was over."

"What happened?" I asked gently.

"It was the drugs," he told us. "The drinking too. The stress, the fast food, everything at once. I became a kind of zombie. Couldn't pay my bills. And then became homeless. And while homeless on the street I got attacked, and hit on the head, and had to have a brain operation, and it went terribly wrong, and when I woke up I could hardly remember my own name. My memory never returned properly. That's why you look at me all funny today. I know I'm not normal."

"That's terrible," gasped Bill.

"And then, while I was homeless, I met Pedro one day on the street and he took me back and gave me shelter and so I began staying at that place of his. Yes I know, it's a terrible dump. But I still live there today. Yes, of course, you know that. Several of my old friends had got jobs at WAI, and when I saw them again they welcomed me in, and we would get together at the cafe there, and they got me a WAI card so I could get all the special privileges, and then

I was given a job too, so I have a desk in one of the corridors now, and I get to coordinate stuff, and organise meetings and so on.

"Plus, you know something?," he added. "Did you realize that many guys living at the squat are official WAI staff? It's always the same story. They became addicts, and lost everything."

We goggled at this. No-one said a word. Now Klaus raised his head. He had a wild look in his eyes.

"And guess what? Now I've been promised my own show."

"That's impossible," snorted Marina, looking at him distainfully.

"Why," Klaus cried. "Why not?"

"You cannot be a program director. You are a tramp," she announced, stamping her right foot on the ground to cement the point.

"What the hell do you know?" Klaus raged. You're just an out-of-work singer, who is often out of tune!"

At that he leapt up and made as if to seize her, but Bill instantly blocked his path. The two men lunged and grappled.

"No!" shrieked Marina. "No fighting! Not in my club!"

The tussle continued. I joined in. Then we all fell sideways down onto the floor, crushing Serge's leg badly as we did so. He let out a wail of pain.

"Get off the kid! Get off Serge," roared Bill.

But it took too long. By the time we had all separated ourselves from each other Serge was doubled up on the floor, holding his leg in agony. We all crowded around him.

"God, are you alright?" I shouted.

"No," he moaned. "It really hurts. Oh, it's agony!"

"Serge, are you all right?" cried Irene desperately.

"Can you move that leg?" asked Bill gently. Serge lay moaning for a while.

"No," he wept. "It hurts too much."

"I think it's broken," Bill said.

"We'd better get him to hospital," I decided.

"I can't move," wailed Serge.

"Don't worry, little guy," Bill soothed. "We'll carry you if we have to."

I now told the others that I would go alone with Serge, but then Irene and Klaus insisted on coming too.

"There will be long delays," I told them.

"I don't mind," Irene said. Klaus shrugged.

It took five minutes to get him into a cab. Then we were off.

At the hospital we lined up for several hours before being seen. Finally we were escorted to a small room, and a doctor appeared. He was in a bullish mood.

"First of all, have you all been vaccinated?" he wanted to know, glaring at us impatiently.

"For what?" I asked.

"The usual list," he said, in an irritated tone.

"Do I really have to reel off the long list of names? You probably wouldn't understand what they are anyway." At this stage he named a few obscure diseases.

"You are risking brain infections, paralysis and blindness if you refuse," he added, in a bored tone.

"I don't know," I said wearily. "Look, the kid's leg is broken. He's in pain. All we want is to get him patched up."

"Nothing without vaccinations," he barked. "It's the law now. OK, come with me." We followed him to another room.

"If you do not have papers proving you've had these shots, then I'll do them all for you right now," he proposed.

"Do we have to," I asked incredulously. "It's just a leg problem, nothing but that."

"Got to follow the rules, or I'll be out of a job," he pointed out.

"The boy needs a wheelchair," I insisted. He ordered one.

As we moved along the corridor a nurse sprayed the air around us.

The injections didn't take too long. Then Serge had his leg X-rayed. Eventually there was good news.

"It's only a sprain," the doctor confirmed. "Just get some rest and OK, I'll prescribe some pain-killers if you want."

"I do want," said Serge.

I looked at my watch. It was nine o'clock. What would Maya think? She had been coming to pick up the kids from Jazzlands hours ago. Now I phoned Marina.

"Maya is here," Marina told me. "She is very worried. Is Serge OK?" I told her it was just a sprain.

"So please tell Maya to pick them up?" I asked. "We will be waiting outside for her." She agreed.

Half an hour later Maya appeared with her van. I tried to explain what had happened. She smiled with relief.

"Yes, it's OK, Marina told me everything," she consoled me. "I will bring them home now. We were quite worried."

Serge was helped into her vehicle, and they drove off. After that I turned round to look for Klaus, but there was no sight of him anywhere. Now a man in a white coat tapped me on the shoulder.

"Are you the one who was with Klaus Vogel?" he asked.

"Yes. Why? Where is he?" I demanded.

"Unfortunately I have to tell you that he assaulted two doctors a few minutes ago. He has been restrained, but we need to ask you a few questions."

"What the hell is going on?" I shouted.

"I was planning to ask you that myself. Does this Mr Vogel have a past history of mental disorder?"

I fought with myself before answering.

"Yes he probably does," I admitted. "But

what did these doctors do to him?"

"They were merely informing him that his laughter was too loud. He was talking with a female mental patient at the time."

"So laughing is banned by your rules now?"

"If it's loud, then yes."

"Can I see him?"

"Not today. He has been sedated and temporarily isolated in the psychiatric wing."

"Locked up?"

"Just for the day. Possibly a few days."

"But you can't do that!"

"I'm afraid we have just done it."

"I saw you talking to Jay," Irene said to Serge, a few weeks later. "Remember that time? When Marina gave us that music lesson? What did Jay say to you? I saw you two outside on the sidewalk. You talked a long time."

The pair were in their local pizza place, not far from the house. Serge threw her a disgusted look, and then grabbed a quick bite from his slice.

"Tell me," she insisted. "I'm your sister." She stroked his hair protectively, but he threw her hand down with a bad gesture.

"It's not what you think," he said, staring into his paper plate.

"Well, what is it then?"

"Do you want to earn some money?" he asked her, suddenly rejuvenated.

"What are you talking about?" she asked,

putting down her pizza slice.

"Well for me, I've had enough," he said. "All this messing around. Dad never gives us any money. Do you want to survive, or not? It's real tough here in New York. I'll explain to you what's going on if you promise not to tell, and also if you guarantee not to stop me."

"How can I say yes to that?" she asked. But then her curiosity got the better of her, and she consented.

"Well, you know the new friends I have?" he asked her. "That gang you say you don't like? I'm making money with them. Selling weed and stuff. Sometimes pills. Sometimes powder. What does it matter? We'll be dead soon if we don't get out of this place fast. We're seeing guns all around. This is East New York. I'm not a kid any more. It's time to get real."

"You're only twelve," she said. "Serge, I'm scared."

"Well don't be. You're just a girl. I knew you wouldn't understand." he looked away.

"But how did all this start," she begged him. "And I think you should stop, right now." There was a silence.

"Serge?" There were tears in her eyes.

"I met Pedro months before we met him that night at the squat with Max," he started out. "But we pretended not to know each other in front of you and Max. Cool dude, Pedro is. He set me up in business. Showed me how to do it just outside the school gate, and also at the gigs. I've got a secret stash already. There'll be enough for a brand new drum kit soon."

"Serge!" Her voice had a quaver in it. "Don't do this, please don't!" She grasped his arm, tenderly. He shook it off in a rough manner.

"See? I knew you wouldn't understand," he muttered.

"And Jay was pushing you into being a dealer too? In that talk you had?"

"Now you've got it all completely wrong," he barked. "Confusion girl! Jay knows Pedro, and buys from him. Pedro is the man with the big contacts. But when Jay found out that day that I was in on the game, he told me to stop. Said I was too young to get involved. Stop thinking you know everything, Irene, and leave me alone! It's my life and I'll do what I want."

One afternoon Maya phoned me as I slept, taking a quick nap before the evening gig.

"Max, please come to the courtroom," she begged. "We need you now. Leo is in jail. He slapped the kids and they ran into the street and called the police. Now can you come and help give evidence? We need witnesses, you know, character testimonials?"

"My god," I yelled, clambering into my clothes, and beating off a roach. "Of course. Hold on, I'm coming!" I raced into the alley and soon leapt on the D train.

At the courthouse the process didn't take long. The room was packed with emotional people begging lawyers for advice.

Soon Leo was lead out from a door on the right. He walked at an even pace, with a slightly resigned expression. His hands were chained in front. There was now a flurry of talk between lawyers and the judge.

"I think it's going to be alright," Maya whispered to me.

Then he was freed. He looked relieved as he exited the place with us. Nothing much was said. I'd heard about him slapping the kids occasionally before. I didn't want to think too much about it. In my time, back in England, kids did get slapped occasionally. I knew Leo loved his kids. That was all there was to it.

Jay was in a good mood. He was partying with the gang. One brother had just been released from jail that day. They had met up in a bar in Manhattan, killed a pile of beers, and were now heading back home. It was wickedly late at night, and the gang were armed and restless, and ready to roll some honkey trash if any chance presented itself. They had girls with them too, and this meant a chance to win some serious p**** if anything real went down.

The car crashed through tunnel after tunnel, as the lights flickered and Jay chewed on a wad of gum.

Marlon and Lee were getting rageful, as they argued over the football.

"Back down you motherf*****," Marlon

roared, taking his knife out.

"Don't try it you bastard" Lee hissed. "One more word and I'll waste you."

"Then you go straight back to the big house," Marlon menaced.

"I'm cool with that. Guess who's comin' back in there with me?"

"Dudes," Tracey begged. "You guys gonna quit this, or what?"

Painfully slowly Marlon snapped his knife back and stove it in his baggies. The train hurtled on.

It was 3am, and Leo also was on the subway heading home. After changing trains he sat down wearily on a bench. Then suddenly tensed up. At the other end of the car six or seven black guys had crashed through the door as the train rocketed down the tunnel. They were heading his way.

He knew he should not be travelling through the most dangerous part of Brooklyn at this time of night. By now the gang had grabbed a few seats quite close to him and were sniggering brutally, and occasionally shooting scornful looks. He stared into space, chanting silently, clearing his mind, getting ready for what might be coming. From their rough snatches of conversation he rapidly understood the worst possible situation. One guy had just come from jail, and from the way he talked about it, Leo recognised that he wouldn't care in the slightest if he went straight back there. The gang were full and ready to roll a white guy, as a kind of macabre victory ritual.

304

Now they were eyeing him swiftly. One spat on the floor with a curse. Another was playing with a switchblade.

"Hey mister," one called.

Another got up and swaggered towards him, an obscene smile on his face.

Suddenly Jay recognised Leo and a curious play of emotions ran through him. What perfect timing! How lucky this was. Now he would see this mofo messed up once and for all. He watched and waited as Marlon gestured and taunted at Leo. Then Jay looked at the girls. Their faces were haunted and desperate. He made up his mind to stop this. It wasn't a fair fight, eight against one. But just as he stood up to go and drag Marlon back to the gang he heard something.

As if in a dream, Leo took out his harp and began to play the blues. He played and played, hard and strong, and it sounded good with the train grinding and shuddering beneath them. The tension broke.

Out of the corner of his eye, Leo noticed for the first time that there were two girls in the group. One was smiling at him, and he saw that it was a true smile. But now the bad guy was looking confused, and one of the gang had grabbed his arm, and roughly pushed him down into a seat. The train rocked on, passing station after station. Leo played all the way to his final stop. As he exited, he saw smiles on the faces of both girls. He put the harp back in his pocket.

But it was only as he climbed the last few

steps up to street level that he remembered who that mysterious face had been, the one who had stopped the bad guy. It was Jay. And he had saved his life.

The cool night air of Brooklyn had never felt so good before.

Marina was starting to lose her sanity. Every time I rehearsed at the club with her and Jay she would explode into a fit of rage.

One evening Jay and I were figuring out how to make the music tight. This was necessary because we were all needing money so badly, and everyone knew that a tight performance was the thing that more people would pay to come and see. I liked free improvisation too, but we were hardly eating any more. As for rent money, that was a constant crisis.

But the moment Marina saw me and Jay agreeing on how to arrange the music she went totally beserk, screaming blue murder and even throwing things at us. I had to exit for Flatbush fast, even though the rehearsal was not complete.

That night I tossed and turned, unable to sleep, worried about how much worse Marina's mental state would get. Then I fell into an unsteady, confused dream.

And she's there. Long dark hair brushing my face. She's talking in many languages. First she sings a ballad with a baby-girl voice, then a blues rocker, and it's a scream of joy and pain, cleaning your spirit, such that afterwards you feel reborn. Finally she's laughing, and it's exactly like the bray of a baby donkey.

"Serge, come here." Leo's iron voice resonated through the silence of the apartment. It was early evening, and the sun was just going down over the Brooklyn skyline.

"My leg hurts," complained Serge, from the sofa.

"Come here!" Serge shuffled over.

"What's this, please?"

Leo was holding up a piece of paper. It contained details of a video shooting schedule.

"Look, I can explain," protested Serge, tearfully.

Leo grabbed him by the arm. He made as if to knock him on the side of the head, but then suddenly froze.

"You have been working, secretly!" he raged.

"Yes, Papa."

"Against my strict orders!"

"We had to do it, Papa. We were desperate. There was no food some nights. You know that."

"Why did you not share this money with the family?"

"Then you would have found out and banned it."

Leo stared and stared at his son. His eyes became round and menacing. His iron hand grasped Serge's arm more and more tightly. Both were now paralysed, staring into each other's faces. Serge began to shiver. He saw a dangerous madman in front of him.

Then suddenly Leo began to laugh. Gradually, tearfully, Serge began giggling too. By this time Irene had appeared and had instantly deciphered the entire situation, and now she was sniggering too. The whole family were engulfed, and had to sit down, tears streaming down their faces. The dog had become excited and was licking any faces he could reach. Maya had finally understood what was happening, and was grinning and chortling to herself as she washed the dishes, while Kira ran around screaming with joy.

"What kind of music is this?" Christo flipped our cassette to the other side. "Which studio did you record at? The drums are no good. Where do you think you're going with this stuff?"

The heat was intense. I had phoned Christo soon after meeting him and Gabriel that day. A meeting had been scheduled. But I was not expecting such a gruff reaction. Clearly we had caught him in a bad mood today.

We were in his office on 57th street at 5th Avenue. Now his Chinese partner pulled the blinds down, dragged a chair up to the desk, and began to interrogate us.

"Do you have a pull? I haven't heard of you. Do you have photos of the band? Are you in the press? Where have you played? What's the story on the band?"

Marina leapt into the attack, smoking heavily, eyes yellow with irritation.

"We were huge in Europe," she asserted, raising her chin and making the New York fish-face mouth.

"*Were*?" the Chinese challenged. "You have to be huge now. What can I do with that?"

"So why aren't you there, if you're so big? What are you doing here?" Christo demanded. The phone interrupted his words.

"Excuse me, I have a call," he shouted. I

kicked my toe into the ground. Marina stubbed a cigarette into the carpet as I started to explain things to the Chinese.

"We have no problems in Italy," I stated. "Our band is kick-ass over there. This I can prove. I don't expect you to believe stuff just because I say it." Marina unzipped a folio of papers.

"Here, look at our CVs and press kit," she butted in.

Now she became a machine, mechanically reciting all the reasons why we were going to make it. She mentioned powerful people back home in Rome. They were in her hand, she claimed. At this point she was quoting a giant list of media connections we had, radio broadcasts we'd done, gigs coming up, management we were negotiating with and then details of recording sessions, and also video projects in the pipeline. As she talked her eyes danced from side to side, and I nodded my head, and occasionally added a supportive comment.

By now the Chinese was interested.

"We cleaned up in Italy," she concluded, adding that her father was big over there. Now she was pointing at me, telling him how I had made it already in England.

A negress raced in with a fax.

"They're stuck in Colorado," she whispered. "They need money." Christo threw it down in disgust.

"Tell them we're working on it," he growled. She departed.

The Chinese guy jumped to the window, adjusted the shades and turned the AC higher for a minute, then lowered it again.

Swiftly he turned back to us.

"I like you guys," he said. "I want to help you. But the image has to change. This jamming stuff has to tighten up too. Listen, I have a song you can try."

"We only do our own songs," Marina hissed, losing patience.

A girl in a bikini and a mauve wig entered.

"I'm busy," moaned Christo. "But are we still on for tonight? They won't let you in dressed like that."

"Did you listen to my demo yet?" the bikini demanded. "And of course I'll have my gown on. Think I'm dumb?"

"No I don't and no I didn't," he admitted.

"So phone me then. I may be busy." And she strutted out.

Marina began to talk, but now the door opened again and a small latin man shuffled in, placed a brown parcel on the side, then turned, and with a shock we recognised his face.

"Pedro?" Marina said. "What are you doing here?"

"Oh, hi," he said. "You guys on this label? You got sorted out?"

"We're working on it," I told him, laughing. He smiled back.

"Gotta go," he said. Christo handed him some cash.

Now a delivery boy entered with Chinese food. He too was paid, and disappeared.

"This is what it has to sound like," said the Chinese guy. He put on a cassette. A roar issued from the huge sound system. It was something familiar. I listened harder.

Where had I heard this music before? The rhythm surged out through the speakers. The Chinese turned the volume up even higher. Who played bass like that? And now some trumpet phrases that I knew so well.

Marina sat up, eyes wide, suddenly horrified.

At this point the sound was engulfing us. A crazy harp solo over a steady groove from the drums. And finally the chanting.

It was Brother Kharma.

"Oh no," Marina muttered, putting her head in her hands.

"See? It's totally in the pocket,' the Chinese guy shouted. His eyes were wild with delight. "Exactly what we want. This is the ultimate groove. They have the killer sound. We may be signing this act. An offer has been made. But they are negotiating with several labels.

Suddenly Christo drew the Chinese urgently to one side.

"What's this?" Christo demanded. "You put in an offer? Without consulting me? When? Can I remind you, you have no executive authority here. I'm the one that calls the shots in this setup."

He waved a hand in our faces. A mock grin.

"Excuse me a moment?"

Then he motioned the Chinese to another room. Once they were out of sight all I could make out were bits and pieces of phrases, amidst the general uproar.

"A cult? What do you mean? What's his name? Yes, the lanky one? Leo? There's a cult around him? Black magic? But can we sell that? Look, dude, you are so out of line. 85 grand? You offered that? You f***ing loser. I should kick your ass."

Then I heard the Chinese mouth off.

"F*** off! I am so out of here."

"You f*** off!"

Then there was silence for a moment. Now they started again.

"He's a maniac, that Leo. A total mofo," from Christo.

"Yeah, but he's gonna make it," the Chinese replied.

"He's armed. He has a gang," Christo argued. "We have enough trouble as it is. D'you wanna get shot?"

"Are you crazy? It's a mystical cult. They all know him down here in Alphabet city. He's like a *shaman* or something?" the Chinese answered.

"Look I don't do this hippy dippy bullshit, you know that. I don't buy into that. Come with something real. Can he sell records?"

"They already have done," the Chinese shouted.

"Anyway watch your mouth, you f***ing

Chink. Remember you work for me. So get a grip."

Then there was silence.

Now Leo and Serge walked in.

Irma, an overweight schizophrenic in Bellevue psychiatric hospital, was munching on a banana, and feeling excited. This was the day that she, plus her new boyfriend, Klaus, were being released. He had a place they could stay and make their love-nest, he had told her proudly. It was a squat in the East Village, not anything luxurious, but solid and basic, and it would be their very first home together. He told her vague details about a friend called Pedro who lived there, and who had a spare room for the two of them.

She took another bite from the banana, and dreamed on happily. He would broom it out, Klaus had told her, and he would give the cupboards and the floor a scrub, and get new sheets for the bed, and put a vase of flowers on the table...

Just as the Russian band were taking off, my cash situation hit rock bottom. The Echoes gig never paid enough. Now I started doing two or three gigs a night, at bars in Brooklyn and Manhattan, playing guitar and singing cover numbers. I'd go through a repertoire of blues, rock, reggae and pop songs, and make just enough money to pay to take yellow cabs from one place to the next, plus a bit more to take home. Then back at Flatbush, a team of crackheads would carry my heavy gear for fifty cents each. These guys were expert at making the freight elevator work, since it was normally locked such that nobody could access the basement. But they knew exactly how to all pile onto the door together with all their strength, and at the same moment I would press the button hard, and in this way the elevator would descend. The spaniel who lived downstairs would moan in agony as I appeared, and as I finally sprawled face down on my sheetless mattress a few roaches would scatter, or maybe one might fall from the ceiling onto my back, but, no matter, I would be unconscious within minutes anyway.

One afternoon I headed right up north to 223rd street, a place called Woodlawn, in Yonkers, since I knew a cluster of Irish pubs were there. I'd already performed in a few pubs, and was just relaxing with a sandwich when a guy called to me.

"Great songs you played," he announced. I thanked him. He offered me a drink, and then gave me a particular look.

"Go to Treasure Island," he told me. I wondered if I was dreaming. Where was this Treasure Island? Did it even exist?

"Treasure Island," he repeated. "The Miami Keys?" Now I had some idea of what he was talking about.

"Key West," he insisted. "Real money gigs." I thanked him. He lit up a cigarette, and stared knowingly through the blue tailstream.

"Hundreds of them," he repeated, dropping his voice to a dry croak. "With what you're doing, you'll clean up. Trust me. Go to Treasure Island."

It was a sign. I knew I would have to get on the road soon.

Around 2pm the following Thursday afternoon, Serge was riding the D train up to West 4, feeling good. He'd successfully skipped school, and now had a plan. Pedro had offered him the chance to deliver a few more packages and earn a bit of extra cash. Serge knew perfectly well that heroin was inside the bundles. He hardly cared. Pedro was a good friend, always laughing and treating him as a good friend, and helping him earn cash. Serge knew that the family always needed more money. And there was more. He needed to prove he was a real man, that he could stand on his own two feet, and not always be mocked or laughed at as the cute little kid. Pedro would help him out one more time.

Half an hour later he was climbing the stairs of the dusty, derelict building. At the top he peered through the gloom. Pedro's door was slightly opened.

"Pedro?" he called. No answer. Just the sound of someone screaming, in the distance. Now he became alert.

"Pedro, are you there?" he called. His eleven year old voice sounded lost and confused.

Pushing through the door he could just make out a figure lying inside, on a bed in the semi darkness.

"Pedro?" he asked. Walking closer, he stopped and stared. Then saw the face. Pedro was on his back, eyes closed, with a needle sticking in his arm.

Serge already knew enough about drugs to know that Pedro was dead.

"Oh no," he gasped. "Pedro, why?" But Pedro just lay there. Then Serge heard the sound of shuffling footsteps on the stairs. He froze.

And now a big man stood in the doorway. It was Klaus. He was staring at the syringe in Pedro's arm.

"No," he wailed. Then he roared. "No! Not him! Not Pedro!"

Now Klaus bent right over Pedros dead body and hugged him, weeping and gurgling with grief.

"No, not you," he moaned. "Not my Pedro. Why? Don't leave me. I'm nothing without you, Pedro. What am I going to do now? Oh Pedro, dear Pedro, please don't go?"

Suddenly Serge felt embarrassed and wanted to run. But now Klaus put an arm round him, and clutched him closer to himself and to Pedro, and continued weeping and gasping, and moaning with grief.

Serge didn't know what to think. He wanted to be home right now. For a while the three crouched and hugged, as Klaus moaned and rocked, and wept on. A small black and white TV was flickering behind their heads. The sound was switched off, but there were advertisements playing on the screen. Suddenly Serge saw that he was staring at his own face. His ad was running on TV for the first time. It shouldn't be doing that. They had told him that it would be foreign TV only. Now Leo would know. He stared at the ad, mesmerised. He saw himself on a skateboard, grinning into the camera before coasting down the hill. Finally he could see himself saying something. Then the ad was over, and was swiftly being replaced by another. So now his parents would know about their secret project, and he would be banned from doing more. He felt sick inside.

Gently he disengaged himself from the huge arm.

"I've got to get back," he confessed. "I'm sorry about Pedro. I don't know what happened. He was a nice guy."

"Don't go!" roared Klaus.

"I'm sorry," muttered Serge. But I've got to get back." He shuffled out, trying not to hear the desperate sounds coming from Klaus.

After he had gone, Klaus remained there close to Pedro for an hour longer, fondling his hair, whispering to him, hugging him, saying goodbye forever, in so many ways.

Then he knew he must get out into the street, find Irma and tell her.

Three weeks later, Marina lost Jazzlands. The rent had not been paid for months. There was one terrible day when the sheriff smashed down the door and the bailiffs marched in, seizing whatever they could find. For a while Marina disappeared totally. Our band ceased to exist.

Then one day I bumped into her in the West Village. It had been raining but now the sun had broken through. The sidewalk was glistening and spar-

318

kling. She was crossing the street just close to West Four subway station when I saw her.

"Marina," I shouted. "What's happened to you?" She walked slowly towards me. Her face was lined and weary. I looked her up and down in sudden alarm. She moved from foot to foot uncertainly.

"Tell me?" I asked. "What's going on?" My voice softened as I realized how her clothes had become rough and a little bit ragged. She sighed and clutched my arm, then sat down on a bench.

"He ran off, just when we got evicted. He was beating me anyway," she said, looking at the sun for a moment. "You didn't help either, Max. Where were you? I'm sleeping on the subway now."

"What?" I said. There was a sob in my throat. "Marina! Are you crazy?"

"No, just broke," she said. "Give me some money. How much have you got?" I went into my wallet and handed her a roll of twenties. She took it silently.

"How about a thank you?" I reminded her. There was a long pause before this arrived.

"Thank you," she said, finally. "But now she pivoted, facing me defiantly.

"Don't think I'm dead yet," she growled. At this she launched into an account of how things were.

"I'm OK, you know. I've got my own TV show now."

"But you're homeless?" I gasped.

"Don't worry. I've got things sorted out," she insisted proudly. "I've just come from the place where I shower," she continued. A taxi blazed past.

"You pay to shower somewhere?"

"Yes, there's a place. And now I'm going over to my storage cubicle."

"You pay to store your stuff?"

"Yes. It's eight blocks down. And then, after lunch, I'll go uptown to where I rent a business desk in a cubicle. Six bucks an hour. I only need an hour. I do all this every day." My eyes were wide with disbelief.

"You have it all worked out, don't you?" I admitted.

"And then at 7pm, after supper, I'll head over to 57th on the west side, to the TV station, to edit my show for an hour," she concluded.

"You really have a TV show?" I gasped.

"Yes I do. And then tonight I'll probably check this great band I know. And after that..." She paused.

"And after that you go and sleep in the subway? Where? Which stop?"

She made a mysterious gesture with upraised hands.

"It's a secret. I've discovered a particular train which stops in the tunnel very late at night, and it rests there for a while. So I get to sleep a few hours."

For a moment I was totally speechless. Now her face lit up suddenly.

"And Max, you don't know the people I've met down there! They're wonderful! We're like one big family! And remember the fire-eater who gave us his room, all that time ago? He's there too!" She was glowing now. Then she looked at her watch, and stood up suddenly.

"Sorry, gotta go," she announced. "I've got my schedule."

And at this she hopped down the subway steps and disappeared.

That night I dreamed the Pied Piper again. This time he was leading all the children, out of the city, and over the hills and far away. I picked up my guitar and followed the procession...

Kathmandu, Nepal

It was 7am in Kathmandu. In the temples the monks were already assembling, and dealing with the first duties of the day, prayer and thanksgiving. Outside in the narrow cobbled streets, a few *sadhus*, old ascetic men with long beards and distinctive orange robes, wandered freely, occasionally begging from passersby.

Inside the temple in Amrit Marg street, Bhavisana, the beautiful twelve year old child goddess was having her feet gently washed by Binsa, her maiden attendant.

"When do we go out to the street again, for a walk?" Bhavisana wanted to know.

"It is every second Saturday, so that would be four more days," Binsa smiled. "Now I must do your hair, and then make your face as it should be. We are a little late today. My fault, I am sorry."

"Bad Binsa," laughed the goddess. "You will not go with me to paradise!" Binsa made no reply, but merely continued to wash the tiny feet.

A thousand miles to the south, the great daily bathing in the Ganges river had begun. Many millions were there, and people laughed with pleasure as the cool waters splashed over them entirely.

Northern Russia

Many hours later, in the Siberian *Sayan* mountains, several middle-aged Shamans were practising their healing skills inside their *yurt,* with its earthen floor. A few logs smouldered gently in the fireplace. Vodka, raw meat and biscuits were on the table.

It was very cold outside and a gentle rain was falling. The mens' hands were resting on ritual canes. Now they started to beat on drums and began to sing their *kalmanie* chants, a long, slow, droning sound. A little thunder struck far away in the distance, behind the mountains. One of the dogs moaned in his basket near the fire.

Rome, Italy

In Rome the street cleaners were at work in Porta Portesi, the ancient winding street where all the antiques and bric-a-brac were haggled over at the open market. It had been a hot, sweaty day of bargaining and wheedling. Barely-clad prostitutes guarded dusty street-corners on the Appian way, just outside town. Cars and motorbikes swerved like crazy, avoiding pedestrians and mangy cats. At the Colosseum, tourist guides were packing up and leaping onto mopeds to get home in time for supper.

London, UK

In north west London two elderly people sat in the sitting room of a house close to Hampstead Heath. The place was packed with books. It was the moment for the couple to watch the evening news. There had been a recent problem with terrorist violence in Finsbury park, the Greek neighbourhood, something connected with Islam.

"Can't think what they have to argue about," the man grumbled to his wife. She nodded sympathetically, absorbed in a left-wing magazine.

"Sometimes I think the whole world is going mad," she commented.

"Have you seen how fast Russia is changing now?" he wanted to know.

"Yes, darling," she replied. "Do you remember how we fought for Russian communism in our student years? How you would get up on a soap box at the market at Cambridge, and give speeches on Marx and Lenin?"

"I certainly do," he replied. "But sadly those days are long gone now."

"Forever?" she asked.

"Possibly so," he replied, making a helpless gesture with his hands. There was silence for a while. Then the man spoke.

"I see there was a letter from Max this morning," he observed. "What does he say?"

"He's alright," his wife confirmed. "But he is thinking of leaving New York soon."

"Thank God," the man sighed.

New York City

A new dawn broke over the east coast of America. The statue of liberty sparkled in the early morning spray, as waves crashed up against beaches and docks from New Jersey to Long Island.

Cars streamed up from the Holland tunnel into New York City. Subway trains exploded across the Manhattan bridge, dumping silent commuters into a multitude of destination stations. Joggers snaked across central park, as stores rolled up shutters, and taxi drivers ferried customers to all possible locations. In the lofts and condos of the wealthy upper west side, men selected shirts, and hustled through their shower and shave routine. Women fussed with microwave ovens, prettied themselves in mirrors, before donning power suits of the latest vogue. Kids ran screaming from room to room, desperately trying to have maximum fun before school.

Cleaners lit up cigarettes and scrubbed. Priests donned their cassocks and prepared their agendas. Musicians lay comatose, and junkies began to organise their first fix.

A million coffee machines chortled into action. In his office, the mayor was checking the football results. Down below his window, in the streets, crowds hustled along Broadway, some on headphones, many in jeans and baseball caps, some in suits with business cases, a few with newspapers.

A couple of tramps and vagrants were arguing in a parking lot on Houston Street.

"Gimme that bottle, Tyler. I had a lousy time last night. Damn cops woke me up four times." His friend passed him the bottle suspiciously.

"Leave some for me, you son of a b****!"

Pigeons soared in formation above Bleecker Street. The news boys were doing big business at their kiosks. A powerful aroma of vanilla coffee coasted along West Four. Two gay professors were chatting on stools inside a bagel bar on MacDougal, peering out at the morning rush with much pleasure.

"Yes, but do you have an *ontological* argument for God's existence, Darius?" one probed the other, before taking a giant bite from his egg and ham bagel.

It was a perfect day. Music poured from the boutique stores on Sixth Avenue. Clouds were flying in the east. There was a cool fresh wind, and the sound of laughter outside the cafes and delis of the Lower East Side.

By now the family were doing even better. At this point they had gained a permanent rehearsal space in Williamsburg. This made a difference. The music was getting tighter, and gigs were coming in. A CD album had been recorded and had already sold out at all the major stores. Brother Kharma were being talked about in the press too, little articles popping up here and there. And then suddenly the band disappeared, to tour Georgia.

I could hardly recognise them when they returned. Suntanned, confident, walking tall. The story was astonishing. The tour had been massively successful. The kids were jumping from foot to foot in the apartment as Leo quietly explained.

"A giant door opens for us," he said. "All concerts booked solidly. Top agent. Owned by one of the biggest corporations." He smiled with satisfaction and Maya beamed too.

This shook me. If anything was the big time, this was.

"I get it," I said. "Here in New York, everything is compressed. You don't see talent clearly because there's so much of it. It's only when you escape this goddamn city that you get the truth. You guys are incredible. I cannot believe it. Well done! Christ, you deserve this, after what you've been through. I simply can't believe it. First the shelter, then the squat. Nonstop poverty, homelessness, fighting for your lives in the most dangerous parts of the town...you know, I'm lost for words." My voice was breaking up a bit.

"Sit down, Max," said Serge. I felt too emotional to talk for a moment. Irene looked at me with big, sad, wise eyes.

"We did OK," she said.

"Well that's it," I announced. "You guys have made it. According to my rule-book anyway. There's just so much going on. I can't forget how we played live on air, at Rockefeller Plaza, and how they beamed it all over the world. And today you kids do commercials all the time. Plus, your gigs never stop. You guys are everywhere at once! That gets my total respect. And now you are touring America. Listen, if you can just get in your van and head for the sticks, and rock them like crazy like that, well, you've made it. You're there! I'm left feeling a bit inadequate. All I really do is play jazz in restaurants."

At this the family raced to reassure me.

"No, no, Max, forget that," Leo said sharply. "Get real. You have incredible talent. You can play anything. And we need you right here. You're part of the band, if you want to be. But I realise you have to do paying sessions with other acts also.

I told him thanks. I felt proud he'd offered that.

Over the next few weeks I saw them go for shopping trips into town, buying musical gear, and expensive stage clothes also. They had passed a major milestone in the music business. Now they were ready for anything. I was glad. They deserved this. I wondered what was coming next.

They had broken every rule of the game, and won.

I felt proud that my friends had made good. But from my side, I soon learned to stay on the move, as the months turned into years. By now I had recognised that New York City had a way to burn people out, if they didn't make it fast enough. Some of my friends had turned into casualties. They had become drugged and enslaved by the city, and could not move ahead, yet were not able to leave.

As time passed, for some reason, the Russian family and I gradually drifted away from each other.

Eventually I started to hustle harder, and play more gigs. This brought results. A few residencies with jazz and blues bands lead to work contracts in other places, Memphis, Montreal and also London, my home-town. Next, a surprise phone call now revealed that the record I had made with Marina and Roman had done quite well, and the label wanted more.

Soon I became used to the relentless travelling, and learned how to live out of one small bag, and always be ready to get on a plane at a moment's notice. Eventually I had fixed up temporary bases in three countries at once. This situation worked for a while, and felt good, but every time I hit New York City again I noticed that something was missing. By this time I was a little older, and I now understood that the insane pace and drive of this city was such that if you disconnected for a while you would soon lose your place and then you would not be able to compete. This realization unsettled me. New York was beginning to bid me farewell.

However the world was opening her arms. From now on, wherever I played would be easy. Such was the power of New York City as a training ground. My head was full of music, and also endless plans and dreams. I was alone, but free, and I would never again lose myself in chaos or madness. Life was beautiful and magical once more, with a kind of innocence that had been hidden for me for many years. I understood that all the wounds and suffering that I had been through now served as a kind of wisdom which was empowering my song-writing and my very soul itself.

But I knew that I would not stay in New York much longer.

One day I discovered that Marina had moved back in with Jay. He was living in Harlem now. Riding the subway up there to visit them I was horrified to find Jay in the process of kicking her out. She was sitting on the steps outside, begging to be allowed to stay. But he was angry, and stayed firm. I was still thirty yards away and they had not noticed me yet.

"One step down," he shouted. Reluctantly she slid down a step.

"You stop right there," he told her.

I could not bear to stay, and turned and headed back to the subway before she might recognise me.

In the meantime I missed seeing Leo and

Maya. They had been the heart-beat of the city for me, and a shelter from the storm. I would be forever grateful to them for this.

Plus, together with their family, they had created a legend. No-one would ever forget their way to make survival fun, and thus turn poverty and desperation into success. Plus the crazy subway gigs, the endless dream, the many songs we sang and the welcoming smiles.

Also, something had changed in America. The spirit of the east had touched this land. For a brief moment, two worlds had come together. This kind of magic might not happen again for a very long time.

I continued to visit and stay in New York City for a few more years, but in the end my path became clear to me, and I understood that I must leave for good. On the very last evening I walked once more to the Seaport, and stared at the grey Atlantic ocean, and then at the dark, glittering skyscrapers, one final, precious time. My heart was full of mixed emotions, and memories of Brother Kharma were in my mind, with all the joy and sadness that could be imagined. As I walked slowly back towards the subway, and as the night wind brushed my hair, I knew that something had changed inside me forever.

THE END

EPILOGUE

New York City - 2018

Twenty years later, Serge was found dead at Maya's apartment in Brooklyn. After being homeless for years, and addicted to hard drugs, he had finally kicked them, moved in with his mother, and found work in construction, checking into two building sites each day, but then something had gone terribly wrong. The family were destroyed by grief.

When I heard the news one evening I was paralysed by shock and disbelief. How could we have lost him in this manner? Were Leo and I to blame? It forced me to search my soul, and desperately try to remember back to those days when we had played gigs together. Serge had always appeared to be OK, often smiling, always happy to play so much music the way we did. What had gone wrong? I had never seen any sign of him slipping downwards in any way. But at this moment, for the first time, I understood how terribly dangerous New York City could be, specially for children, and also how very blind we had been. And I knew I must now carry this heavy weight with me forever. Little Serge would never be coming back any more, never laughing, never playing the drums, never ever greeting me with shining eyes, or playing a game, or giving me a hug the way he used to. In my heart I blessed him and prayed for him, and then I thought of all the other children of the world whose lives had been made dark by a combination of music, drug addiction and homelessness, and with a great sadness in my soul I prayed for them too.

AFTERWORD

America has finally become saturated with deserted factories, bulging landfills, eerie ghost towns, sprawling, lifeless deserts and toxic rivers, coast to coast. Many of the immigrants have returned to their native lands as the US economy falters. Many others are now jobless, living in debt, and sometimes homeless. Far too many mistakes have been made. Corrupt politics has ravaged the country, such that education and health care have been gradually eaten away. Ignorance and decadence are now widespread.

Many artists are leaving New York City. They are following the Pied Piper, searching for new lands and clearer skies elsewhere. The miraculous American dream of freedom and democracy is no more.

Yet Liberty Avenue cannot be forgotten. The Russian family play on. Their music pours out of the wasteland as strong as ever. Listen hard and you will hear something. Occasionally it may sound like the wind gusting in the night, or the waves beating on the shore, or birds singing in the sunshine of the valley, but it's always them, calling out to us.

And sometimes in my dreams I search for those familiar skyscrapers of Manhattan Island, and imagine that I am back there on the horizon once again, hand in hand with a dancing gorilla and a beautiful lizard.

POSTSCRIPT

Jay came off drugs and worked as a truck driver for many years before becoming a Born Again Christian and teaching yoga in Boston.

Marina eventually returned to Rome, where she became a successful TV actress, specialising in horror TV serials.

Leo returned to Russia, where he received an honorary degree from Moscow University. He now runs the Blues Factory, a not-for-profit establishment in the South of France.

Klaus became the manager of a diner cafe in the Bronx, and today collects antique military uniforms.

Gabriel became a major player in the free jazz world, performing and recording in many countries.

Marcello and Kaspar were both killed in a mysterious plane crash in Bogota.

Irene still tours internationally, fronting her own band, which is a continuation of the Brother Kharma band, and also its street-wise philosophy.

Serge's funeral in Brooklyn was attended by hundreds of loving friends and fans, and he is sadly missed, both for his majestic drumming skills and his dynamic, optimistic spirit.

Bill established himself as one of America's top session drummers, and now runs a production company in New York City.

The rest of the Russian family have settled down in different parts of America, except Kira, who at the time of writing works as an engineer on a container vessel making trips in and out of the port of Dubai.

Maya remained in New York City, where she continues her musical career.

I relocated to Montreal, where I manage a recording studio today.

Lightning Source UK Ltd.
Milton Keynes UK
UKHW020644040722
405345UK00008B/386